Raves for 'SO MANY DOORS' by OAKLEY HALL!

"Tells its story with the smashing impact of a pile driver."
—*Chicago Tribune*

"Tough, sexy, combustible…a violent, almost visceral, talent."
—*Kirkus*

"A rough, tough, brawling novel…not for the squeamish."
—*Houston Press*

"Writing with the force and pungency of a master of the suspense story…he tells a story highly charged…of a completely recognizable America hitherto only lightly touched."
—*San Francisco Chronicle*

"Relentless…revealing…compassio⟨ W9-BZZ-374
—*New York Journal American*

"This is a serious and ambitious book."
—*Reading California Fiction*

"With the advent of this novel the broad realm of contemporary fiction will certainly acknowledge the mature writing stature of Oakley Hall."
—*Denver Post*

"When I began writing fiction, I was blessed to have Oakley Hall as a mentor. Having read many of his books, I was delighted to see this reissue of *So Many Doors*. As in his other novels, he proves he is the master of characterization, narrative immediacy, and the art of luring you into a gripping story."

—*Amy Tan*

So Many DOORS

by **Oakley Hall**

A HARD CASE CRIME NOVEL

A HARD CASE CRIME BOOK

(HCC-137)

First Hard Case Crime edition: November 2018

Published by

Titan Books
A division of Titan Publishing Group Ltd
144 Southwark Street
London SE1 0UP

in collaboration with Winterfall LLC

Print edition ISBN 978-1-78565-688-0
E-book ISBN 978-1-78565-689-7

Design direction by Max Phillips
www.maxphillips.net

Typeset by Swordsmith Productions

The name "Hard Case Crime" and the Hard Case Crime logo
are trademarks of Winterfall LLC. Hard Case Crime books
are selected and edited by Charles Ardai.

Printed in the United States of America

Visit us on the web at www.HardCaseCrime.com

'Twere sure but weaklings' vain distress
To suffer dungeons where so many doors
Will open on the cold eternal shores
That look sheer down
To the dark tideless floods of Nothingness
Where all who know may drown.

FROM *The Man Against the Sky*
BY EDWIN ARLINGTON ROBINSON

For Barbara

CONTENTS

PROLOGUE 11

PART I: BAIRD 17

PART II: BEN 69

PART III: MARIAN HUBER 157

PART IV: GENE 181

PART V: JACK 233

EPILOGUE 317

Prologue

They stopped between two of the orange-glowing bulbs that lit the long corridor at intervals, and the turnkey leaned over to fit a key into a lock. He swung the door open. "In here," he said.

The lawyer went in and the door clanged shut behind him. The squeak of the turnkey's shoes and the jangle of the keys he carried faded off into silence.

The cell was small and square, with yellowish-white walls. In the ceiling a recessed light was covered by a wire cage, and high on the wall opposite the door a barred window split a square of blue sky into six rectangular segments. In the center of the floor stood a three-legged stool and against the wall was a cot on which the man, Jack Ward, sat, leaning forward with a cigarette in his hand. As the lawyer looked at him he raised the cigarette to his lips, squinting, and then he lowered it again. He stared back.

The lawyer nodded to him and changed his briefcase to the other hand. Ward didn't move; he looked in his early thirties, with dark, unkempt hair, a high forehead, heavy brows. His eyes were narrow and slanting, deep-set above broad, high cheekbones.

The lawyer felt himself being inspected in return, and finally Ward rose and stepped forward. He was tall and heavy shouldered, the shoulders slumped now, and his arms hung loosely at his sides. His dark sport coat was too small for him and his khaki trousers were rolled at the top. They had taken his belt, the lawyer saw, and looking down he saw that the laces of his shoes were gone as well. The neck of his shirt was tieless and unbuttoned and beneath a dark fringe of hair the pulse in his throat flickered gently.

"Did my wife send you?" he said. His voice was deep, and there was a note of anger in it.

"I'm your lawyer. The Court appointed me."

"I know you're a lawyer. Did she send you?"

"The Court appointed me."

Ward's eyes searched his face. They were hostile and suspicious, and he rubbed the back of his hand over his chin. "I don't want a lawyer," he said.

"I'm aware of that."

"Beat it, then."

"When the defendant refuses to obtain counsel, the Court…"

"Okay," Ward said suddenly. "You're my lawyer." His shoes slapped flabbily on the floor as he stepped back to the cot and sat down again. "Go ahead and sit down," he said, jerking his hand at the stool. "But you're wasting your time. I'm pleading guilty. I shot the bitch and I'd do it again."

The lawyer leaned his briefcase against the stool, sat down and pulled his trousers' legs up on his ankles. "This is just your first reaction," he said. His voice was thin and nervous, and he coughed and said, "You'll get over it, and there are a great many angles to this sort of business, insanity, or…"

Ward laughed, tipping his head back. But it was a strange laugh, completely mirthless and unsmiling. "Hell," he said. "I'm not nuts." He laughed again. "Look, I'm not going to try and cheat the bastards. I signed their confession. I told them why I did it and how I'd been meaning to for a long time, and how I'd do it again if…"

"You'll have to tell me the whole story," the lawyer interrupted.

"Why?"

"Maybe I can help you."

"No," Ward said. He dropped his cigarette to the floor, scraped his foot over it, and then he took another cigarette from the pack beside him on the cot and tossed it up and down in his hand. "No," he said.

"Do you know what it is to die in the gas chamber?"

"Yeah," Ward said. "I die in there all the time. But I wish to hell they'd get me to it."

The lawyer stared at him. Ward's face was flat and expressionless as he tamped the cigarette and put it between his lips and lit it. Suddenly the lawyer said, "How'd you happen to have the gun?"

"I brought it with me to shoot her with," Ward said carefully. "Listen, they tried all that on me already. I told you you're wasting your time."

The lawyer leaned forward. "Ward," he said. "I see good reason to believe you didn't bring the gun with you. If you didn't, we might be able to prove this was unpremeditated. Was it your gun?"

"Yeah," Ward whispered. He paused, and then he whispered again. "What if it was unpremeditated?"

"It might not mean the death sentence."

Ward stared back at him silently; his shirt front was trembling. Finally he looked down, and, as the lawyer watched, snuffed the glowing end of the cigarette between his fingers. No expression of pain crossed his face but when he looked up again his yellow eyes were blazing and his mouth was stretched tight across his teeth in a hard grin. The lawyer's breath came faster as he saw the cigarette fall from between Ward's fingers.

"I hate to see a man commit suicide," he said angrily. "That's the coward's way out."

"You ever try it?" Ward said. Then he said, "Well, they fixed that, anyway. They wouldn't let me do anything as easy as that."

"Why do you want to die?"

"I'll tell you. It's simple as hell. I killed her and I want to die for it. Do you think you can understand that?"

"Yes, but you see, you'll feel differently in a few days. This is just…"

"No," Ward said, shaking his head. "You don't know."

"Tell me, then."

"You'll never know," Ward said. "I don't want any help. Forget it; tell them I don't want a lawyer."

"But you'll change your mind. In a day or so…"

"Goddamn it," Ward said. "Listen!" He was trembling, and his voice was hoarse and shaky. "Look at V; I killed her. Look at my wife; what the hell's she got now? Look at a lot of things you'll never know about." He stopped and cleared his throat and slapped his hand against the iron rail of the cot.

"Listen!" he commanded. "A man's got to take stock of himself sometime. Like now. What he's got and what he's done and all, see? Well, I don't have any credits on my sheet and the nearest I can come to squaring up is to get the hell out. Out!" he said again, jerking his thumb as though he were an umpire saying it.

The lawyer took off his glasses and blinked his eyes and put them back on again. The gesture seemed to startle Ward; his hands clenched on the rail of the cot.

"Your wife doesn't want you to die," the lawyer said.

Ward didn't say anything. He stared at the lawyer with a kind of grim and detached intensity. He sat perfectly motionless but the pulse beat visibly at the base of his throat and after a moment he pressed his lips closed. After a long time the lawyer sighed and said, "Why did you kill her?"

Still Ward did not answer. He rubbed the sleeve of his coat across his eyes. The silence in the cell was deep and heavy. From somewhere near came a soft, Negro laugh; a man's voice called out, then drifted off and the silence closed in again. "Had you known her before you came to San Diego?" the lawyer asked.

Ward rose slowly. He took a step forward, holding his right hand rigidly open, the fingers pressed together, and suddenly the hand flashed out. It slapped the lawyer's cheek with a sharp report; the lawyer's head was jolted to one side, his glasses flew off and tinkled when they hit the floor. He gasped and opened his mouth to cry out, half-rising from the stool.

But Ward's hand grasped his shoulder. "Wait!" Ward said. "Don't yell. Wait. I didn't mean to do that. Don't yell. I'm sorry." The lawyer stared up at him through watering eyes; finally he gulped and nodded and Ward's hand left his shoulder.

Ward moved across to get the glasses. One foot came half out of one of his shoes and he stumbled and stepped on them. Then he picked them up and pressed the frames into the lawyer's hand, saying over and over again, "I'm sorry. I'm really sorry."

"I got upset," he said. "Look, I'll buy you another pair. I can give you a check." He grinned reassuringly as he retreated to the cot. The lawyer raised his hand to his cheek.

"Look," Ward said. "Maybe you better come back tomorrow. Maybe I am nuts. I don't know what happened to me then. Come back tomorrow and we'll talk it over, will you?" His face had a tight, strained look, as though he were rigidly controlling its expression, and finally he covered it with his hands, rubbing his hands slowly up and down over his mouth and eyes. "Look," he said in a muffled voice. "I'm sorry I scared you."

The lawyer licked his lips, picked up his briefcase and rose stiffly. "All right," he said, slipping the horn frames into his pocket. "I'll come tomorrow afternoon. Would you mind if I brought an alienist with me?"

"What?...Sure, bring three of them." Ward got up and stepped forward, but as he did so the lawyer instinctively retreated. Ward stopped and said, "Well, thanks. Thanks a lot. You come back tomorrow."

"I will," the lawyer said, and he moved sideways to the door.

When the turnkey had let him out, Jack stood motionless in the center of the cell, staring down at the tiny points of light where the sun from the window caught the shards of glass upon the floor. He listened to the clatter of the lawyer's black shoes and the squeak-jangle of the turnkey fade away down the hall. He was panting now.

Suddenly he put his hands in his hip pockets and stretched, pushing down on his hips and curving his chest out, trying to keep himself from trembling. Exultantly he flexed his shoulders and yawned, squeezing his eyes closed, and then he stepped across to the door and gripped the bars so tightly the steel seemed to contract under his hands. The long, yellowish corridor was empty and silent, lit at intervals by the caged lights. He could not see the man in the cell opposite him; he could see no one anywhere.

He gripped the bars tighter and pulled his body against them, straining his body tightly against the bars, and when he returned to the cot he was laughing silently and breathlessly. Sitting on the edge of the cot he laughed into his sour-smelling hands, thinking that in a minute he would stop laughing and smoke one more cigarette.

Part I
BAIRD

1

Baird sat on the porch of his house staring out at the orchard that fell away down the hill. The leaves of the apple trees were dull and dusty, but beyond, the wide flat floor of the San Joaquin valley was bright in the sun, extending off into bright haze, from which rose the dark mountains of the coast range.

He lowered his eyes to his hand, which was clasped tightly on the chair arm. The hand was thick, arthritic, spotted, roasted by the sun until it looked like the back of a toad. He saw himself now as too old, an old rancher in faded levis and a khaki shirt frayed white at the cuffs and collar, with thick white hair and hooded, deeply pouched eyes—and all in him worn harsh and sucked dry by age.

He tried to think of the things he could be doing now, the never-ending round of chores about the ranch: the broken mailbox, the weeding in the orchard, the pump, the chicken house. He might go into Bakersfield to see about getting the alfalfa cut....And he should be going in to see the lawyer, as he had promised to do when the lawyer had talked to him on the telephone. He thought of that for a moment, because he could not help it, and then he tried not to think.

These years since he had sent her away he had forbidden himself to think about his daughter; even when she had been living on the next ranch and he would see her sometimes on the highway, driving the long, black automobile, or on Sundays when he would see them riding together, or just hearing the distant crack of a shotgun, knowing who it was hunting rabbits. When the lawyer had phoned, he had not understood at first because it had not been in the Bakersfield paper. So it had been the lawyer who had told him and Baird had promised to come in to see him and had hung up, gasping and pressing his crossed arms against his chest where his heart had turned to a piece of crumbling, aching stone. His legs had turned to sticks which would only carry him to the door of her room, where he had stood gasping and blind with tears.

He wasn't going to San Diego. Already it was too late, and now there was no point in going. But he absolved himself of not having gone. She had been his daughter, but when he had sent her away and forbidden himself to think of her or even to recognize her existence, she had been his daughter no longer. That was what he had decreed to himself that night, and stubbornly he had held to it. She was no longer his daughter; he would not think about her anymore.

As he stared out at the orchard he saw Juan, dark and lean in dungarees patched at the seat with lighter blue, come around the corner of the house carrying a shovel and a hoe. He didn't look toward the porch as he slowly walked down among the rows of trees. Baird took his watch from his pocket; it was one o'clock.

He pushed himself to his feet and thumped down the steps and onto the baked dirt in front of the porch, squinting into the sun. He turned and stared back at the house, angry that his will was not strong enough, for the house he saw was the house that had been his and hers after her mother had died. She had lived here with him. She had grown up here, and he had tried always to do the best thing for her. His eyes were watering, and in them the house shimmered and sparkled.

The house was old too, the paint cracked and scrofulous from the valley sun. The porch covered the entire front and behind it were three narrow windows with the shades half-drawn. On the porch were two rockers and the marble-topped table, the legs of which were scaling with rust. Between two of the windows a batten had come off, leaving a dark vertical scar.

He leaned against the weatherbeaten rail. The sun was too bright, too hot and his eyes would not stop watering. He could feel his heart pounding in his chest.

When he felt stronger he went into the house, and stopped again in the parlor to look around him, his hand resting on the high back of the leather platform rocker. Slanting wedges of light from the windows shivered across the room, across the army blanket that covered the old davenport and across the brown linoleum and the base of the tall floor lamp with the faded satin shade.

Finally he stepped forward and threw open the door of the little room that had been hers. In it were an army cot, a tall dresser, a table and a chair, and on the wall a faded color photograph of Bridal Veil Falls. He slumped down in the chair, one elbow resting on the table, hand braced against his cheek, the other arm lying loosely across his lap. His eyes fell on his dusty boots, and then moved upward to the cot, which was rectangular and flat under its white coverlet, like a cement slab.

He felt his hands clench so tightly they ached. "Why?" he whispered hoarsely. Why had the Lord willed it this way? He thought of the Denton ranch that would now be his; the eighty acres of potatoes, the grazing land, the fancy quarter-horses, the stone house; all of it his, given him as nothing else had ever been given him in his life, without his having to pay for it. But he had paid for it, and paid for it as he had never paid for anything else, paid what a price, taken what a loss. But the loss had been nine years ago, and could he say that what he had thrown away was lost?

He put his hand over his face, remembering another time he

had sat here like this—with her suitcases in front of him. But she had been bad, a bad girl, a bad woman, evil, like her mother, abandoned, a————. His mind refused to frame the word.

He was fighting against it, fighting against the remembering, but too strong, too powerful, the remembering rushed up, like hot sour vomit in his head. All of it, all the cruelty of it, came back with a vivid rush that throbbed in his brain and ached in his throat, and the forbidden closet of his memory burst and overflowed.

2

Some part of it, he supposed, must have started the year Alf Landon was defeated. It was a year when the words "parity income" meant that the government paid the farmers money not to plant crops when people were starving. Young men in fresh khaki came around to tell him what to plant, and how to plow, and to explain lengthily about soil conservation. Each month he took the government check he got for doing what they said down to Bakersfield, to cash it and buy supplies.

Juan carried the boxes of canned goods back to the truck while he went into the lingerie store. A girl with lip rouge on her mouth and a dead front tooth came to wait on him, smirking at him across the glass-topped display case. She giggled when he told her what he wanted.

"What size, sir?" she said.

"She's sixteen. I guess about medium size."

She reached under the counter and brought out a pink one, holding it up by an end. "Like this? Or we have them in white."

"That's all right. How much is it?"

"One fifteen."

He snapped open his leather purse and took out a dollar, opened the other compartment and counted out the change while she wrapped the parcel for him. Outside he walked quickly toward where he had left his truck. A Greyhound Bus and a big red truck and trailer passed him with a sharp smell of exhaust fumes, and he saw Roger Denton and Mark Schuford come out of the Rancher's Bar and Grill and cross the sidewalk to Denton's automobile.

He averted his face so he wouldn't have to see Denton, but then he heard Denton call his name and he looked up and nodded.

"Can I give you a lift, Baird?" Denton said. Schuford was smiling and holding the door open, an unlit cigarette tilted upward in his mouth.

"My machine's right here," he said. "Thanks." As he hurried on with the package clenched tightly in his armpit he watched the new, shining automobile drive by. His face felt flushed and when he saw Juan lounging in the front seat of his old truck he gestured angrily at him. Juan leaped out with the crank, started the motor and they drove silently out the highway to the ranch.

Juan followed him up from the shed, carrying the boxes of canned goods. They passed the shack with the slanting, tar-papered roof that had been on the land when he had bought it, thirty-five years ago now, where Juan and Mary slept; passed the outhouse covered with the dead morning-glory vine Cora had planted after their marriage, the chicken coop where the old rooster herded his six hens out of the way, the mint bed beside the pump in the shade of the house. Jill scampered out of the shadow, barking and wriggling and looking up at him with eyes that were like clear glass marbles.

"Down, Jill!" he said sternly, and then the back door banged open against its stop and V ran out.

"Did you bring me anything?" she cried. She was wearing levis that were too tight and one of his old white shirts, the sleeves turned up on her brown arms. Her face was plump and clear and she wore her blonde hair in two fat pigtails that danced when she tossed her head and tried to pull the package from under his arm. He stopped to let her take it and Juan stepped around them and went up the back steps into the kitchen.

"What is it, Papa?" V said, but he put his hand on her arm when she started to tear the paper.

"Not here," he said. He watched her run up the steps. She was growing up; she was shaped like a woman now, and she was almost as tall as he.

In the kitchen Mary had dinner on the stove and Juan was standing on a chair stacking cans in the cupboard. Baird walked past them and into V's room. She had the package open and the paper had fallen to the floor. She looked up at him and smiled.

"It's a nice one, Papa. Do you want me to put it on?"

"Yes," he said. "You'd better start wearing it all the time."

She unbuttoned the two top buttons of the shirt and stripped it off over her head. Her flesh was white above the sunburn of her arms and below that of her throat, and her breasts were surprisingly full, the nipples tiny and pink. For the first time it embarrassed him to see her like this. It seemed wrong. His tongue thickened in his mouth and he looked away as she slipped her arms into the straps of the brassiere and turned around, holding the two ends in her hand.

"Would you fasten it, please?"

He snapped the ends together, trying not to touch her back with his awkward fingers. He remembered the day four years ago when he had driven her to Manteca so that Cora's sister, V's Aunt Elizabeth, could tell her the things she ought to know and the things that would be happening to her soon, and the awful, silent, embarrassment of the trip home again, when he had known what V must be thinking, and she must, in turn, have known that he knew. Now she was looking at herself in the mirror, full front, and then in profile, holding her shoulders back and thrusting her chest out.

"I'm awfully big," she said.

"Does it fit all right?"

"Yes," she said. "It kind of binds a little but I guess it's all right."

Her head was cocked to one side, her lips pursed. He cleared his throat and tried to say lightly, "You're growing up, V."

She giggled and looked at him shyly, covering her breasts with her hands. "Did it embarrass you to buy it, Papa?"

He shook his head. He felt strangely angry. He wished he knew how to talk to her. He never knew what to say. She put her shirt back on and pushed the tails down into the top of her levis. "Can I go over to see Mr. Denton?" she asked.

"I don't guess he's home. I saw him in town just a little ago."

"He said he'd be home."

"Did you get all your chores finished?"

"Oh, I finished mending the stockings this morning, and there's nothing more to do in the kitchen and I won't be very long. Mr. Denton promised to let me ride Romer."

"All right," he said. "Don't be late for supper, honey."

"I won't. Thanks, Papa." She kissed him on the forehead and ran out. He watched her go, jealously; he watched her through the window as she ran down through the orchard in the sun. It seemed such a short time ago that she had been a little girl, and not much before that a baby, and he and Cora had taken her to Cora's church in Bakersfield to be baptized. Vassilia Caroline Baird; she had cried when the water touched her. Today he had had to buy her one of those things and it would probably not be long before she married and went away somewhere and he would be more completely alone than after Cora had died.

When September came V had to exchange her levis and work shirt for black skirt, white blouse and black neckerchief, and return to the Priory, where she boarded five days a week. But on the weekends she was often restricted and could not come home; she did not do well in her studies. He missed her desperately during the school year. It was lonely on the ranch without her, but even when she was home for the weekend he did not see much more of her; she was always gone, out with Jill the dog, or over at Roger Denton's.

Denton had eighty acres of land which he had put into potatoes some years before, and he had prospered raising them, and raising horses. He had a big stone house, a large stable and ring, horses for V to ride, three collie dogs and often a new litter of puppies. Denton was a bachelor almost as old as Baird, but from the few times he had spoken to Denton, Baird knew him to be an educated man. He had money, a new car every year, and Baird realized bitterly that there was nothing on his own little ranch to entertain V, or even that V liked or felt attached to, and there were many things at Denton's.

3

The next summer when school was out V came home on the Greyhound Bus. Baird picked her up at the highway in the truck. He left her in her room to unpack and went into the kitchen to tell Mary to bring some iced tea out to the front porch, but then, through the kitchen window, he saw V come out on the drive and set off through the orchard toward Denton's.

He felt sick, knowing she had slipped out the front way to avoid seeing him. He hurried to the porch and called her back, and when she came slowly up the steps he motioned her into a chair. She had changed her clothes. The legs of her levis were rolled up on her ankles. She didn't speak or even look at him, and hurt and angry, he wondered why.

He said, "Don't ever go off without telling me, like that."

She bit her lip. She was sitting in the rocker and she rocked back, bracing the tips of her toes on the floor and looking down at her hands. Mary came out on the porch with two glasses of tea.

"Oh, Mary," V said, "please could I have some mint in mine?"

Mary nodded. She was huge in a red-and-white-checked Mother Hubbard, and her laceless men's shoes squeaked softly as she went back into the house.

"How were your grades this time?" Baird asked.

V slumped down in the rocker and hung one leg over the arm. She would not meet his eyes, silently stirring the ice in her glass with a forefinger. When Mary returned with the sprig of mint, she crumpled it and dropped it into her glass, again stirring her finger in the tea and staring down at it. Baird remembered that Cora had always liked mint in her iced tea—and suddenly, in his mind's eyes, he saw her here. He saw her sitting on the front porch with Mr. Burgess, who had been principal of the Tyler Union Elementary School when she had taught there; he saw Cora and Mr. Burgess sitting on the front porch over iced tea as he and V were sitting now, discussing poetry and books, Mr. Burgess talking in his eastern voice about Shakespeare and Keats and Shelley, with his red mouth like a slash in his long white face, his slender white hands making continual lifting, circling motions; Cora watching him with her head tilted to one side like a bird, her knees and feet held together as she rocked, her dark eyes big and happy with interest. And he saw himself sitting with them, wearing his ignorance and inferiority as Juan wore his dark skin, ashamed to remain with them because he was so completely and irrevocably outside their conversation, restrained from leaving by the suspicion and jealousy that had sickened him.

He shook his head savagely. "V!" he said.

"Yes, Papa?"

"I asked you about your grades. Did you fail Algebra?"

She shook her head without looking up. "D."

"What else did you get?"

"I got a B in English." He looked at her steadily and she fidgeted in the chair and finally said, "I got a B in Ancient History, a C in Sacred Studies, and a D in Latin."

"I didn't know you were doing so poorly in Latin."

"I failed the final. We had to conjugate a whole lot of verbs nobody knew and a lot of girls cheated, but I didn't." She looked up at him defiantly.

"Take the ice out of your mouth when you talk," he said. "I'm glad you didn't cheat but that's no excuse for getting such a low grade." He had tried to explain to her that he had spent the money necessary to send her to the Priory instead of to the public high school so that she would have a good education, as her mother had had; so that she might be able to teach school if she ever had to go to work, instead of having to get a job in a packing plant, or becoming a waitress. He watched her spit the ice back into her glass. The rocker squeaked as she leaned forward to place the glass on the floor. She said in a low voice, "I'm sorry I'm such a disappointment to you, Papa."

"V…" he began, but then he said instead, "You could work harder. There's no reason why you shouldn't get better grades if you'd work harder."

"I do work hard!" He saw that her eyes were wet and hurt. "I guess I'm just stupid," she said.

"Don't talk like that, honey. You know you're not stupid."

"Well, I guess I am. I guess I'm no good. I don't like school. Maybe I ought to quit going."

"You finish school!" he said angrily. "You study harder. There's no reason why you can't get better grades."

She got to her feet and turned away from him. "I'm going over and see Mr. Denton," she announced.

He looked at her silently, helplessly, as she stood with her back to him, waiting for him to tell her to go, or to send her to her room. He knew he should punish her for this rudeness. But it was her first day home from school and he said, "Don't be late for supper, honey." It did not sound the way he had wanted it to, and she walked down the steps without glancing back. He wondered if she were crying.

He sat on the porch for a long time, sipping his iced tea and looking out on the dusty orchard and the rutted dusty road, feeling sorry and helpless and inadequate and, at the same time, angry. He knew she didn't like the Priory, but he couldn't let her leave school, and he knew the discipline at the Priory was good for her.

It wasn't just that the public high school was coeducational; he told himself he was not afraid of that. He wanted her to marry and be happy. But there was a wild bunch at the high school; girls who wore short skirts and tight sweaters and too much lip rouge, riding around in open automobiles with young men who drove too fast, who smoked and probably drank and he didn't know what else. He had had to run a couple out of his orchard once, youngsters in a convertible coupe who were lolling all over each other. He was pretty sure they had been drinking; when they had driven away the boy had shouted back, calling him an old hick, the girl laughing and leaning against his shoulder and looking back and waving. The youngsters were wild nowadays—it was because of the depression, the paper said—and the Priory was the place for V.

V was late for dinner and he went out on the porch to wait for her. The sun gone behind the coast range, the land was silent and beautiful in the fading day, the alfalfa in the bottom creamy green, streaking and darkening in long finger strips with the warm wind that rustled through the orchard. Tule fog was forming low along the valley floor.

Above the rustling of the trees he heard the sound of hoofs, and then he saw the horse. V was crouched forward on its bare back, her hair streaming out behind her, the copper-colored gelding smoothly running up the slope from the bottom. She pulled to a stop on the drive and, holding the reins in her hand, led the horse up to the porch. The face she raised to Baird was flushed and excited.

"Papa, meet Tony," she said.

"You're late for dinner."

Tony's small fox ears flicked upright and he stamped a foot. Still smiling, V licked her lips and started to speak, but Baird said, "Supper's on the table. Now take him home and get back here quick as you can. I don't want you out after dark."

She didn't move.

"V!" he said. "Did you hear me?"

"Tony's my horse."

"What do you mean?"

"Mr. Denton gave him to me." She was smiling again. "Oh, Papa, isn't he beautiful?" She pressed her face against Tony's muzzle, her arm encircling his neck. Baird put his hands on the porch rail and leaned forward, looking down into the horse's short, dark intelligent face. It was the finest quarter-horse he had ever seen, with heavily muscled hindquarters and a deep chest heaving slightly from the run up the hill.

"You'd better take him back," he said tiredly.

"Oh, no! He gave him to me!"

"You'd…"

"Oh, please," V cried softly. "Oh, please, please, Papa!"

"I'll buy you a horse if I can. We can't afford anything like that."

V buried her face in the copper neck. "Oh, please," she whispered. "He's so beautiful. I want something to be mine." Baird didn't speak, licking the dryness from his lips. Then he heard her whisper, "He's the only beautiful thing I ever had," and he almost cried out with pain. He wanted to tell her that he himself had never had anything beautiful; except the land, which was beautiful only at this time of day, and only then if he could forget what it had taken out of him; except Cora, who had died before he had ever known her and of whom he had been jealous and suspicious until the end and even after it; except her, V, who somehow did not belong to him.

But he could not tell her, and he said, "You'd better take him back," and turned and went inside. Mary was filling the glasses with milk from the dented tin pitcher. She looked up sullenly as he came in. "Put some supper in the oven for her," he said, and outside he heard the clop of hoofs, slow at first, then hastening, and fading to silence at a gallop.

It was almost an hour before V returned. She went into her room through the kitchen and through her closed door he could hear her crying. He cursed Denton. He couldn't accept a favor like that, and he couldn't afford to buy Tony. Finally he went to sit on the porch in the darkness, where he couldn't hear her crying.

The next morning he was helping Juan clear out one of the irrigation ditches when Denton drove up from the highway in his new Ford pick-up truck. Baird put down his shovel and wiped his mud-caked hands on his trouser legs before they shook hands. Denton was a short, spare man with bushy, iron-gray hair and eyebrows and a long neck. He wore a chamois jacket and tan breeches, and there was a cigarette in a yellow holder between his teeth. Baird had disliked him from the first time they had met, ten years ago now, when Denton had first bought his ranch. He had seen Denton, with one look at Baird's clothes, ranch buildings and house, decide Baird didn't amount to much. That first day Denton had talked about his heart trouble, his ranch and the peach orchards near Marysville he had sold to buy it, and about why he had never married. But since he and V had become friends, Denton had dropped his superior manner and seemed strangely anxious that Baird should like him. Baird always had the feeling that Denton had something important to say to him, but could never get around to it.

"Weather's been fine," Baird said.

"Hasn't it? Though I could do with a little less sun." Denton spoke with a soft, slow, slurring sound, the esses leaking out the corners of his mouth. There was a silence; Baird looked down at Denton's gleaming riding boots.

"About that horse," Denton said.

"Yes."

"I'd like her to have him. I had him broken for the kid, Baird. He's gentle."

"It's not that."

Denton was silent. He took the holder from his mouth and tapped the cigarette with a yellow-stained forefinger.

"I can't afford a horse like that," Baird said. "I wish you'd talked to me first, because…"

"You don't need to buy him."

"Well, I couldn't let you do that."

"I don't know why not. Oh, I know how you feel, but… Well, she loves that pony and I'd like to give him to her."

Baird shook his head. "That horse is worth a lot of money. I can't let you do me a favor like that." He shook his head again. But maybe the horse would serve to keep V at home, he thought. He pictured her if he told her he had changed his mind and she could have Tony. He took off his hat and smoothed his hair back.

"I'm not doing you a favor, man," Denton said. "It's for her. Why, hell, I'm a lonely old bachelor; it gives me a lift having the kid playing around my place." He stopped and tapped the cigarette again. They both watched the ashes drift down. "I'd really like to do it for her," Denton said.

"Well, maybe I could pay you for him after a while. I don't like to be in debt to anybody."

"You're not in debt to me!" Denton protested. "And if you'll let me I'll hustle a couple of men over here to put up a corral."

"No," Baird said. "Don't do that. Juan and me…Juan can rig one up."

He got the tin of Copenhagen from his shirt pocket and bit off a corner of tobacco. "That's a fine-looking horse," he said. Looking up, he saw that there were spots of color on Denton's cheeks, and he was dabbing at his forehead with a handkerchief. His mouth was half-open, as though he were going to speak.

But he closed it again and looked away. Finally he nodded and said, "Out of one of my mares by Copper McCloud. The kid'll take good care of him."

Baird said awkwardly, "Well, I sure want to thank you. V'll be happy, I know."

"She's a great kid. The best there is. She deserves that pony."

"I wish I could do more for her," Baird said, as they walked to the pick-up and shook hands. Denton's eyes suddenly jerked up to his, almost pleadingly.

"Baird…" he began.

Baird looked at him and after a moment Denton smiled foolishly. His cheeks were red. "I wish you'd let me build that corral," he said.

"No," Baird said. "Thanks," and Denton nodded and got quickly into the pick-up. Baird watched him, puzzled, as Denton backed down the hill. He stood for a moment watching the bend in the road where the pick-up had disappeared, then he walked slowly up to the house to tell V.

4

The corral went up quickly. They built it out next to the shed and whitewashed it, set boulders around it and whitewashed them. At the juncture of the shed and the corral they built the stall and V nailed a horseshoe over the door and painted TONY beneath it with blue enamel. She was happy and it made him happy to see her so. He knew Juan and Mary felt it as well. The house and the dingy, sunbaked little ranch buildings seemed more alive.

But the horse did not keep V at home, as he had hoped. She spent all her time with Tony now, riding him, or currying and petting him, and she was long hours over at Denton's. She was learning to jump and teaching Tony tricks, riding in Denton's ring on one of Denton's English saddles. Right after breakfast she would be gone, usually not to return until lunch time, and then she would be gone again until supper. And one long, summer evening she went out after supper and returned at dark, laden with packages. Baird heard her snap the lock when she went into her room.

He was sitting in the platform rocker by the window, reading the paper in the funnel of light from the floor lamp. He didn't look up when he heard her come out but after a moment she turned on the ceiling light and called softly, "Papa!"

He put down the paper. He gasped when he saw her.

She was smiling, turning slowly around, standing directly beneath the dim, dangling light bulb. She had on a jacket and short skirt of white buckskin trimmed with gold, and tasseled white Hessian half-boots. She carried a huge white Stetson in her hand.

He stared at her legs. Bare from thigh to calf, ivory, full-fleshed, they were woman's legs. He was shocked, and suddenly frightened.

"How do you like me?" she asked in a little voice.

He licked his lips. "What have you got on?"

Again she turned around self-consciously, her free hand on her hip, one leg slightly bent. Her hair, brushed until it shone, hung down her back in two blonde braids.

"Isn't it beautiful?" she cried suddenly, and she ran and knelt beside his chair. "It's my costume for Frontier Day." Her hand clutched his arm and he could feel its warmth through his shirtsleeve; her eyes shone. "Oh, Papa, I'm going to ride Tony in the Parade!"

"Not in that!"

"Yes, I am."

He cleared his throat. "Not in that, you're not!"

"But Papa, why not?"

"You know why not." He took off his glasses, folded them nervously and laid them on the window sill. V's face had paled, but she still smiled, the smile set and meaningless.

"Did he buy that for you?"

She nodded. Her eyes searched his hopefully.

"He ought to know better than that. You're not going to put on a show for those people down in Bakersfield." He felt her hand leave his arm. "You look indecent," he said.

V slowly got to her feet, looking down at her legs. There were goose pimples on them and she was shivering, and when she put the hat on he saw why she had not worn it before. It was too large. The brim slid down almost to her eyes, and when her eyes met his, he looked away.

"Go put your clothes on," he told her harshly. "Take that outfit back tomorrow."

She turned away. The boots clumped on the linoleum as she walked to her room. He saw her looking at herself in the mirror and she took off the Stetson hat before she closed the door.

He put his glasses back on, shook out the newspaper and tried to go back to his reading, but he could not concentrate. The lines of type were wavy and jumbled together.

He put the paper down. He wished he had not spoken so harshly. She couldn't be expected to know such a costume was improper. He supposed he was always too harsh with her, but that was his way and he couldn't change it. Yet he had hurt V, and that hurt him, and his foot caught in something and he looked down. It was a tear in the rag rug that covered the worn place beneath the rocker.

He could remember when V's mother had made that rug, and now it was worn out. His throat ached with shame as he remembered Cora, who had been dead twelve years now; a tall, thin schoolteacher with beautiful dark eyes and hair and a consumptive chest. He had met her during the war; somehow he had known that if he asked her to marry him she would accept, and he had never known why. But he had suspected many reasons why she should have married him; he had invented cruel, calculating, insidious reasons, and then for seven years he had been tortured and wrung by emotions he had not known existed and which now he looked back upon as some terrible, secret, shameful disease.

When he thought about it he could almost recapture the ache of the jealousy, so intense had it been; his suspicion of Mr. Burgess, of young John Schuford, who had come to visit with Cora sometimes, of still others whose existence he knew he only imagined. He knew them now as only fantasies of his mind, but he could still feel the torturing emotions that had shaken him. And after each of his outbursts at Cora, when his rage had died, he had had a moment of clarity in which he realized that his imagination had deceived him, only to be enraged again with the surety that he was driving Cora to the very thing of which he had accused her.

He could recapture the ache of jealousy because now he felt it again. It hurt him that he and V could not be friends the way she and Denton were but he could not blame V. It was a lonely, dull life for her with no one her own age within miles; only a horse and a dog for playmates, and both of them somehow unnatural because they had been deprived of the right to reproduce; an old man for her only friend, and a father who was still older and who was harsh and worked out.

He supposed he should go in and talk to her, but what was there to say? He couldn't let her ride in the Frontier Day Parade in that outfit. It *was* indecent. He couldn't have those Bakersfield people ogling his daughter, thinking her a bad girl. It was Denton's fault, and anger at Denton welled up in him and left him shaking. He pushed the paper from his lap, rose and strode across to V's door. He knocked. "V?" he called, and he turned the knob and entered.

She was sitting on the edge of her bed, her elbows on her knees, hands supporting her chin, staring at the blank wall opposite her. She had taken off the boots; one of them lay flat on the floor and the other stood upright, the top bent limply to one side.

"Put the things back in the boxes, honey," he said, and he tried to say it gently. "I'll take them back for you."

She jumped to her feet. "Papa, you're not..."

"Hurry, honey," he said. Boxes and brown wrapping paper and tissue paper were scattered across the table. He picked up the boots and put them in one of the boxes.

"Papa, you're not going over there and be mad or anything…
Papa, listen, please…"

"No," he said. "I'm just going to take them back." He packed
tissue paper in around the boots and put the cover on the box.
V took off the jacket and handed it to him, unzipped the skirt
and let it fall in a circle around her feet then picked it up and
handed it to him, looking at him with round, frightened eyes.
He started for the door carrying the two boxes. At the door he
turned. V was holding out a huge hatbox to him. He could see
the print of her teeth on her lower lip.

He went out to the shed, stacked the boxes carefully on the
front seat of the truck and cranked the motor to life. The truck
lights jumped and shivered weirdly over the outbuildings and
the house and the trees as he guided the truck out the drive
and down the hill to the highway. On the highway he took a
deep breath, clinging to the wooden steering wheel with both
hands.

A single electric lamp beneath a metal reflector illuminated
the stone front of Denton's house and a stocky Japanese, wearing
a white singlet and a long white apron, came to the door. Behind
him was a foyer with a concrete floor, and on the wall opposite
the door hung a Navajo blanket. "What you want?" the Japanese
asked, studying Baird expressionlessly.

"Tell Mr. Denton I'd like to see him," he said, and then he
saw Denton standing in the hall behind the Japanese, wearing a
dressing gown and a green eyeshade.

"Good evening," Denton said. "Come in, won't you?" He
darted a look at the boxes, then smiled nervously at Baird. "Come
in, come in," he said.

Baird handed the boxes to the Japanese and followed Denton
down the strip of fiber matting that covered the concrete in the
hall. Denton turned into a small office. In it were an enormous

roll-top desk, two leather chairs, and a glass case in which two rifles and two shotguns stood upright. A ledger lay open on the desk, and beside it was a decanter and a glass containing an inch of yellow liquor.

"Sit down, won't you?" Denton said. He was still smiling, and when Baird had seated himself, he said, "Can I give you a drink?"

Baird shook his head. As he looked around the office he was angrily aware of his dusty boots, the worn cuffs of his trousers, V's imperfect mending of the tear in his shirt sleeve. He said, "I brought back that outfit you gave V."

"I see," Denton said. He had taken off his eyeshade and now he closed the ledger and pushed it to one side. He swallowed the remainder of the liquor, and when he lowered the glass his right eye was blinking nervously. Surprised, Baird realized that he was frightened.

"She's not going to put on a leg show for those people down in Bakersfield," he said.

"I see," Denton repeated. "I seem to be in the wrong. I'm sorry." His smile was fixed, his eyes anxious. The eyeshade had flattened the hair at his temples, but above it sprouted loosely, like a topknot. Baird felt mollified, and then, suddenly embarrassed; he was sorry he had come. He didn't speak, watching Denton pour more liquor into his glass. "I suppose I stepped out of line," Denton said, almost to himself. "I should have thought…I didn't know you would object."

"Well, that doesn't matter," Baird said. "But you see…" He paused and took a deep breath. "I think V's spending too much time over here. It's not right. But I don't want to…"

"Yes, yes," Denton said. "I understand. You want me to discourage her from coming here so often." He nodded and raised the glass to his lips and when he looked at Baird once more one side of his mouth was still smiling but the other was not. "I'm sorry, but I can't do that," and then he was not smiling at all when he said, "You see I love her."

Baird gasped. His hands tightened on the arms of the chair, and weakly he tried to raise himself. Denton seemed to whirl in front of his eyes. "Like a daughter," Baird heard him say.

He subsided. The leather arms of the chair felt cold to his bare wrists, and he was afraid now. He didn't know what to say, what to do.

"Wait!" Denton said, and he passed his hand in front of his face as though he were brushing away a spider web. "Wait," he said. "I'm afraid I put that badly. But I may as well tell you this now—I've been thinking about it for a long time." His face was drained of color and the eyelid twitched violently. Baird wondered if the man were drunk.

"You must see I'm very lonely here," Denton said, "and that girl's the only thing that…Here, I'll tell you what I'd like to do. She's what? Just seventeen now? Next year she'll finish high school. I want to send her to college. To the University at Berkeley, or to Fresno. Or San Jose. For a year or two, or more, it doesn't matter. But she'll be in her twenties then. And of course there will be no mention of this till then…."

The voice sank, the slurred words came slower, but Baird could not concentrate on what the other said. He felt his mouth gape open; his lips felt dry as he stared at Denton, who was hunched over the desk, hands clasped, lips moving. And then he caught the words, "She won't have to marry me, of course. There'll be no compulsion of any kind. But…"

"You're crazy!" he shouted, half-rising again. "You're crazy! She's too young." Denton must be drunk. "You're too old!" he cried.

"Wait, now," Denton said, lifting his hand in a jerky gesture.

The half-smile returned to his lips. "I thought of asking you if I could adopt…But of course you'd never permit that. But I want her company very much, you see, and I'd like her to have an education. She might feel better about this if she had. And of course I'd like her to feel she owed me something. Wrong of me, I guess. But you see, I'm lonely, very lonely, and I've had one bad heart attack already. The next one, or the one after that…" He snapped his fingers savagely, grimacing, and with the gesture he seemed to recover his composure.

"She'll be company for me," he continued, more reasonably. "A kind of nurse, and when I go she'll have everything. Do you see now? I'm afraid I haven't explained this very well."

Baird stared at him, shivering, his shirt twitching over his chest, his hands clenched until the knuckles seemed about to pierce the skin. He couldn't think. He looked around the office with quick jerks of his head. His thoughts shamed and revolted him. In his mind he had seen V as he, her father, should not see her; she was printed there as Denton, her lover, might see her. And then it was wrong that Denton see her so, for Denton must somehow see her with his eyes, and he was seeing her with Denton's. It was wrong, unnatural, evil, and he tried to shake the sight from his head as wildly he looked back at Denton.

Denton's head was lowered, his lips pursed, and he was gazing at Baird from under his heavy brows. All the confused nervousness seemed to have left him. "I'm a well-to-do man," he said. "I imagine you know that."

Yes, Baird thought, and he thought of Cora, thinking that Cora would be happy to have V be comfortable, well-off, married to an educated man, but instead he saw Cora walking with young John Schuford, just back from Germany. He had seen them walking in the orchard, and he had followed so as to come upon them when they were not expecting him. But they had

not even been surprised to see him. He remembered the things
he had said that night to Cora; suddenly he realized the complete hell he had made for her.

He squeezed his eyes painfully shut and shook his head
again, trying to think: *Denton has money. He can give V so
much. If V marries this man and comes to live on this ranch I
can see her often—better than having her marry and go away
somewhere.* But she was so young, and Denton was almost as
old as he.

"You're too old," he said hoarsely. "You're too old for her."

Denton didn't move. There was no expression on his face.
He didn't speak.

"Have you said anything to—her?"

Denton shook his head. Finally, he said, "I don't know if she
would consider it. Now, as you say, she's too young. I thought
after some college…In a few years…She'd have matured then,
you see." He leaned forward and looked at Baird keenly. "I can
give her a lot. I have no relatives. There's no one else I care for
at all. If she married me she'd be a companion and nurse, she'd
be near you, and when I go she'll be able to do almost anything
she wants to."

"I don't know," Baird said. "I don't know what to say." He
had stopped trembling and he felt as though unsolvable problems were going to be solved for him. But he said, "Well, it'll
have to be up to her. But now she's too young."

Denton nodded. "I'm not going to mention it to her. Maybe
next year when she graduates from high school you'd better
sound her out about going to college. She may not want to. If
she doesn't, I thought I'd ask her to marry me then."

"Yes," Baird said slowly. "I suppose that would be the way. I
don't know. I'll have to think about it a little. We can talk about
it again."

"It sounds a little feudal, I know. I suppose I'm very selfish, but I know she likes me."

"Yes," Baird said. "I think she does." He watched Denton's hand shake as he fitted another cigarette into his holder. Suddenly Baird felt superior to him; this man, educated, well-to-do, almost as old as he was, and to whom he had always thought himself inferior, wished to court his daughter. He almost laughed aloud. He got to his feet, and Denton rose with him, smiling.

They shook hands and Baird squared his shoulders as he marched down the hall. The three boxes were stacked beside the door. As he cranked the truck and got behind the throbbing steering wheel, he saw Denton in the lighted doorway of the stone house, one hand clutching the edge of the door. He looked small and forlorn.

5

In the fall when V returned to the Priory she was permitted to come home every weekend. Evidently she was studying harder, and Baird realized it was because she wanted to be with Tony. "I want something to be mine," she had said, and he would remember her saying it always. Tony belonged to her and she loved him because he was hers.

Her affection for Tony disturbed him, and he wondered again if it would be right for her to marry Denton. But there was no one else for her, no way for V to meet anyone but the pimply faced high school boys he had seen. He could not bear to see her waste her life with one of these, for what could they offer her to compare with what Denton had to offer?

He had forbidden himself to worry about how she would react when he spoke to her about college, or, if she rejected that, what she would do when Denton asked her to marry him. But as her graduation day approached he lay awake in bed at night, wondering; watching her gallop through the orchard on the shining copper horse, he wished he knew what was right and what would be best for her.

In the spring he had other problems. He had dug into his precious savings to buy an adjoining sixteen acres of bottom land from one of Mark Schuford's sons. He was not sure he could afford it, but it had been a forced sale and a good buy.

There had been a grove on the land. The trees had been cut down long ago, but the stumps remained, and would have to be bulldozed out. He made arrangements to borrow Denton's little D-4 tractor and bulldozer blade. Denton offered also to lend him a man to run it, but Baird refused, and the next day he went into Bakersfield to see about hiring an operator. The state was building a new highway south of Bakersfield; he had seen them grading and paving, and it was likely he would find some one there who knew of a cat skinner who wanted a job.

From the highway he could see the clouds of dust that marked the trails of the earth-moving equipment, and there was an intense, overlying roar of Diesel engines, loud and popping as they strained, smooth and catarrhal when idling. He turned off the highway and onto a rutted road, jolting and slithering through the thick dust. He had to pull to one side as a huge dump truck pounded past him, black-stained and heaped with black, steaming asphalt.

He passed a water truck and two motor graders working up on a levee, and then beside the road a bulldozer and a pick-up truck were drawn up together. Two men were bent over the bed of the pick-up, in which engine parts were spread. Baird pulled off the road behind them and got out. A cloud of dust caught up and settled over him, and he wiped his sweating, dusty face on the sleeve of his shirt. The cat skinner and the mechanic nodded to him. The cat skinner wore a sweat-soaked singlet and a striped cap, and his face and arms were burned black. The mechanic, in stiff, greasy overalls, squatted and hunted through his tool chest. He brought out a socket wrench and bent over the bed of the pick-up once more. Baird spat a mouthful of tobacco juice. "You run this machine?" he said to the operator.

The other grinned and nodded. He didn't look much over twenty—a snub-nosed boy with a streak of grease on his sweating forehead. "When it goes," he said. "It's got a bellyache, right now."

"I'm looking for one of you fellows wants to work for a couple weeks."

"What kind of work?"

"Bulldozing. Knocking up stumps."

"Gee, I don't know…Hey, Willie, you know anybody'd want a job dozing stumps?"

"How about Jack?" the mechanic said, without looking up.

"Oh, yeah. Hey, you know where this guy could get hold of him?"

The mechanic grunted as he broke a nut loose with the wrench. "He's got to go through your union anyway, don't he?"

"Oh, yeah. Listen, Mister, you go on down to the union hall or call up or something. Tell them what you got and say you want Jack Ward."

"It ought to be a nice change for him," the mechanic said. "Knocking up stumps." The cat skinner laughed.

"Jack Ward," Baird repeated. It was an easy name to re-member. "Well, thank you," he said.

"Okay. He's a good skinner and I don't think he's working right now. You ask for Jack."

"Thanks," Baird said as he moved away. When he had turned the truck around he drove back to Bakersfield and left a call at the union hall for a bulldozer operator for the next morning at eight o'clock. He drew a map of how to get to his ranch on the back of the job slip, and had a notation made that he would like, if he was available, Jack Ward.

6

During the night it rained heavily and in the morning a thin drizzle still persisted. At eight o'clock Baird went out to stand on the brow of the hill above the new bottom land to wait for the cat skinner to show up.

The edges of his slicker were cold and wet on his wrists and around his neck, and the slicker crackled as he walked up and down. Against his will he was worrying about V; she would be coming home from school at the end of the week, and he would have to speak to her then about college.

He had told Denton that if she did not want to go to college, to wait until the end of summer to ask her to marry him. The end of summer—September…He walked slowly up and down. The rain had almost stopped. Below him the bottom was gray and liquid and he could see the dead stumps clinging tenaciously to the land, here and there a lonely green shoot spearing up from the dark wood.

He heard the roar of an automobile mounting the hill, and then a topless yellow roadster shot around the corner of the house and pulled to a stop beside him. Jill ran out of the shed, barking furiously. The cat skinner opened the door and heaved himself out; a tall, thick-shouldered youth with black hair plastered down over his head. His dungarees were soaked dark.

"Damn wet," he said, wiping his face on the sleeve of his jacket.

"You were supposed to be here at eight."

"Sorry." He looked at Baird boldly. "Car conked in the rain."

"You can put your machine in the shed," Baird said. "This ought to let up after a little."

"It's not going to get any wetter'n it is," the operator said. He had a broad face set with eyes that slanted curiously upward, and he stood with his legs braced wide apart and his arms held out from his sides. Grimacing, he shook his arms and body and pulled at his jacket where the wet cloth stuck to his chest. He was just at the age, Baird saw, where a boy becomes a man, and he was a big man. Suddenly Baird distrusted him.

"Those the stumps?"

"Yes. There's about ten acres of them."

"That the cat? What is it, for Christ's sake, a D-4?"

"Don't you think it'll do the job?"

"Oh, sure. But that's little boy's work." The operator turned and grinned at him. It was an honest grin, and Baird's distrust faded.

"I think we'll have to shoot some," he said. "Leave those till last, unless they get in your way. I'll get some powder tomorrow."

The operator nodded and gazed down at the stumps, running his fingers through his wet hair. "Got a chain?"

"There's one in the shed. There's a new cable in the shed, too. You'll have to string it; the one on the cat's broke. You Jack Ward?"

"Yeah." He grinned again, showing wide white teeth, and extended a wet hand to Baird. "Baird, it said on the job slip."

"I'll expect you to work hard, Ward. You can start up on my time, but shut down on your own. Eight to twelve and one to six."

"Fair enough," Ward said. Baird watched him saunter off toward the bulldozer, and then went to tell Juan to go and help him with the cable.

Baird unobtrusively watched Ward for a few days. He told himself he was doing this to make sure Ward worked faithfully from eight to six, but he knew it was also because he loved to watch the cat skinner work. He was good at his job. He had the operation of pulling the stumps down to a minimum of time and effort; first he hit a stump with the blade raised, to tip it and break the roots, and then on the second pass he would pry it loose by hooking the blade under the lifted edge, raising the blade and easing the cat forward at the same time, until the stump toppled free. On hot days he worked part of the time with his shirt off, and the muscles rippled on his broad flat back, which was burned a dark red.

He found himself watching the cat skinner whenever he could get away from his own work; watching him from the shade of the shed, or going down to help him dynamite a stubborn stump, talking to him when there was no need. But there was something strong that drew him to Ward. He liked to watch him not only when he was running the cat, but when he sat against a stump to eat his lunch, or sauntered up the hill to the pump to fill his water bag, or walked more slowly to the car at night after he had shut down the tractor, carrying his lunch pail and slapping his cap against his thigh and whistling cheerfully. He recognized Ward as being of his own particular class and kind, but somehow lifted beyond it by a sense of power over blind mechanical power immensely greater than Ward himself. It was casual and taken for granted, that feeling of thousands of hours of dust and sweat and deafening noise, but in those hours an accumulated sureness and capability he himself could never possess. But he could feel it vicariously, and he came to watch Ward with silent absorption, whenever he could take the time.

V came home that weekend. Baird put on his black suit and polished his boots and drove in to the graduation exercises, and afterward brought her home. When he had carried her suitcases in from the truck they sat on her bed and looked at the diploma together. It was a black leather folder lined with red satin, and in the folder was an oblong of heavy paper that bore her name, a beribboned gold seal and three signatures. When he handed it back she stood it proudly on the dresser next to the framed picture Denton had taken of her on Tony. Suddenly she cried, "Through! Through! Through!" and pulled the black neckerchief from around her neck and hurled it into the closet.

Baird pointed to the two boxes he had put on her bed that morning. In them were gabardine riding pants and a pair of fancy Texas boots—her graduation presents. He saw her flush as she pulled the boots out of the tissue paper. Quickly she kicked off her school shoes and pulled the boots on over her black cotton stockings.

"Oh, they're pretty," she whispered, tracing a finger over the tooled designs in the leather. "Butterflies." She looked up at him, smiling with her lips pressed together. "Thank you, Papa!"

"If they don't fit I can take them back, honey."

"They fit fine. They're beautiful. They're just what I always wanted." She had cut her hair to shoulder length and the blonde hair parted cleanly up the back of her head as she leaned forward, inspecting the boots. He realized with a start that she was an attractive girl. She had her mother's good features, her mother's mouth and eyes, hair blonder than his had been, and the rather short, thick, Baird nose. There were spots of color on her cheeks as, smiling, she ran her hands over the boots.

"Did you get better grades this term, honey?"

"Better. Three Bs and a C." She took the pants from their box and brushed the material against her cheek. "I got a D in geometry, though."

"That's too bad."

"I'm sorry, Papa."

"I think you sat in class and dreamed you were out riding Tony."

Silently V rose and held the riding pants up to her waist, looking down at them with her lips pursed. Baird said, "Well, I don't guess you'll ever have much use for geometry, anyway. You can always ride Tony."

He saw her cheeks redden. She glanced at him out of the corners of her eyes and the corner of her mouth jerked up. She looked down again at the pants she was holding to her waist. "They're awfully nice," she said. "Thanks, Papa." And when she looked up at him he saw that she was crying.

He wondered why. Then he knew; the outfit he had bought her didn't compare with the one Denton had tried to give her. He felt the smile that had been warm inside him freeze as she put the pants on the bed and stooped to open her suitcases. He would speak to her about college now. He had to tell her Denton wanted to send her to college. He would do it at supper. Abruptly he got up and went to sit on the porch.

At the supper table he tucked his napkin into his belt and sipped his milk, waiting for V. She had been riding Tony and she was in her room combing her hair. When she came out her hair was tied back with a blue ribbon; she was wearing her riding pants and boots, and the chocolate-colored cowboy shirt he had given her for her birthday.

When he had finished eating he crossed his knife and fork on his plate and pushed the plate away. V was cutting open the center of her tamale. "Glad to be through school, honey?" he asked.

She smiled and nodded. He watched her take an olive pit from her mouth and put it back on her plate. He cleared his throat.

"Well," he said. "What do you think you'll do now?"

Her eyes grew round and serious and she held her fork poised over her plate, looking up at him. He said quickly, "Would you like to go to college, V?"

"We can't afford it, Papa."

"Well…" he said, and stopped, and then he sighed and said, "See here; Mr. Denton's offered to pay your way through college. If you want to go." He waited for her to speak, and when she did not, said in a lower voice, "If you want to go."

"Oh," V said.

"You could go up to Berkeley. Or to Fresno, if you wanted to come home weekends."

"I don't know," V said. She picked at the food on her plate. Baird could feel his heart beating. He put his hand across the table and took hers in it. He felt her hand tense and she looked down.

"V, you'll have to decide. He's offered to do it. He asked me to ask you." He paused. "I guess if it wasn't for the depression I could send you myself. But I guess—I guess I haven't been a very good father to you," he said.

He felt awkward, holding her hand. He released it and she dropped it quickly into her lap. When she spoke her voice was little and young and she did not meet his eyes. "You have too been a good father," she said, and he felt she meant the words sincerely. But he knew they were not true. He felt old and lonely and worried, more removed from her than he had ever been.

"Well, you'll have to decide," he said harshly. "I want you to tell me, not him. I don't want you to talk to him about it till you tell me what you decide. Do you understand?"

"I don't want to," she said.

His breath whispered hot and dry through his lips. "Why?" he said.

"I just don't want to."

He didn't say anything more. His head felt hot and he rubbed his hand over his eyes. He had not felt this way since Cora's death, and he hated it. Now at the end of the summer Denton would take V away from him; he was afraid of it as he had been afraid Mr. Burgess or John Schuford would take Cora away from him, jealous as he had been then. He had thought this kind of jealousy was gone forever with Cora's death, and now it was back.

Shamefully he remembered the terrible, continual awareness he had had that he had been old, and Cora young. And Denton was old, and V young. Shamefully he wondered if Denton would treat V as he had treated Cora. But somehow he knew that Denton would not, because, of all the terrible insufficiencies he himself had, Denton had only this one. Denton was only old. Denton would take his daughter away.

But what else was there for her? When Denton asked her, she must realize there was nothing else. In a way she was trapped. He glanced at her quickly and then down at his empty plate with the knife and fork crossed upon it. What else was there for her?

"What's the matter, Papa?" V said.

"Nothing," he said. "Why?"

"I don't know," she said, and after a moment, "Papa, who's that running the tractor?"

"Fellow named Jack Ward."

"Is he any good?"

He nodded.

V laughed nervously. "Jill was riding up on the seat with him this afternoon. It looked awfully funny. She acted just like she was helping him."

When they left the table she clumped around the house in her new boots, admiring herself in the mirror in her room from time to time. She was restless and talkative. After she had kissed him good night he sat up late, rocking in the leather rocker beside the floor lamp, worrying.

Now he would have to go over and tell Denton she did not want to go to college, and he hated the prospect. Denton would ask his advice, and he didn't know what advice to give. He wanted to see the best thing done; the only thing of importance now in his life was that the best arrangement be made for V, and he only knew what her life would be like if she married Denton, and knowing that, he was afraid to think what it would be like if she did not.

He could not bear to face Denton now. Denton would have to wait, at least until Ward had finished knocking up the stumps in the bottom. He would not be able to avoid speaking to Denton when he returned the tractor.

7

On Monday, just before one o'clock, Baird went down to the bottom to find out when Ward thought he would be able to finish. Ward was sitting against one of the stumps with his cap pulled down over his eyes and his long legs crossed, tossing crusts of his sandwiches to Jill. When Baird squatted beside the stump and spoke to him, he pushed his cap back on his head and snapped the lunch pail closed.

"About another three days," he said. "I'm leaving the rest I got to shoot till last."

"There enough powder left?"

"Oh, yeah."

Baird nodded, rubbing Jill's back. Jill stood rigid, grunting contentedly.

"Say, how you going to get rid of those stumps?" Ward asked.

"I thought I'd rig an A-frame to get them on the truck. Juan can take them out and dump them somewheres."

"I'll tell you what might be better. I'll doze up a ramp you can back up to. I can push them right onto the truck."

Baird frowned, removed his hat and ran his fingers through his hair. This, he knew, would be much faster than using a block and tackle, which would require all of his and Juan's time for at least a week. This would be better, even if he had to pay Ward for two or three extra days. "Good idea," he said. "You might as well get on that right away. How long'll it take you to make your ramp?"

"Hour, maybe. I can do it this aft. You want to start loading in the morning?"

Baird nodded. He pushed Jill away and gazed down the smoothed track the dozer blade had made to where the stumps were herded together, looking like huge pulled teeth. "Good," he said. He saw V riding down the hill toward them on Tony, the horse jerking his head up and down as he picked his way over the broken ground.

"That's pretty good land," Ward said. "Pay much for it?"

"No," Baird said. "Yes, it's all right." He saw Ward grinning at V, who had pulled the horse up close by. She was smiling self-consciously and patting Tony's neck as he cropped the grass. Ward got to his feet, slouched across and cupped his hand over Tony's muzzle. Tony snorted and jerked his head away.

"This is Mr. Ward, V," Baird said. "That's my daughter." Ward grinned up at her and put his hands in his hip pockets.

"I thought she was a timekeeper or something," he said. "She's been out here watching me every day."

V flushed. "I'm glad to meet you."

"That's a lot of quarter-horse," Ward said, teetering back on his heels. "Where'd you get him?"

"His father's Copper McCloud."

"Yeah? He's got his old man's color, all right. How about riding him sometime?"

V looked startled. "Oh, I don't think...Nobody ever rides him but me."

Ward shrugged and said, "Does he know any tricks?"

"Oh, sure. He's awfully smart."

Baird watched them silently, chewing on his tobacco and listening to them talk and wondering what V thought of Jack Ward. Finally he spat a stream of brown juice, rose, and walked over to them.

"Well, see if you can get that ramp up this afternoon," he

said to Ward. "I'll run Juan down with the truck first thing in the morning."

"Right." Ward was laughing at something V had said. They watched him start the cat and climb into the seat, where he paused to light a cigarette. Walking up the hill beside the horse, Baird saw V looking back over her shoulder, sitting up very straight.

But at dinner that night she was angry and silent. "What's the matter?" he asked.

"Oh, that Jack Ward!"

"What's the matter?"

"Oh, I let him ride Tony and he ran him all over the ranch. I'll bet if I hadn't caught him he wouldn't have let him cool down even. Oh, he's so conceited."

"Tony needed a good run. You baby him too much."

"I don't either! And I wish you'd tell him to stop riding Jill around on that old tractor, Papa. She's going to get hurt."

"She'd more likely get hurt if he left her on the ground."

V set her mouth in a tight line and said nothing more. She pushed her fork at the potatoes on her plate, and then without taking a bite, put her fork down and rubbed the back of her hand hard across her lips. She took a drink of milk.

"He's a good cat skinner," Baird said placatingly. "He's the best I've ever seen around here."

"Oh, yes, and doesn't he know it!"

"Well, he'll be through this week."

"Oh," V said. "Will he?"

"I think I'll let him go Saturday."

"That's good," V said.

And by Saturday Ward had pushed the last of the stumps onto the truck for Juan to take out and dump, and was knocking down the ramp he had built. V had stayed at home all afternoon and when Baird came up to the house from the bottom, she made him go down again and ask Ward to have some iced tea with them before he left.

Baird had been meaning to have Ward take the tractor back to Denton, but instead he had him park it beside the truck, and they walked up from the shed together. Ward stopped to wash his hands and face at the pump, then caught up with Baird again, wiping his hands on the front of his shirt, and running them over his hair.

V was waiting for them on the front porch. She had crushed mint in the glasses, and she poured tea from the sweating pitcher as they came up the steps. She handed them each a glass and Baird sat down in his rocker across the table from her. Ward leaned against the porch rail.

"Thanks," he said. "This'll go good." He grinned at V.

"It's been a hot day," Baird said. He looked keenly at Ward, wondering how old he was; in his middle twenties, he imagined. Probably he had been brought up on a farm, as he himself had been, and probably he had never finished high school either. He wondered how Ward had happened to become a cat skinner. He wished he knew more about Ward, watching him leaning against the porch rail with the glass of iced tea in his hand and his legs crossed, sure of himself, and relaxed and self-contained. Baird turned to look at V, who sat stiffly in the straight chair she had brought out from the parlor, rattling the ice in her glass.

"Plenty hot," Ward said. His yellow eyes were inspecting V boldly, but after a moment he turned to Baird and his face became serious.

"Say, you got plenty of water for irrigation?"

"Yes," Baird said. "There's plenty and it's not very deep. I've got a new pump."

"I was looking at your ditches. They're in pretty foul shape. But I guess you know it, unh?"

"Well, I've had Juan working on them," Baird said.

Ward and V both laughed, Ward mirthlessly, without smiling, rubbing his hands over his cheek. "That poor old Mex," he said. "He's a natural for the WPA, isn't he?"

"He's awfully hard on hoe handles," V said. "Papa, remember the time he broke the hoe and cut his leg and you were so mad?"

"Why don't you get those ditches dug out while you still got the cat?" Ward said.

"Juan'll get them finished after a little."

"You can do a good job, little rig like that. It's going to take that Mex till 1951, the way he's going."

"Could you do it in a week?"

"Say ten days. I maybe could do the worst part in a week, but you might as well get it all done at once."

Baird rocked back, clasped his hands behind his head and computed ten days wages. Denton did not need the cat back yet, he knew, and this would mean he could put off talking to Denton. "All right," he said. "Why'n't you stay and take care of that for me?"

"Sure."

There was an uncomfortable silence. Finally V said, "Where are you from, Jack?"

"Lodi."

"Do your mother and father still live there?"

"They're dead."

"Oh," V said, in a little voice. "I'm sorry."

"You don't need to be. We didn't get along too good. I don't even remember my old man."

"Don't you have any relations?" Baird asked.

"I've got a bud in the Marines. I don't know where the hell

he is, though." Baird frowned and Ward pushed himself upright and placed his glass beside V's on the marble-topped table. "Well, I better be going," he said. "Thanks a lot for the iced tea."

"Do you have to go?" V said.

"Got a date." He grinned at her and shook hands with Baird. "See you Monday." They watched him go down the steps and around the corner of the house and in a few minutes he drove past in the yellow roadster. His black hair stood upright in the wind and he waved as he started down the hill.

V poured herself another glass of tea and took a cookie from the untouched plate on the table. Baird was staring at the dust settling in the curve of the road where the roadster had disappeared. "Cookie?" V said.

He took one. "Nice young man," he said.

She shrugged and looked at him coolly over the top of her glass. "Oh, he's all right. He hasn't got very good manners."

"Well, I'll be glad to get those ditches dug out," Baird said, but he was strangely disturbed. Would it be better if V married someone like Jack Ward? Suddenly he began to dislike Jack Ward, and at the same time to feel fiercely loyal to Denton. The cat skinners, he knew, were a wild bunch; Ward was probably a drunkard. Maybe he should let Ward go, tell him he had changed his mind about the irrigation ditches.

But then he told himself that this was foolish; he had seen no evidence that Ward was attracted to V, and he had tortured himself over this kind of thing with Cora, too many times. Still, he thought V liked Ward, and it would be because he was the first young man she had known at all.

And his idea that V was interested in Jack Ward confirmed itself day by day. She began spending a great deal of time out where the dozer was working, and soon she was packing sandwiches for herself so she could eat with Ward in the orchard at noon. Baird would see them down among the trees in the shade, laughing and teasing Jill, sitting against the side of the cat while they ate their lunches. He began to wish he had not let Ward stay to dig out the irrigation ditches, that he had let him go instead when he had finished the stumps. He hated Jack Ward.

And V began neglecting Tony. One evening Baird found the feed trough in the corral empty, and he had to fill it himself. The second time it happened he meant to take her to task about it, but he did not. He had never seen her so happy and he did not want to spoil it, for Ward would be gone soon enough.

She seemed happy as she had been when she had first had Tony. He would hear her singing in her room sometimes, and there was color that was not merely from the sun on her cheeks. One night she made him take her in to Bakersfield to a Marx Brothers movie, and they had such a good time he would always remember it; Jack had told her to be sure to see the movie, she said. And finally he realized with a terrified, outraged jerk at his heart, that she was crazy in love with Jack Ward.

8

Then one evening V was not at the house in time for supper and he went outside to see if he could find her. It was a long summer dusk, with the mountains to the east purple and black with shadow, and the hot wind sighing up the valley from the desert. He looked down through the orchard where the D-4 was parked, a dark mass among the trees, and then he walked slowly back to the corral. Through the kitchen window he could see Mary's bulky figure silhouetted above the stove, the tall rosy glow of the stovepipe beside her. Juan's black head was pressed against the glass as he sat leaning back on the stool between the stove and the kitchen table.

Jill let out a single, sharp bark as he entered the corral, and jumped up on his leg. Tony's feed trough was empty again; he set his lips and shook his head; he would speak to V this time. Tony stood patiently at the trough. His coat, dull copper in the fading light, felt rough and uncurried, and he made a muted sound as Baird patted him on the muzzle.

Going around the shed to get some feed, he halted, frowning, as he came upon Ward's roadster. Then he stepped inside the shed door, halting again to let his eyes accustom themselves to the darkness.

He heard the sounds before he could see. The sound hit him savagely in the face, but still he did not know what this was he had come upon. Then he knew, and the darkness cleared from his eyes like settling dust and he saw. He saw V's face turned up toward him, a white triangle in the darkness. Ward's face, a dark one, and he could hear V's terrified uneven breathing.

A husky sound swelled in his throat and forced its way through his lips. He staggered a step back; he could have torn his eyes and ears from his head for what they had seen and heard, to punish them, to prove them horribly, monstrously wrong. He almost cried out to her, but the cry was muted and drowned in the surging sea of outrage that swept over him.

He was panting, his body convulsed, his chest pounding, as he hurried toward the house. He passed Tony, who was stamping and snorting, he passed Jill, who whined at him. But he didn't hear. He could not think; he only knew what he had to do, for the white triangle of face turned up to him from the shed floor had been Cora's face, confirming past all doubt diseased and crazy suspicions that had been dying now for thirteen years. His boots grated harshly on the path, were noiseless as he cut across the grass, sounded sharply again as he ran up the steps. He paused for a moment before the door, trying to control his breathing, the nauseated, raging fist within him clenching and unclenching with the beating of his heart. "Whore!" he whispered.

He went in and crossed the kitchen without looking at Juan or Mary. The door sprang shut behind him. In V's room the panting broke loose from him again, like an animal clawing and leaping from his arms. He looked around him, gasping for breath; he dug the heels of his hands into his eyes. "Whore!" he whispered. He saw the white triangle of Cora's face staring up at him from the dark floor of the shed, above it Mr. Burgess' face, above it John Schuford's face, above it the face of the man who had helped him cut the alfalfa that year, above it the dark face of Jim Lewis, who had brought them milk and ice, and who was dead now, above it myriad, nameless, unknown triangles of faces. He saw Cora tumbling with them all on the floor of the shed. But they did not look up at him in terror, there was no uneven, terror-stricken breathing. They looked up at him and laughed and called him an old hick, throwing at him, like stones he could not dodge, his age, his poverty, his ignorance; looking up at him and talking about poetry and cuckolding him and shaming him and laughing.

With furious haste he pulled V's suitcases down from their shelf in the closet. He jerked open the drawers of the bureau and blindly dropped her things into the suitcases, mouthing harsh, self-pitying words. And now Cora's face had separated itself from V's and was dead and gone, and now it was V who was cuckolding him, lying on the filthy floor of the shed like an animal with Ward.

The suitcases were almost full. He threw in the Texas boots and the gay diploma and the photograph of V on Tony, a diary he had given her for her birthday once and she had never used, a half-eaten box of candy he found in the back of the bottom drawer—and he sank down in the chair and looked wildly around the room once more.

His eyes were blind. He had never known he could hate like this. He had never known rage and madness and somehow terror like this. He knelt and closed the cases on the tumbled clothes, and cinched them fast with the worn leather straps. Carrying them he walked heavily through the kitchen and down the back stairs. He dropped them in the middle of the drive. There was no movement, no sound, from where the squat darkness of the shed loomed, but it was now too dark to see.

He strode back into the kitchen. Mary looked at him enquiringly, then her black eyes knew. Juan sat at the table, staring at his half-emptied plate in carefully arrested motion. A hoarse, unfamiliar voice said, "Put my dinner on the table!"

Mary brought his plate and put it down between the knife and fork that marked his place. Half-rising, he reached across the table and pushed together the other knife, fork and spoon, and pushed them toward her. He saw the fat brown hand pick them up.

He heard Ward's car start up, stop. When it drove past he didn't look up from his plate. Frozen in bitterness and hate like a block of ice he thought with a kind of brutal triumph that after supper he would go over and tell Denton.

And he did. And after that he never spoke to Denton again, trying to drive his daughter from his mind as he had driven her from his house. For nine empty, wasted years he had tried, and then one afternoon even the emptiness was gone, when her lawyer telephoned from Bakersfield to tell him she was dead.

Part II
BEN

1

All his life, Ben Proctor had tried to understand people. He had always tried to understand why they were the way they were, what made them that way, and what they thought, and he believed he understood people better than most. Growing up, becoming a man, in a period when there was much anger and little understanding, he knew he had been seldom angry, and that he had mostly understood. He knew this quality was the reason he had the job he had, and was the reason he was good at his job.

When he had been elected general secretary of the local, he had known it was because everybody liked him. At first he had been hesitant to accept the post, because he was not sure of himself. He knew himself too well. He believed he was a better than fair grader operator, but he did not think he was qualified for union work.

He had succeeded, however. The members instinctively trusted him; in a way, he was still one of them, and they knew he was doing his job as one of them. It was possible that he might rise to be president of the local, if anything ever happened to Johnny Keefe, which was not likely, but he knew it was impossible that he ever rise further than that, and he even doubted that he could make good in the presidency. He did not have the personal drive. He was not pushing or hard-boiled enough. It was too easy for him to see the other fellow's side of a matter; it was impossible for him not to see the other side, and seeing it, he must consider it.

When Slim Farley had sent him the clippings from the San

Diego paper, he had been so profoundly shocked that for a time he could not breathe. He had set out to get drunk. He had stayed drunk and had not come to the office for two days, and he had immediately gone to look for Harry and Push. He had new friends now, but Harry and Push had been his friends in the years when he was seeing a lot of Jack Ward and V. Next to Jack, he had always counted them his best friends, and he had sought them out.

He was ashamed now that he had felt he had to get drunk and that, drunk, he had insisted upon talking about Jack. He had not wanted to talk about Jack, but he had, and of course they had talked to Red Young, too. For the first time he had felt that he was an outsider, that Harry, who was a cat-and-carryall operator, and Push, who was a grade foreman, were on one side of some kind of fence, and he, Ben, who worked for the union, was on another, and all they had in common now was that years before they had all been cat skinners working on the same jobs. Their conversation had been restrained, almost apologetic, and he remembered that he had done most of the talking himself, drunkenly. Push and Harry had not said much. They had seemed to know how he felt, and they had been careful not to say anything against Jack. And he supposed they must have known how he felt about V. With embarrassment he remembered that it was he who had done all the talking about Jack and V. Push and Harry had tried gently to confine the conversation to reminiscing about Red Young.

Now he was sitting in his swivel chair, hunched forward with his elbows on the desk, his mind crowded with Jack Ward. A warm wind came in the open window behind him and ruffled the papers on his desk and turned cold the sweat under his arms. He was freshly shaved, he had had a Turkish bath, he had been told off by Johnny Keefe, and he was trying to focus his thoughts on the lists of dues delinquents he held in his sweating hands. But he could not. He was thinking about Jack.

He was surprised it was not V who tormented him, but he knew he had first to try to understand Jack. He knew too that this was impossible, because he had not seen Jack since the war, and Jack must have changed. But his mind would not let it alone, and finally he surrendered and tossed the blurred lists of names on the carbon-smudged flimsies into his in-basket.

The chair squeaked as he swung around and leaned back. He clasped his hands behind his head, his eyes fixed unseeingly on the black-bright street outside his window, remembering the CCC camp where he had first met Jack.

2

He had not liked Jack at first. He had already been in the CCC almost a year when Jack joined. Jack had been immediately accepted into the circle of oldtimers, like Ralph Mogle and Campanelli, from which Ben was still excluded. But they had been in the same tent once, when they were up in the mountains fighting a fire. Ben had brought a stack of *Fighting Aces* magazines with him and Jack borrowed them to read at night. They were both still in their teens then and they talked together about the airplane fighting in the late war, about Eddie Rickenbacker and Raoul Lufberry and von Richthofen's Flying Circus, and Jack bragged a little about how Mogle was teaching him to run the bulldozer.

They were camped in their squad tents in a little high valley, the tents lined up in three rows behind a stone cabin, over the door of which hung a sign that said "U. S. Forest Service." The cabin stood at one end of a rumbling wooden bridge and all along the road and up the sides of the mountain the trees were burned. A few had fallen but most of them still stood upright, without branches, like tall, charred poles. The underbrush was burned into a low tangled black carpet, and soot hung heavily in the air.

Ben walked slowly along the road with his shovel over his shoulder looking for smouldering wood. When he found any he broke it up with the shovel and smothered it with dirt—sometimes a fallen log would smoulder for days before it blazed up. He was hot, dirty and tired, and the soot in the air itched on his sweating skin, around his collar and under his belt. He had walked the mile up and down the road above the foresters' shack three times since lunch, and he had buried all the embers he could find. Here and there on the slope above the road a tree was still burning but these had been isolated, the under-brush cleared away in a wide circle around them.

As he rounded a bend in the road, Ben came upon Jack sitting on a charred gasoline can, scraping his shovel back and forth across the soot-covered surface of the road. "Hi, Ben," he called.

"Hi," Ben replied, squatting beside him and bracing himself on his shovel. Jack was smoking, holding the cigarette cupped in his hand. "How's it going?" Ben asked.

Jack rolled his eyes and groaned. "Oh, Christ, I'm shot. This gets old after a while."

Ben grinned, wiping his hands one after the other on his pants' legs. "When do you suppose we're going to haul out of here?" he asked.

"Beats hell out of me. We pull out of here it's just to go out on another one. Big bastard going up by Yosemite, I hear."

"Yeah, I heard that too," Ben said. When they were silent, everything was silent; it was necessary to listen to hear the distant clink of shovels and from somewhere up on the mountain, the steady cough of Mogle's bulldozer.

Jack finished his cigarette, snubbed it on his shoe, shredded the butt and threw the paper over his shoulder. He jerked his head toward the sound of the dozer. "Boy, that's the life," he said. "That's a white man's job. To hell with this rooting around with a shovel."

"Yeah," Ben said. He sat down on the ground, straightened his leg out and rubbed the knee. It still got sore if he walked too much. Through the damp, taut cloth that covered the inside of

his knee, he could feel the long, jagged, tucked and bunched
scar. He ran his fingers gently along its length.

"You should have come up with me this morning," Jack said.
"He would have let you run it."

"Aw, I don't know him. I guess I don't like him very well. He
talks too much."

Jack glanced at him quickly and grinned. "Yeah," he said. "I
know what you mean. He's the greatest cat skinner and woman
skinner there ever was. Just let him get started telling you
about it, unh?"

"I guess it's kind of all he's got."

Jack frowned. "Sure," he said finally. "He gripes me too, but
what the hell, it's a good chance to learn to run a dozer. That
bastard Campanelli wouldn't ever let anybody run his."

Ben didn't say anything.

"I don't want to swing this God damn thing the rest of my
life," Jack said. He pushed himself up with the help of his
shovel, scratched his chest and stretched, yawning. "Hell," he
said. "Let's get at it again, unh?"

Ben nodded and rose, still massaging his knee with his hand.
"You got a gal at home?" he asked, as they walked up the hill
together.

Jack shook his head. "Nope. Women give me a pain." He
screwed up his face and swung his shovel like a baseball bat at a
charred bush. "You?" he said.

"Well, kind of," Ben said. "You know. We write all the time,
but what're you supposed to do about it? Can't get married."

"To hell with getting married," Jack said. "To hell with that.
Slip it to her till you get sick of it, then check out."

"Aw, she's not that kind, Jack."

"Stop it!"

Ben halted abruptly. He felt the blood rush to his face. "I
said she's not, God damn it!"

Jack looked surprised. "Okay, she's not. Okay, she's some new kind. Sorry! Jesus!"

"You been talking to Mogle too much," Ben said as they walked on, but he wasn't angry anymore. He liked Jack, and he knew Jack liked him, and somehow, that day, they began to be friends.

The next fall when Campanelli left the camp, Jack was assigned to his dozer. Jack began giving Ben lessons, and when Mogle quit to get married, Ben and Jack were the two bulldozer men, and as such had an important place in the CCC camp. Then, in March, Jack's mother died of cancer, and Jack asked Ben if he would come to Lodi to the funeral. "I don't think many people're going to be there," he said embarrassedly, without looking at Ben. "I'd kind of like to have you come along with me. If you'd want to."

So Ben got permission to go to Lodi with Jack. At the funeral were several old people, and Jack's brother Sterling, a pimply faced Marine several years older than Jack, in blues and a sway-backed barracks cap. Afterward Ben and Jack and Sterling went out to get drunk, and the next day Jack and Ster sold Mrs. Ward's lunch wagon for seven hundred dollars, split the money ceremoniously and Ster took the train back to San Francisco.

That night Jack suggested they go to a hotel, have call girls sent up, his treat, and have a party. At first Ben hadn't wanted to. He was ashamed for anyone to see his scarred leg and he had never been with a woman, but then he thought he might as well get it over with. So Jack bought a bottle of bourbon, rented two rooms in a shabby hotel with cracked yellow paper on the walls, and they had their party.

Ben got drunk as quickly as he could and he didn't remember what his girl looked like, except that she had frizzy, ginger-colored hair and white shaved legs, and once in the night when he woke up he had smelled her breath and it almost made him sick. In the morning when she left he pretended to be asleep.

They had only been back at the CCC camp a short time when they heard about the Public Works jobs in Bakersfield. They left and took a room there together. Jack was hired to operate the bulldozer that pushed the carryalls scraping in the cut, Ben as a grease-monkey, and after a month or two the grade foreman had Ben take over the cat and tampers.

When the job was finished they moved up the valley to Visalia for a while, then to Fresno, then Porterville, and back to Bakersfield again. In Bakersfield they lived in a run-down apartment house near the railroad yards. They were both just twenty-two then, and they talked a lot about what they had done and what they wanted to do, making a bargain that they would shut up and go to sleep when they heard the long, keening rattle of the milk train in the yards.

For a while Ben was jealous of Jack; not because Jack was the better cat skinner, but because Jack was more successful with the girls they knew. Jack was tall, well-built, and, Ben supposed, handsome in a way. He had a hard, flip, confident manner with women, while Ben was quieter; and he was shorter and thinner than Jack, with thin brown hair and jug ears. After a while Jack settled down a little and did not brag so much about his conquests. It was then that he and Ben began to accept each other fully.

Then V turned up. That was in the early summer of 1938. One night when Ben came home from the state highway job, she was alone in the room, sitting on the edge of Jack's bed and looking very young and forlorn. Instantly Ben was sorry for her.

3

She sat on the edge of the bed watching him as he came in. He stopped just inside the door, pulling it closed behind him so that the doorknob punched him in the back and he had to take another step forward.

She sat stiffly, her knees close together, her hands folded in her lap. One corner of her mouth twitched, as though she wanted to smile but could not, and there was no lipstick on her mouth. On the bed beside her was an old leather suitcase, and another stood upright on the floor at her feet.

"Where's Jack?" Ben asked.

"He said he was going out and get something to drink." Her voice was young and frightened, and the smile she finally managed was frightened. She had been crying, he saw, and he wished he had stayed down at the Hitching Post, drinking beer with Harpy and Petey Willing and Red.

"I'm Ben Proctor," he said. "Jack's roommate."

"Oh, he's told me about you. I'm Vassilia Baird. Everybody calls me V, though."

"Okay, V," Ben said. "Any friend of Jack's." He picked up an armful of clothes from the rickety straight chair, dropped them on his bed, and sat down facing her over the back of the chair. Blonde hair grew low on her forehead and curved inward almost to meet her eyebrows at the sides of her face. She hesitated when Ben offered her a cigarette, then took one; her fingernails were unpainted and cut short. Ben lit the cigarette for her and she drew on it intently and exhaled a huge cloud of smoke.

"I haven't been smoking very long," she said. Her smile grew a little more sure of itself. Her brown eyes looked directly into his, seeming to demand he keep the conversation going.

Ben jerked his head at the suitcases. "Leaving town, V?"

Her eyes dropped. She shook her head. Ben said quickly, "Well, it's sure a lousy night."

"Oh, is it?" V got up and walked to the window with quick, nervous steps. She stood gazing at the dark pane. Ben could see the reflection of her blouse, startlingly white in the mirror of the window. He looked her over, remembering what Jack had said: *She's cute as hell, and I don't think she's ever even seen a man before. And she's really stacked.* And she was: long legs and high breasts and just enough flesh around her hips. Ben watched the curve of her cheek as she rested her hands on the sill and stared out the window. Her face was very young. Jailbait, he said to himself, but it did not express what he was thinking. He wondered if Jack had slept with her yet. Somehow he knew Jack had, and he hated it, because she looked young and fresh, and she did not look like that kind.

"It isn't very nice, is it?" V said. She came back to the bed and sat down again, resuming exactly the same position. "Is it going to rain, Ben?"

"Yeah, I guess so." He flicked ashes from his cigarette into the cuff of his pants. "I guess it will," he said angrily.

"What do you do, Ben?"

"I run a cat. Like Jack."

"Are you working now?"

"I'm working on the new highway. Down south of town."

"Have you known Jack a long time?"

"Three or four years," Ben said.

Her smile was strengthened again, as though she were glad of this, and he knew that now she was going to ask questions about Jack. He tried to think of something to say so that she wouldn't, but then he heard footsteps on the stairs, on the landing, the door opened and Jack came in, carrying a paper sack. Ben glanced at him quickly.

"Hi," Jack said. "What do you know, Ben?"

"Not much." He got to his feet and said, "Well, I guess I'll go out and get some dinner."

"Stick around," Jack said. "Have a drink." He put the sack down on the table beside the washstand, and took from it a bottle of bourbon and a bottle of ginger ale. The empty sack toppled over and fell to the floor. Jack brought down the two glasses from the shelf, rinsed out the glass their toothbrushes stood in, half-filled the three with liquor and ginger ale and handed them around.

Ben watched V watching Jack. Everything she felt was on her face for him to see. She was smiling, still sitting stiffly, but when Jack sat down beside her she stopped smiling and looked up at him. Ben turned his eyes to the window; his face felt frozen and stiff. In the railroad yards he could hear a string of freights sliding by, the yard engine going, "Huh-huh-huh." The window was black and depthless, reflecting the ceiling light like a white, artificial moon.

"Well, here's to every damn thing," Jack said. He raised his glass. Ben watched a strained expression come over V's face; her throat worked as she took a drink, and he knew it was the first she had ever had. He felt the expression on his own face change slightly to become the same as hers. He saw her shudder, and then she tried to smile.

"What's the matter?" Jack asked, grinning crookedly.

"Ugh!"

"That your first drink, V?" Ben asked, and when she nodded, he said, "Jack should have got you some good stuff, instead of feeding you this cheap junk."

Jack frowned, turned, and looked steadily at Ben. "Hey, Ben."
"Yeah?"

"Hey, do you suppose you could go over and stay with Red for a couple days?"

"Oh," Ben said. "Okay. Sure, Jack." He looked at the suitcases, then at V, then at Jack. Jack winked. V's eyes were fixed on her lap. She crossed her legs and tucked her skirt in around them.

"Sure," Ben said again. He finished his drink in silence, rose self-consciously and went over to the bureau. He could feel Jack's eyes watching him as he pulled some underpants and socks and shirts and a pair of clean levis from his drawer and stuffed them into his canvas bag. Carrying the bag he took his shaving gear and toothbrush from the washstand and walked to the door.

V was drawing a circle on the bed cover with her forefinger and Jack's arm lay around her waist. Somehow Ben knew she was crying. He heard her whisper, "Goodbye, Ben, I'm glad to've met you," and Jack said, "So long," and then he stepped outside and pulled the door closed.

As he did so he dropped his toothbrush, and stooping to pick it up, he felt furious; at the toothbrush for falling, and at Jack and V. In his car driving over to Red's, he grumbled aloud at this imposition, but he knew what angered him was Jack, at whom he did not want to be angry, and V, because he was sorry for her, and there was no use being sorry for her. But he could not force from his mind the picture of V sitting on the bed with her knees and feet close together and her hands in her lap, and in her eyes fear and loneliness, and in them too the hope for something for which she had no right to hope.

4

"Well, well," Red said. "He's got a set of brass guts. Kicking you out for a shack-up."

"Aw, I don't know," Ben said. "I'd just like to know what the score is. That's all."

"Sure, stay here if you want to," Red said. "Plenty of room." He had just come out of the shower and was sitting in his green upholstered armchair in fresh BVDs, clipping his fingernails. The skin of his barrel chest and bulging calves was milk white, but his arms were burned and his face was a mass of dark freckles, which were almost solid across the bridge of his nose. His eyes were green and narrow, and reddish blonde hair was plastered wetly over his skull. He had dropped his towel on the floor in front of him, beside his dusty boots and a pair of stiff, stained sweat socks.

Ben knocked the ash from his cigarette into the cracked saucer that rested on the windowsill. He leaned back in his chair, listening to the steady clipping sound of the scissors. He wished now that he had not told Red about V, but he had been angry and he had felt he had to tell someone. But it was none of his business, and it was none of Red's business.

"Yeah, hell," Red said. "I won't boot you out when I got some dame up here. Share the wealth, I say." He looked up and grinned, and Ben knew he was welcome to stay. Red had two grins: one was friendly, the other mean and sneering, and this had been the friendly one. Ben had known Red less than a month. Red was working on the new highway job, running the push-cat that boosted the carryalls in the cut, and he and Ben ate lunch together every day. Evenings, the three of them, Ben, Jack and Red, had been seeing a lot of each other.

"Well," Ben said, "I guess I shouldn't have talked the way I did. I don't really know what the score is. But I got kind of sore. You know. She's young and she looks kind of nice, and there was Jack giving her the first drink she ever had, and I bet I gave her her first smoke, and I bet Jack got her cherry. You know. It made me want to puke."

"Somebody's got to get it," Red said.

"Yeah, I guess so."

"Share the wealth, I say," Red said. He tossed the scissors over onto his dresser and scratched his head. "Maybe you should've stuck around over there, Ben."

Ben didn't say anything. He ground out his cigarette, borrowed Red's towel and soap and went to take a bath. When he returned he put on a clean white shirt and clean levis. Red was already dressed and was standing in front of the mirror, rubbing his hand over his bristling jowls. He turned his face from side to side, then jutted his jaw and patted himself under the chin.

"Say, what's this gal look like?" he asked.

"Blonde. Brown eyes. Pretty cute."

"Built?"

"Yeah," Ben said. "You eaten yet?"

"Damn that Jack," Red said. He was still contemplating himself in the mirror, but after a moment he turned, picked up his wallet and change from the dresser and put them in the pockets of his levis. "Yeah, let's go out and eat," he said.

5

It rained lightly during the night, harder the next day, and the highway job was shut down. Late in the morning Ben went around to get the rest of his clothes.

When he knocked, Jack's voice told him to wait a minute. Bedsprings creaked, footsteps sounded, the door opened a crack and Jack's face appeared. He grinned and swung the door open. "Want the rest of your stuff?" he asked. He had on blue-and-white-striped shorts and his broad face was puffy and bleary-eyed. Looking over his shoulder he beckoned Ben to enter.

V was still in bed. Her face was turned away from the door and she seemed to be asleep, but as Ben passed she opened her eyes and smiled at him. Her hands clutched the blankets tightly around her neck and she pulled her knees up. "Hello, Ben," she said.

Since he had seen her last she had put her hair into two fat braids, one of which was crumpled under her head. There was a spot of color on either of her cheeks and she clutched the bedclothes tighter as Ben looked at her. Then he looked away, biting his lip. "Hi," he said.

Jack leaned against the washstand, yawning and scratching his sides as Ben pulled his bureau drawer open. "No work today, Jack?" Ben asked.

"Nope. All through."

Ben stacked the shirts and socks and shorts he had taken from the drawer into the canvas bag he had brought with him,

and straightened up. Out of the corners of his eyes he could see
V looking at Jack. Her hands were out from under the covers
and she was smoothing her hair back and rearranging the twisted
braid. A yard engine grunted past outside, butting three refrigerator cars, and rain splattered in fat drops against the window.
In a gust that rattled the pane, the rain broke harder, as though
someone had turned a hose against the side of the building.

"Say, Ben," Jack said. "They don't happen to be shorthanded
down on the highway job, do you know?"

"Why don't you come down and talk to Push?"

"I guess I will. You staying over at Red's?"

Ben nodded silently. He took his raincoat and suit from the
closet, wrapped the suit in the raincoat and picked up his
bulging canvas bag. "Well, I'll see you," he said. "Come on
down and see Push tomorrow."

"Maybe I'll see you at the Hitching Post tonight," Jack said.
He yawned again and sat down on the bed next to V. "You going
to be there?"

"Yeah, I guess so." Ben walked quickly to the door. V's skirt
hung over the foot of the bed and her blouse was draped over
the back of a chair. "So long, Jack, so long, V," he said hurriedly,
as he went out. He stamped down the stairs, his raincoat drag-
ging on the steps. He was angry again. His teeth were set tight
together and the muscles of his jaw ached.

That night at the Hitching Post he was sitting at a table with
Red and Push and Harry Franco when V and Jack came in. He
saw them first outside the window, and then they were in the
doorway, V in a black dress that looked new and was too tight,
and with too much lipstick on her mouth. Her blonde head
came just below Jack's shoulder. Ben saw Petey Willing and
Fred Banks, and Willie, the mechanic, who were sitting at the
bar, turn to look at her.

Red put down his beer and whistled softly. "Jesus," he whispered. "What a set of cans." Harry screwed up his mouth and nodded approvingly. Push leaned forward toward Ben.

"Who's that?"

"Jack's girl. Her name's V."

"New, unh? She's right cute."

Jack waved to them and walked with V toward a table across the room. He stopped and put a coin in the jukebox, which suddenly glowed with red and yellow lights. Peggy went over to get their orders, walking stiffly and not looking at Jack.

"Oh, that damn stud," Red whispered. "Oh, my bare feet."

"These damn young cat skinners," Push said. "New girl every day, and I can't even hold onto my wife." He laughed softly. "Say, get a load of Peggy."

Harry whispered something Ben couldn't hear.

Push poured beer into his tilted glass. "Pretty young, pretty young," he said. "I don't know. You met her yet, Ben?"

"Yeah," Ben said. V seemed aware they were discussing her. She was talking rapidly to Jack, a set smile on her face, which was turned slightly away from them.

"How about it, Ben?" Red said. "I got to meet that. How about it?"

"Ah, leave them alone."

"Keep that! I'm going over there." He pushed his chair back. Ben quickly rose with him.

"You guys want to come?"

Push shook his grizzled head. "Some other time. This angle'll do right well for me."

"Yeah, me too," Harry said.

Red hitched up his pants as he and Ben walked over to the other table. Jack grinned at them as they came up, and Ben said, "V, this is Red Young."

"Hello," V said.

"Hi," Red said. "What do you know, Jack?"

"Not much. Sit down and have a beer." He unzipped his leather jacket and drew a pack of Luckies from his shirt pocket. Red took the chair next to V and Ben lit the cigarettes Jack had passed around.

"Say, where'd you get this, Jack?" Red asked. "Pretty damn cute." V flushed and looked down. Her dress was too tight around the top and she held one hand to her neck to cover it. Jack grinned, and then he looked seriously at Ben.

"Push got a job down there for me?"

"I didn't ask him yet. Why'n't you go buy him a beer?"

"I guess I better." Jack tilted his chair back, stepped over it and set it on its feet again. Walking across to Push's table he met Peggy with a tray of beers, stopped her and let his arm go carelessly around her waist. Peggy wriggled away and she was scowling as she passed their table. Ben saw V moisten her lips and her eyes were round.

"Two more beers, Peg," Red called. He was chuckling.

"Jack was saying you just got out of high school," Ben said quickly. "Where'd you go, V?"

"The Priory." She licked her lips again. She had licked all lipstick away and only a thin line of scarlet remained around the edges of her mouth. Ben wondered if Jack had bought the black dress for her.

"You're Catholic, unh?" Red said. "I knew a…"

"Episcopalian," V said.

"How'd you like the Priory?" Ben asked.

"I didn't like it very well. They were awfully strict." She took a drink of her beer, trying not to make a face, and then she licked away the moustache of foam the beer had left on her upper lip.

Red said, grinning, "How old are you, V?"

"Eighteen."

"Come on!"

She turned and smiled at him. "Yes I am. I was eighteen in April." Ben saw Red's arm move, the smile left V's face, and she looked down at her lap. Ben kicked Red as hard as he could.

"Oooook!" Red cried. "God! Damn!" He half-rose in his chair, but then Peggy came up to the table with two bottles of beer, and behind her were Petey and Fred Banks. Ben rose without looking at Red, introduced them to V, and they pulled chairs up to the table.

They all sat in uncomfortable silence for a moment. Then Ben asked Petey when he would have his dozer working again, and then he asked Fred how the grading was going on the levee, and when he had started them talking, sat back and looked Red coldly in the eyes. Red glanced away and poured beer into his glass, but he was scowling and his lower lip protruded. V was saying she hoped Jack would get a job down on the new highway with them.

"Here he comes," Petey said. "He got it, all right. Hey, Jack, how'd you make out?"

"Got it," Jack said, rubbing his hands together.

"When do you start?" Ben asked.

"Tomorrow if it clears up," Jack grinned, and Red said, "What'd you get? Dozer?"

"They're getting a new grader. Push's putting me on it."

"Where the hell'd you do any grader work?"

"He was on one for a while up at Fresno," Ben said. "He's pretty good at it."

"It's about time they got another blade," Fred said. "Mac and me've been busting our guts trying to stay caught up."

Red rose abruptly, his chair scraping on the floor. "Let's go," he said.

"Well, I'll see you tomorrow, Jack," Ben said. "So long, V."

"Get Peggy to bring us a couple beers, will you?" Petey said. Ben nodded and followed Red across to the other table, signaling to Peggy on the way. Push was leaning back, a cigarette drooping from his lips, his eyes half-closed against the smoke. Harry looked up at Red with one eyebrow raised, sipping his beer.

"That's pretty good," Red said, jerking back his chair. "How come you give that bastard the new blade?"

"Because he knows how to run one," Push said. "Why'n't you tell me you wanted it?"

"You knew damn well I wanted it. You think I want to gather piles on that push-cat the rest of my life?"

Harry said, "Jack ought to be a good blade man."

"If we get another I'll see if I can put you on it, Red," Push said.

Red's eyes were little and mad. "You know damn well you won't get another."

"All right. Go to hell then."

"That bastard," Red said. He looked angrily at Ben. "And Goddamn you," he said. "I ought to break your tail for you."

"Any time you want to try," Ben said.

"Ahhh, you little shrimp." Red's eyes flickered from Ben to the others and he swung around in his chair and waved an arm at Peggy, who was standing at the end of the bar. "What's the trouble?" Harry asked.

Ben didn't say anything, and Peggy brought four beers to the table. Her black eyes were sullen.

"Hey, Peg," Harry said. "Your boy's got himself a new baby."

She glanced at him woodenly and started away, but Red caught her arm and pulled her back to the table. He sneered up at her as she threatened him with the tray.

"How about it, Peg?"

She didn't speak. Her upper lip curled back over her teeth and she shook her arm loose. "Yeah, she's sure stacked," Harry said. "We been sitting here wondering how Jack does it."

"She's fat," Peggy said scornfully. "She's just a fat little high-school girl." She stalked away, and Ben saw her looking at Jack and V as she went up to the bar. Petey and Fred were back at the bar with Willie again, and Jack and V were talking, their heads close together.

"I think I could use some of that Peggy," Red said.

"Well, tonight's the night," Harry said. "She's off Jack."

"To hell with that. I'm taking no leftovers from that bastard." Red was scowling darkly and he raised his glass and let the beer drain into his mouth. Ben watched him, his anger gone; five minutes before he had felt he could have killed Red, but now he knew Red had just acted the way he was used to acting.

He could understand Red being mad because he had been kicked on the shins, and he could understand Red being mad because Jack had got the new grader. In the matter of seniority on the job, Red had the more right to it, but Ben knew, too, that Push had been right in giving it to Jack because Jack would be the better grader operator.

But it was a monotonous, dusty job, pushing the carryalls in the cut, and almost every cat skinner aspired to be a blade man. It had the highest prestige of any cat-skinning job, the pay was better, and it was a necessary step to becoming a grade fore-man, if a man didn't want to eat dust and bounce his kidneys to pieces all the rest of his life. He would like to be a blade man himself.

He sighed and looked up at Red, who was grinning now, lis-tening to Push tell about his wife leaving him. Ben had heard the story many times and each time it was a little funnier, but he didn't want to hear it now. His eyes moved across the room to where Jack and V had been sitting.

They were leaving, and Jack had his arm around her waist as they walked to the door. She was smiling up at him and Jack was making motions with his free hand, grinning and telling her something. Ben watched them. He watched them go out and pass the window, again feeling angry and uneasy. She was too young for this. She was too young, and there was an innocence and a frankness about her that was unlike any girl he'd met since he had gone to CCC camp. And she looked completely unprepared and defenseless, when she had to be prepared, had to have a defense. He scowled and drank his beer. Red and Harry and Push were laughing about something he hadn't heard.

Suddenly, for no reason, he thought about Doris Rasmussen, and he put his hand down to feel the puckered, lumpy scar on the inside of his knee. Even under his levis it was sensitive to his touch, but he did not remove his hand, squeezing the scar and kneading it and frowning, thinking about San Jose and his mother and father, and his brother and sisters, and thinking about Doris Rasmussen.

In 1932 Ben's father had bought the grocery store near the college in San Jose. It was a narrow, two-story building, and the second story was an apartment into which they moved. Ben's older brother, Jake, who was nineteen, had a job in San Francisco driving a delivery truck and so did not live at home, but Ben's mother and father slept upstairs in one bedroom, and Martha Lee and her husband, George, had the other, so that Ben and his other sister, Arlene, made a little bedroom for themselves out of a shed in the back of the store.

He and Arlene always talked for a long time after they had gone to bed at night. He liked Arlene better than anyone else in the family. She was a year and a half older than he, a senior in high school, a thin girl with ears that stuck out like his, which she tried to hide by wearing her hair in a long bob; but she had a sweet, big-eyed face and freckles across her nose.

Arlene was in love with Bill Rasmussen, whose father owned the hardware store down the street. She liked to tell Ben what a big basketball star Bill was, although Ben went to the same high school and knew well enough, and how Bill was going to get a basketball scholarship to Stanford and be a lawyer. The night Bill asked her to go steady she woke Ben when she came in and talked about Bill, about how in love with him she was and what he had said to her, and she turned on the light to show Ben the little gold basketball Bill had given her. In the light her lipstick was smeared all around her mouth and the top button of her blouse was unfastened, but her eyes were bright and she looked beautiful, even with the pink tips of her ears showing through her hair. She kept him awake almost all night, talking about Bill.

That was the way he met Doris Rasmussen. Doris was thin too, even thinner than Arlene, with jet black hair like her brother's, and blue eyes that looked rimmed with black because of her long eyelashes. She was in Ben's class at school and none of the boys liked her because she was quiet and never talked to anybody and she didn't seem to have any girl friends. "Doris Rasmussen doesn't have any buddies or any bubbies," the boys said.

One day after school Arlene asked Ben if he would double date with her and Bill and Doris. Mrs. Rasmussen had told Bill he had to get Doris a date, Arlene said. Ben said he would and the four of them went to a show and after the show to a place on the highway for hamburgers and coffee. Ben was shy and Doris even shyer and so they did not say much, riding home in the rumble seat of Bill's car, both embarrassed to look at Bill and Arlene necking in the front seat. And after that about once a month Arlene would talk around and talk around, until finally she would have to come right out and say that Mrs. Rasmussen had told Bill he had to get a date for Doris again. And then they would all go to a show in Bill's car, and afterward out for a hamburger, with Bill and Arlene necking in the front seat, and Ben and Doris sitting in stiff and uncomfortable silence in the rumble.

The night after the basketball team won the tournament, there was a beach party at Half-Moon Bay. More than ten couples were going, most of the first string of the basketball team and some of the other seniors. Ben and Doris went along too, riding in the rumble seat of Bill's car with their feet on two cases of beer and a cake of ice sliding and bumping around in a washtub, listening to Arlene and Bill and Harry Brooks and Edith Klineschmidt singing in the front seat.

At the beach party they built a fire and cooked hot dogs, and then sat around in a circle and sang and told ghost stories and a few faintly dirty stories, and drank beer. Ben sat next to Doris on the blanket he had brought, not singing, but watching the others, watching Arlene and Bill who sat across the fire from him drinking beer out of the same bottle, and from time to time he tried to think of something to say to Doris.

It was a dark night, with clouds over the moon and a breeze coming up from the ocean. When the fire died down and the stories and songs wore off, it was decided, after a great deal of giggling and protesting from the girls, that they would all go in swimming naked.

Ben withdrew with the other boys, who were talking loudly for the girls' benefit and whispering among themselves. He undressed a little apart and when the girls shouted from the water that they were in and now the boys could come, he did not go down to the beach right away.

When he did go, he went far to the left of the others, walking slowly along the beach, which was faintly white in the darkness. The ocean was black, and the sky was black, with the moon glowing coldly behind a scud of cloud. Behind him he could hear the shouting and the laughter fading into the steady whispering of the surf. Then he heard someone coming out of the water, and he almost ran back into the bushes. But he did not, watching the white figure detach itself from the darkness. It looked like one of the boys. The figure came toward Ben along the beach, looking down and scuffing its feet in the sand. "Hi," Ben said, and then he saw that it was Doris.

She halted. Her face jerked up toward him and he thought for a moment she was going to run away. He said, "It's Ben," but she did not move, standing stiffly with her arms at her sides. She was very white, with slim legs and flat hips like a boy, and her chest was flat as a boy's. She stood a few yards from him and a little lower on the beach. They stared at each other, but finally she bent her head so that her black hair hid her face. "I didn't mean to see you," Ben said. "I was just walking along here."

"That's what we undressed for, isn't it?" She whispered it, and he could hardly hear her, and then she raised her head again and stared back at him defiantly. It seemed to him that they stood there for a long time, silently, without moving, except that he could feel himself trembling and goosepimples came out on his arms and legs. The wind off the ocean felt cold, the sound of the surf seemed very loud. Suddenly Doris stepped forward, and with her head bowed and scuffing her toes in the sand, moved past him. When he turned, she was running, swiftly and gracefully, and she disappeared once more into the darkness, as though she had never been there at all.

In the rumble seat on the way home he kissed her. He kissed her passionately, with his arms tight around her, and although she was cold as ice and shivering, she pressed her lips to his viciously, her hands locked together and digging into the small of his back, her body arched up against him. Edith and Harry had stayed at the beach and were going to ride home with somebody else, and in the front seat Bill and Arlene were singing, and looking back from time to time, and then laughing and making cracks. When they sang Bill swung the car back and forth across the road in time to the song.

He never did know what happened, and afterward he never wanted to ask. He heard Arlene cry out, and with the cry there was a long scream of brakes, and then an enormous grinding crash that seemed to fill the world and jerked him away from Doris and out of the rumble seat into darkness with a terrible tearing pain in his leg.

When consciousness came back to him he was in the hospital.

His skull was fractured and his leg broken in two places, and Bill and Arlene were dead.

He was in the hospital six months and they had operated five times before they were able to tell him they could save his leg, and by then he hardly cared. At first his mother and father came every day, and his mother always cried and had to go out. His father looked very old and very puzzled and never knew what to say. Martha Lee and George came a few times before they went up to Portland where George was to go to work for his uncle, and sometimes on weekends Jake would come down from San Francisco.

But after she got out of the hospital, Doris came every day. One side of her head was shaved and there was a thick white pad taped to the shaved place. They would talk for a few minutes and then she would read to him, and when she was tired of reading they would sit silently until it was time for her to go.

When he was released from the hospital he did not return to school. His father had had to sell the grocery to one of the chain stores and had bought a little house on the outskirts of town and a small grove of orange trees. Ben was still on crutches so he could not do much to help, and there was the cruel, ugly scar on the inside of his knee. He walked as much as he could, but that leg was smaller than the other now and sometimes he sat alone in his room with his pants off and stared down at the scar and thought about the night at the beach when he and Doris had looked at each other.

He saw Doris almost every week. They went to a show whenever he had any money, which was not often, or else sat in the living room talking if the Rasmussens were not at home, or went for walks if they were. But he was ashamed of his leg, especially when he was with Doris, and he could not bring himself to touch her now.

It was Jake who talked to him first about the CCC, saying it might be good for him; he would gain weight and get his color back. At first he did not like the idea, but then he thought of the money he could send home every month, and he decided he would do it. He did not tell Doris until the last minute, and she did not say much except that she would write him, and he promised to write her. But he was afraid to kiss her; even when she took hold of his arms and raised her lips to him, he only pecked at them, and then he left abruptly and limped home. In bed that night, he cried.

But they wrote each other religiously, his letters stiff and formal; Dear Doris, and Yours, Ben; her letters short and badly spelled and written in a weak, spidery script that made him come to think of her not as flesh and blood but as a kind of ghostly memory; Dear Ben, and Yours, Doris. For two years they had written. But when, after he left the CCC camp he did not go back to San Jose, she did not write anymore, and after a few unanswered letters he stopped writing too.

Almost a year later he got an announcement of her marriage to a John Rudolph Castle, and the next day a letter from his mother which contained a clipping from the newspaper, a terse two inches of print and a picture of a dark girl he could not recognize in a white wedding dress. He was hurt that Doris had not written him herself, but he sent her for a wedding present a set of eight individual silver salt and pepper shakers that cost him thirty-two dollars.

7

The next morning was clear and Jack came down with the new grader about nine o'clock. He had driven it from the dealer's in Bakersfield, a big orange-painted Adams. He waved as he passed Ben's dozer, standing up and leaning forward against the controls, and Ben watched the Adams jolt down the temporary road beside the levee, to where Push sat in his pick-up, watching the surveyors setting stakes.

At noon Ben and Jack shut down their rigs together, Push drove up with Harry in the front seat, and Red and the two blade men, Mac and Fred, standing in the back and clinging to the top of the cab. They sat around Push's pick-up to eat their sandwiches and drink their coffee, Ben and Red together on the ground, Jack leaning against the running board with his long legs spread out in front of him, Push sitting behind the steering wheel, and Mac and Fred beside Jack on the running board.

"That's a nice blade, Push," Jack said.

"Yeah? How do you like an Adams?"

"Good. I never was on one before, but it handles damn good."

"I'll take a cat blade every time, though," Mac said. "I don't know why, but I just don't like them Adams."

"It's the color," Fred said. "That damn orange. Reminds me of some damn doctored-up orange juice I got sick as a dog on one time."

"I suppose you'd got sick on lemonade you'd want to paint your cat blade some other color but yellow," Harry said.

"You can get on that grade this aft," Push said to Jack. "The surveyors got the stakes about all set." The door was open and one of his feet rested on the running board next to Jack's shoulder. He was eating a piece of apple pie and Ben watched the juice run down his fingers. Just before it dripped off his wrist, Push stuffed the rest of the pie into his mouth and carefully licked his hand.

"You going to get me a stake runner?" Jack said.

"I got one coming down after lunch. You mind a nigger?"

"Who you got?" Ben asked. "Toussaint?"

"Yeah. You know him?"

"He was on my rig up at Fresno," Jack said. "He taught me how to run a blade, he says. He's a good boy."

"I'd rather have a colored boy than a Mex any day," Mac said. "That Mex I got's a no-good bastard. Damn him."

"I don't know what you got him for anyway," Fred said. "You knock up all your damn stakes just the same." Mac kicked his legs out from under him and Fred plumped down off the running board. Red was grinning sneeringly.

"You guys know Jim Poston?" he said. "He was on a job I was on once. He never needed a stake runner. He could see right through about two inches of dirt to where a stake was and just skin the hairs off the top of it."

"Red sounds pretty grouchy," Harry said. "I guess he's hungry. No dust to eat down in that cut today."

"Yeah," Red said. "I lose ten pounds every time it rains."

Ben dug down in his watch pocket for his dice and rolled them between his hands. He got to his feet. "How about some craps?"

They all got into the back of the pick-up and spread a gunny sack on the ribbed metal bed, and rolled for high man. Push won the dice and made a little. Ben lost a dollar and the dice traveled around the circle. When Jack got them, Red said, "How about shooting for that V dame, big boy?"

Jack grinned crookedly and rattled the dice against his ear. "What you got to cover with, Red?"

"I'll just take a piece of it," Red said.

"How much is she worth?" Harry said quickly. Ben felt his eyes narrow as he looked at Red. Then he looked at Jack. Jack's grin had faded and his cheek muscles were bunched up like fists. He ran his hand over his hair, watching Red silently. Red was stacking and pushing over a pile of silver. Ben could see the curl of his lips as he looked down at his thick fingers moving among the coins. No one spoke.

"Yeah, well, maybe it's better if she isn't covered," Red said. "Have to ask Jack about that sometime."

"You going to keep that up?" Jack said quietly. His body looked very stiff to Ben, and he was sitting up straight, resting his clenched fists on his knees. He stared steadily at Red, and Red flushed, laughed, and pushed a quarter out on the gunny sack.

"Go ahead and shoot, blade man," he said.

When the game finally broke up and Ben rose, he saw Toussaint plodding down the grade toward them, carrying a shovel. Stiff black pants that were too big for him hung from his thin shoulders on yellow suspenders. A wide white grin blossomed on his black face as Ben waved to him. He stopped and pulled a stocking up out of his shoe.

"Hi you, there, Jack!" he called. "Hi you, Ben!"

Jack jumped down off the pick-up and walked across to meet him. He knocked the crumpled felt hat off the Negro's head and slapped him on the back. Ben could see him grinning. "How the hell are you, Toussaint?"

"Pretty good," Toussaint said. "Boss around here?"

"You go run stakes for Jack," Push called, as he got into the pick-up. "Don't you let him knock any out, hear!"

"Jack don't knock but very few," Toussaint said. "I taught him good." Ben watched Red walk stiff-legged back toward the cut, and Push drove off in the pick-up with Harry and the blade men.

"Get your britches up on that Adams over there," Jack said to Toussaint. "You'd stand around here all day, gabbling like an old rooster." He stood with his back to Ben, his hands in his hip pockets.

Toussaint winked broadly. "That Jack mean," he said. "You going whup me, Jack?"

"I'll whup you you don't get up on that rig," Jack said, and Toussaint turned and hurried over to the Adams, as though he were terrified. He walked jerkily, his knees lifting high, his trousers flapping loosely around his ankles. Jack sauntered after him, without looking at Ben.

That evening Jack shut down the grader next to Ben's cat, and they went in to make out their work slips together. They walked silently, but outside the timekeeper's shack Jack touched Ben's arm.

"Say, Ben," he said. "I haven't had a chance to talk to you before." He pushed his cap back on his head, avoiding Ben's eyes.

"Yeah?" Ben said. He saw Jack look up expressionlessly as Red passed.

"About V," Jack said. His narrow eyes looked for an instant into Ben's, and then down at his feet. He rubbed his hand through the hair that protruded from under his cap. "Listen, Ben," he said angrily. "I know you're sore about the way I booted you out."

"I don't give a damn about that."

Jack's eyes flickered at him again. "See," he began. "The poor kid…" He scowled and kicked savagely at a pile of dirt. "Hell, here's what happened. Her old man threw her out."

"Why?"

"Aw, you know."

"How'd he find out?"

"He caught us out in the shed. What the hell you want, a written report?"

They both looked down.

Ben saw Jack's heavy boot kick at the pile of dirt again. *Slip it to her till you get sick of it and then check out*, Jack had told him once. He thought of V, sitting on the bed in their room, looking scared and lonely and trying not to cry.

"See?" Jack said. "What the hell am I supposed to do? I guess it's kind of my fault."

"Jesus Christ!"

Jack looked up.

"You're Goddam right it's your fault!" Ben said hotly. "Goddam it…"

"Christ, I know that, Ben," Jack said. "But I don't know what I'm supposed to do. She hasn't got any money or any other folks or any place to stay. It's just…"

Ben jerked his hand up between them, and Jack stopped. "Just a minute," Ben said. "You don't know what you're supposed to do, unh?"

Jack was silent.

"Yeah," Ben said. "You know what you ought to do."

"Aw, cut it out, for Christ's sake!"

Ben felt suddenly weak. His right leg was trembling as he turned away, and he reached down and hit his fist against his calf. "You bastard!" he said, and he meant it.

He walked quickly into the timekeeper's shack, made out his

work slip and caught a ride into town with Push and Harry. But already the rage had begun to leak out of him. In a way he understood what Jack was thinking. Jack must feel he had been trapped. He knew that Jack recognized his responsibility, but he knew too that Jack was going to refuse to accept it.

And he thought of Slim Farley, who had quit the job at Visalia to go to Los Angeles when he had knocked up a girl. They had talked about it a lot after Slim left, laughing over it, and Ben realized that it was he who was out of step, not Jack. Jack was going to work this out according to his lights and his lights were the same as those of the others they knew. It was he who was out of step, and he wondered why he saw it differently.

He tried to remember what Jack had told him of his boyhood in Lodi. Jack had talked about his mother and his brother Ster and he had talked a lot about a girl named Margie Watson. But there was probably not much difference in the way he and Jack had been brought up. They had both been poor, they had both been in the CCC, they had known each other throughout the period when they were changing from boys to men. Yet somehow, without pride, without righteousness or conceit, he realized that he had retained something Jack had lost, or else he had come into possession of something Jack had never had a chance to possess.

8

"She was really cute," Jack had said. "Really cute, damn her. A little hefty in the tail, but nice legs and a nice set of cans. She always wore a sweater that buttoned up the back and some kind of girl's-club pin right on the end of her left one. Real thick kind of dark hair in bangs, and those big blue eyes that looked good to everybody else except she couldn't see anything with them. She was a song leader and she used to come talk to me when I was on the bench during the football games. I used to always sit on the end of the bench whenever I came out so she could come over. If that bastard Bud Greene didn't get there first. She sat next to me in the sixth period English class too. Ward and Watson.

"Margie Watson," Jack had said, laughing and shaking his head. "She always sat there in class with one leg under her, like she was trying to hatch her saddle shoe or something. I'd lean up to scratch my knee, trying to see where it went. But I never could, damn her. She put some kind of oily stuff on her legs so's they'd shine, and when she got up after class there'd always be a red place on her calf from sitting on it.

"I used to walk her home after school. She lived over on Pine Street in a pretty new big house because old man Watson was vice-president of the bank. And Jim Grant's station where I worked after school for twenty damn cents an hour was way down that way too. We'd stop and have Cokes at the Owl Drug Store. Bleeding my nickels out of me. I didn't have many nickels, either.

"It was in Miss Counselman's class she asked me to go to her party. The old biddy had a business letter or something up on the blackboard and she was pointing at it with a pointer and yapping away and everybody was scribbling it all down. I thought Margie was, too, but she tore a sheet out of her binder and folded it up and stuck it under my elbow. I remember what it said: 'I'm having a birthday party next Friday night. Would you like to come?'

"Well, I almost came right then. My old heart was going budoingg, budoingg, budoingg. I thought sure as hell she'd hear it, so I said 'Sure' so loud old Counselman heard me and turned around and gave me the beady eye.

"After school when I was walking home with her she told me all about it and when to come and all. But I was getting pretty scared. I knew damn well they were going to dance and I didn't know how, and I'd never been to any kind of party like that before. I was beginning to wish to hell I hadn't snapped at it in such a hurry. Aw, and—you know—I'd always felt real big and clumsy and stupid in front of Margie—you know how you do— but I kept thinking, this is it, man, this is it, this is the big deal. But then I kept worrying did she know about Ster being kicked out of school for getting caught in a gang-bang with May Pearl Jackson in the boiler room a couple years before, and I kept worrying about did she know Ma ran the Sacramento Diner.

"Aw, hell," Jack had said, grimacing and shaking his head and avoiding Ben's eyes. "I was *really* screwed up. Well, and I didn't tell Ma till the last minute I was going to Margie's party. I was getting so I hoped the Watsons' house would get struck by lightning or Mr. Watson'd walk in front of a truck or something. Or that maybe I'd better go walk in front of a truck. Just a little one, with fenders that bent easy. Jesus, Ben, I was sweating. But then Friday night came around and I had to tell Ma I was going out and I knew damn well what she was going to say."

Jack said, in a strained, tremulous voice, " 'Oh, now isn't that sweet of her, dear? Is she a nice girl?' " and then he laughed and rubbed his hand over his mouth. "I said damn right she was a nice girl. Her old man was vice-president of the bank, how could she help being a nice girl? Well, then she took hold of my hands and told me she was sure I'd be a gentleman and have a nice time. She told me to be sure and be a gentleman about ten times. She'd been going on like that ever since Ster got booted out of school. When that Goddam Ster got caught and Mr. Prentiss called her up about it, it just about killed her, and she was half-sick all the time anyway. She kept getting fatter all the time till she could hardly walk for being so fat. Her face was real fat and white except kind of gray under the white, and her hair was all coming out gray where she parted it.

"Anyway, I went on upstairs and got dressed. I had a pretty decent pair of green pants I always saved for good, and I'd shot a day's pay on a black-and-white-striped Filipino tie at Marchand's. And I spit on my shoes and polished them up with some toilet paper. And then I put on my letter sweater.

"You remember it, don't you? It was bright red with a big old H.M. on the front and a white stripe on the sleeve and white buttons down the front. Sure, you remember it. Well, it was new then and I thought it looked pretty slick, and, hell, I'd never had a coat or a suit. We never had any money to buy crap like that and what the hell would I have done with one anyway? I told you I'd never gone to any parties before and we'd stopped going to church when Pop got killed. Well, anyway, I put on the damn sweater. I was sorry Margie'd seen it so many times, but, what the hell, I thought I looked pretty slick.

"So then I went to the party. Somebody's told me you ought to always get to a place about fifteen minutes late, so I walked real slow and I had a box of candy for Margie all wrapped up in tissue paper and pink ribbon and stuck under my arm. Oh, I was the boy that night, all right. When I got up on the Watsons' front porch I combed my hair again and unbuttoned my sweater and then buttoned it up again and unbuttoned the bottom two buttons. There was a whole slew of nice cars lined up in front of the house and I felt sorry for these poor dumb bastards didn't know enough not to come right at eight. But I could hear music from inside the house and I knew they were dancing and I damn near chickened out right then. Margie came to the door and she really looked good. She had on some kind of long blue dress left lots of bare around her neck and shoulders and she had a gold locket on a chain around her neck. She smiled at me kind of funny, like she'd gone into an unlimed backhouse on a hot day, and she kept pulling at the locket. But she told me to come on in.

"Well, you can see what a big clown I must've looked like, with my letter sweater and my green pants and my Filipino tie and a box of four-bit candy under my arm, and I was beginning to know it. I could see inside the house and guys were dancing. Bud Greene in a dark-blue suit and that bastard Chuck Ensminger in one of these black jobs with the shiny lapels they wear in the movies. And the girls all had on long dresses like Margie. Oh, Jesus, and the floor was all polished to hell and there was ribbons strung from the chandelier to the corners and the band was going at it, and I knew damn well I wasn't going in there.

"So I stood there with my teeth in my mouth and my shoes full of feet, gawking and unbuttoning my sweater, and buttoning it up again, and fixing the box of candy under my arm, and Margie kept saying wouldn't I come in, Jack, like she didn't mean a word of it. I wasn't going in there. I felt like I got sucked on some big joke or on a snipe hunt or something and I was blushing and sweating and…Damn!

"Well, I gave her some crap about my Ma being sick with the doctor there and all, and how I'd just come by to tell her I couldn't come. And I'll bet she'd said, oh, she was sorry, Jack, and had the door closed before I could even turn around, which was doing pretty good.

"I ran down the steps and out onto the sidewalk, because another car'd just pulled up and I didn't want anybody to see me. I didn't know till I got down to the end of the block I'd forgot to give her her box of candy, and I turned around and heaved it as far as I could down the street toward Margie's, like I'd dropped way back from scrimmage and was heaving one fifty yards to a fast end. I didn't even hear it hit. Jesus, I was miserable and mad at everything and everybody and I was wishing there was some way I could go back there and spit in their eye, but what the hell could I do? I was really the big clown, and I ran all the way home and climbed up to my room over the shed roof because, honest to Jesus, I would've took off for China if I'd had to talk to Ma right then."

When he had finished he had lain back on his bed, laughing, and he had seemed to enjoy telling it, as though by the telling, by making a joke of it, he was able to rid himself of the embarrassment that was within him.

Ben supposed that Margie was a mark on Jack; how much of one he could not know. It had sounded like a small thing, but for Jack it had probably not been small. Then there was the life they led, a life where there was not much place for marriage, and women had always been easy for Jack. But he knew there was no simple reason why Jack looked upon V in one way and he looked upon her in another. It was just that fundamentally their viewpoints were different, and Jack's was more like that of the others they knew than was his own.

The next day when they were coming in from work he apologized to Jack. Jack grinned at him embarrassedly and did not speak right away. Then he said, "Aw, forget it, Ben. I know how you feel."

"Well, I'm sorry I blew like that," Ben said. "It's no business of mine."

"It is, in a way. You kind of got slung out of your room."

"You'd do the same for me, I guess." Ben paused, and then he said tiredly, "I don't know. It's just that…It's just that she looks like a good girl and all that, and she's kind of too young. I guess you know what I mean."

"Sure," Jack said. "Yeah, I guess it looks kind of poor, unh? But—you know—it kind of got tossed at me. I don't like it, either. I know it stinks."

"Yeah."

"It's tough, all right," Jack said. "She's only eighteen and I hate to see her slugged around before she gets to know the ropes."

"Too bad she has to get to know the ropes."

"Yeah, well, she's sharp as hell. She'll be all right. I'm just the first guy she's ever known very well, is all."

There was a false grin on Jack's face, and Ben nodded tightly and moved away from him. He rubbed his hand across his eyes. His eyes felt hot and dry.

It was no business of his, he told himself, no business of his at all, but he had never felt so bitterly and furiously rebellious; at the injustice of life, at the monstrous heedlessness and cruelty and dog-eat-dog of the world. It was not merely at Jack now, it went past Jack, and, too, it was that he felt so profoundly sorry for V. And not merely sorrow, but an enormous, impotent, resentful pity; for he could see what was ahead for her as though it were written in a book for him to read and memorize.

9

Although he tried to keep away from them, he could not. Jack and V came to the Hitching Post several nights a week, and twice in the three months that followed Jack asked Ben over to the room for a drink. The room had not changed much, except that now the beds were made and the clothes that had usually been strewn around, put away. On the bureau were a large bottle of cologne, several jars and boxes arranged neatly beneath the mirror on a white handkerchief, and a framed photograph of V on a horse, looking very young and squinting into the sun. In the corner behind the closet door stood a pair of Texas boots.

Once he went to a movie with them, and once swimming, sitting beside the pool with his shirt off but with his trousers still on, so that V would not see his leg, watching them laughing and splashing in the big public pool, as Jack tried to teach her to swim.

When they came out they sat down, one on either side of him. Jack had on a pair of tight blue trunks and V was wearing a skirted gray wool bathing suit with a number 28 stenciled on the front that Jack had rented at the pool.

"This is such a funny bathing suit," V said, grimacing and loosening it around her legs.

"You look great," Jack said. "You look like Miss America of 1910."

"I wish you'd buy me a bathing suit."

"I'll buy you a bathing suit when you learn how to swim."

"How's she doing?" Ben asked.

"She was doing fine till she swallowed about half the pool. See how it's gone down? About a foot."

"You shouldn't have let go of me," V said. "I got scared. I told you not to go away like that." She leaned back and grasped the arms of her deck chair, closing her eyes against the sun. Her color was high and her face shone with drops of water. Water dripped from the skirt of her bathing suit onto the concrete beneath her chair.

"You should have come in, Ben," she said. "The water felt awfully good."

"Oh, I just like to sit in the sun," Ben said. Jack glanced at him quickly, and then the ice-cream man came by. Bells tinkled on the front of his white cart.

"You want an ice-cream bar, V?" Jack said.

Her hands relaxed and turned over, palms up and half-open. "I don't want anything," she said.

Ben sat watching her out of the corners of his eyes. Even though it hurt him to be around them, he loved to watch her. In the dozen times he had seen her he had come to know every one of her mannerisms: the way her eyes would widen and she would lick her lips when she was afraid she had said the wrong thing; the way she took Jack's arm and bent her head to one side to look up into his face, as though she were asking a question; the self-conscious awkward grace with which she moved; the way she talked, straight and honest, like a man, her emotions told exactly in the sound of her voice, with no attempt at concealment.

Once, when Ben was with them at the Hitching Post, she spilled her beer in her lap and broke out with a stream of curses, and Jack laughed in his peculiar way, heartily, with his head tipped back, without smiling, because she had obviously not known what she was saying. Then Jack became serious and told her that women were not supposed to swear, that men swore because they were stupid and didn't know any proper words to express what they meant, and that he would paddle her tail if he ever heard her do it again. She listened to him gravely, surreptitiously mopping at her lap with a napkin, watching him with round eyes. When he had finished, she nodded and smiled nervously at Ben, sitting silent and very straight, with her chin drawn back. It was then that Ben felt his heart go out to her, as though he had taken it very gently from his chest and offered it to her, and she had accepted it and thanked him with the little smile, and had carefully put it away somewhere so it would not get damaged.

Ben remained at the table when they left, and, watching them go, he felt a strong current of emotion running through him. Suddenly, in his eyes, they had both gained a profound and mysterious stature, which appeared to him so strongly he gasped. Watching them as they walked past the front window and disappeared, he was breathless, his eyes staring, his mouth dry, for clearly he had seen their capability together, and clearly he had seen their doom, and the sight remained indelibly printed inside his head.

He did not understand it, it shook and confused him, and after that he always tried to refuse whenever Jack asked him to go somewhere with them. He did not want to see happen what he knew was going to happen, and he tried to watch them from a distance, detachedly, grieving as it began to work out the way he had known it would.

The first time Jack and Petey Willing came by for Red, to go out and get drunk, Ben tried to tell himself this did not mean anything. But he knew it did. And then he heard that Jack was seeing Peggy again. Then a month or so later he saw Jack at the Hitching Post with Ruth Adams, and one day a redheaded girl picked him up after work in a black Ford coupe.

Ben tried to stay out of it, he tried to consider it none of his affair, but he was Jack's best friend and they were thrown together every day on the job, and there came a time when he knew he was going to say something to Jack, knowing it wouldn't do any good, knowing it would just cause trouble between Jack and himself. But he had to say something.

The two of them, with the blade and the cat and tampers, were working together almost a mile south of the others. Sometimes Push and Harry would come down to eat lunch with them, but most of the time there were just the three of them, Jack and Ben and Toussaint.

One Monday when they had finished lunch, Toussaint had taken their water bags to try to find the water truck, and Jack was lying in the shade of Ben's cat, his head on his bunched-up jacket, his cap covering his face. Ben sat beside him, his arms around his knees, leaning against the track. The metal of the track was burning hot, searing through his shirt, but he did not move, staring down at Jack.

Finally he licked his lips and leaned forward. His voice sounded stiff when he spoke. "Well, how's she taking it, Jack?"

"Who taking what?" Jack's voice was muffled under his cap.

"V. How's she taking it?"

Jack grunted and raised one knee.

"Has she learned the ropes yet?" Ben said huskily. He picked up a handful of dirt and let it sift through his fingers into a pile between his feet. Heat shimmered off down the smooth grade to where Harry's roller loomed, far off, and to the right he could see the tops of the cars speeding along the old highway.

"She's not bitching," Jack said.

"No, I guess she wouldn't."

Jack removed the cap from his face and slowly raised himself to a sitting position, pushing down with his hands and sliding his hips back. "Now, just what the hell's it to you?"

"I told you," Ben said. He spat on the ground and kicked a

pile of dirt over the spit. "I just hate to see you taking her over the jumps. I think it's pretty Goddamn miserable."

"Okay. I'm a heel."

Ben didn't say anything, feeling Jack's yellow eyes searching his face. He removed his cap and ran his hand, hard, over his hair, and then pulled the cap low on his forehead.

"Aw, Jesus, Ben," Jack said. "Quit the Christering, will you?"

"Sure," Ben said. Jack was still staring at him and he made a second pile of dirt. He made this bigger than the first. "You just don't know what you've got!" he said suddenly, loudly. "You don't even know what you're doing!" He wished he could tell Jack what he thought, but he would not permit himself any more sloppy talk. He knew he was wrong already in even talking seriously about this. He grimaced and scraped his boot over the second pile of dirt.

"You hot for V?" Jack asked gently.

"I just don't like what you're doing to her," Ben said. And then he said, "It gripes me because I like you, and I don't..." He stopped. He could see Toussaint plodding down the grade toward them, dust pluming around his feet. He was carrying the three water bags, bent away from them to balance their weight.

Jack was silent for a long time, but finally he said, "I'm no good for her, Ben. You ought to see that. I've got to let her down some way, and I'm doing it the easiest way I know."

"Sure," Ben said. Sure, he said to himself, as he got up and stepped around to the front of the cat. He cranked the starting motor and it caught with a series of small, vicious explosions. He shifted in the cat engine too soon, and turned to look at Jack, who was walking slowly across to the Adams.

Ben took the water bag Toussaint handed him and tossed it into the cab. Toussaint stood watching him as he climbed up on the tracks, frowning.

"How come you mad at Jack, Ben?"

Ben sucked at his lower lip and kicked the friction brakes loose. "Nothing," he said, knowing that Toussaint could not hear him in the roar of the engine as he opened the throttle. Toussaint put his hand to his ear and squinted up at him.

"How?"

"Nothing, Goddamn it!" Ben yelled. He watched Jack climb up on the Adams, then he savagely jerked up the dozer blade, shifted into gear and let the clutch slam out so that the cat lurched spastically forward. Then the tracks bit into the ground and the cat settled down, the tampers rolling and jolting behind, the knurled feet spiking into the soft earth under the weight of the water-filled drums. Ben sat, half-turned, with his shoulders slumped and his hands resting on the dozer control, watching the feet bite deep, bruising and scarring the earth.

That night Ben heard Petey's car honk out in front, and Red hurriedly stuck a pack of cigarettes into his shirt pocket, ran his comb through his hair, and went out and down the stairs. Ben had been asked to go along, but he had said he had some letters to write, and now he stepped to the window to see if Jack were with them. He was, and Ben saw Red hurry out the door and get into Petey's coupe. The door slammed shut and the coupe sped off down the street, the exhaust pipe crackling and popping.

He was lying on his stomach on his bed, with a tablet in front of him and a pencil gripped between his fingers, wondering what to say to his mother, when there was a knock on the door. He sighed and got up to open it. V stood there, holding her purse in both hands in front of her.

"Hello, Ben," she said. "Could I talk to you a minute?"

"Sure," he said. "Sure, V." He turned quickly, pulled the covers up on the beds and pushed his and Red's work clothes off the green armchair. "Sit down, V. I'm sorry it's such a mess."

"Oh, that doesn't matter." She sat down and smiled a stiff smile at him, sitting as she had when he had first seen her, knees and feet close together, hands clutching the purse in her lap. Her brown eyes watched him gravely as he got her a cigarette and an ashtray, and lit the cigarette for her. She wore a black, pleated skirt and a sweater that was too big for her, the sleeves rolled into fat lumps around her wrists. Her hair was clean looking, long and loose and dark-blonde.

Ben blew out the match and sat down on the edge of the bed, one hand uncomfortably in his pocket. "It's good to see you," he said nervously. "You look good, V." He started to say, How's everything? but he caught himself. He knew why she had come.

"Thank you," V said, and they both looked at the open window at the same time. The night was dark and warm, and a warm breeze came in and ruffled the pages of the tablet beside him on the bed.

"I'm not keeping you from anything, am I?" V asked.

Ben shook his head. "I guess you want to talk about Jack, don't you?"

The smile was fixed tightly on her lips, as though she held it there only by a terrific effort, and when she looked back at him he bowed his head and smoked his cigarette with quick, short draughts, waiting for her to speak. "Go ahead," he said finally.

"He doesn't love me, does he, Ben?"

"Jack's a funny guy," he began, and then he stopped. He wasn't going to lie to her. He tasted something hard and metallic in his throat.

"You're his best friend," V said.

"Yeah, I guess so."

"Ben, I've got to talk to somebody about it and you're the only one I know. Please tell me the truth."

He drew savagely on his cigarette, snubbed it savagely out. "All right," he said. "I don't think he loves you."

He didn't look at her to see how she had taken that. It was private and he would not intrude. He waited silently until she said, "Is he trying to get rid of me?"

"I think he is," he said wearily, and then he looked up. Her face was ugly and creased, but she didn't move, her eyes fixed on his. Finally she shut them. She dropped her head slowly, and he saw that she was crying, silently, only her shoulders shaking slightly, and he could see no tears. When she raised her head again, her eyes were open, helpless and scared, containing nothing but helplessness and fear, and one hand crept up the side of her face, the fingers working and tugging at her hair.

"V…" he said. "V…" He wanted to tell her that the word love didn't mean anything. It was only a word used in movies and books and magazine stories that covered an infinite number of variations of emotions and feelings and sensations, but it did not really mean anything. He wished she had not used it. It was a word from poems and a million popular songs, but it did not mean anything. But he did not know how to explain this, and he did not know how to explain what he felt, somehow, should exist between her and Jack; did exist because, although she did not understand it, she must feel it intuitively; did not exist because Jack neither understood nor recognized it; and that he, Ben, only understood because he could see it in the round, detached from it because he could never have it, watching like a spectator at a game where the players were blind or blindfolded. But he could not formulate in his mind what he wished to express, or convert his confused thoughts into words, and so he did not speak.

"I don't know what to do," V whispered. She rose abruptly and walked over to the window, turning her back to him. He watched her back as she looked out, watched her hand holding the gray purse, the blurred and indistinct curve of her cheek. The room was silent. After a moment he heard the faint, lonely hoot of a train. He heard footsteps on the sidewalk; he could hear his own slow breathing.

"V," he said suddenly. "If you want to hang onto him...Listen, you've got the tools. You've got the tools if you just learn how to use them." Then he paused and said, "It's too bad you have to."

"I don't know about things like that," V whispered.

"You've got to learn fast. You've got to hang on and learn fast." He watched her, there at the window. The train whistled once more, and he knew she had been listening for it, too. "You've got to learn fast," he said again, but she did not answer.

At last she took her lipstick from her purse and painted her mouth, using the dark glass of the raised window as a mirror. He watched her as she applied the lipstick slowly and carefully, and then, sick, he watched her walk to the door.

As she passed him he saw her face. It shocked him. It was as though it had been, for a moment, agonizingly contorted into the shape of everything inside her. But there was no grief there now, no fear; there were only the hard, cold, angular lines of complete determination. It was as though every quality but this had been suddenly wrenched out of her; as though all there was left was an iron and single-minded resolution. Revenge, he thought, and with the glimpse of her face, the thought frightened him; but then he knew it was not revenge. Knowing what it was he felt tired and wrung, and all at once the feeling welled up in him that he had to get away from this. He was going to get away from this.

When she opened the door, she paused. She did not turn around and he did not rise, but she said coolly, "Thanks, Ben," and then she went out.

When he heard her heels rapping down the hall he wanted to call her back, to tell her to give Jack up, not to tear herself to pieces in the trying. "V," he said, but he said it softly, and she could not have heard him.

The next day Ben quit the highway job and went back to San Jose. He got a job running a bulldozer for a contractor named Rex McLean. He wanted no more of Jack and V.

10

Ben was working at the new naval base on the Peninsula the Monday the Pearl Harbor news started coming in. The next day he tried to enlist in the Navy. He was already 4-F, and the Navy wouldn't take him, nor the Army, nor the Marines. He knew he was never going to be part of this, because of his leg.

In February they finished the grading at the naval base and moved down to Hamilton Field, where new air-strips were being installed. He knew Doris was working as a secretary in one of the offices at Hamilton Field, because his mother and Mrs. Rasmussen had mutual friends, but he made no effort to look her up. He saw her a few times, riding around with a fat captain in a new Chrysler convertible, seeing only her small white face above the car door, her black hair piled high in a bunch in front, and waving low on her shoulders in the back. He knew she was doing a good deal of partying and drinking and sleeping around with the officers at the field, because the mutual friend had told his mother that too. Her husband was a pfc down at Camp Callan.

But evidently Doris had heard he was working at Hamilton Field, because one Saturday afternoon she came out to see him, and when he was through work he took her home. She lived in an auto court which, because of the housing shortage, had been converted into a row of one-room apartments and in her apartment were large photographs of four men in Air Corps caps, all of whom looked very much alike, and a picture of her husband in his Army uniform, signed in a scrawling hand, "Your Johnny," under the inscription, "To My Dear Baby Deer."

On the bed were three large, cloth-covered animals, a rabbit and a pink dog and a black-and-white dog, and on the bedside table were two glasses, one of them containing an inch of liquor in which a cigarette floated soggily, and a bottle one-third full of good bourbon.

They sat down on the bed and drank the rest of the bourbon without saying much, and then Doris cooked some chili on the hot plate and made some toast while Ben took a shower. After dinner Doris brought out another bottle of the good bourbon, which she said Hughey had given her. When they were drunk she sat on Ben's lap and put her arms around his neck and cried drunkenly on his shoulder. That night he stayed with her.

He slept with her often after that. It didn't matter to him that there were others as well, and although he felt badly about her husband, Doris said he knew about her and was going to get a divorce when he came back to San Jose. One night the fat captain came when Ben was there, and barged in past Doris and tried to hit Ben. The captain was drunk and when Ben pushed him away, trying to defend himself, the captain fell down, and Doris screamed at him and kicked him till he got up. The captain tried to hit Ben again, but Doris screamed, "You touch him and I'll kill you! You touch him and I'll kill you, you fat bastard pig drunk dog son of a bitch!" Ben held her as she tried to claw the captain, and the captain looked confused, and suddenly very young, and began to cry. When he had gone Doris had hysterics on the bed. Ben sat beside her until she quieted down, then he went out and got into his car. Down the road a way he stopped the car and sat for a long time with his face in his hands.

He had intended not to see Doris again, but a few days later she was waiting at the sentry box at the gate when he drove out of the field after work. When he stopped for the sentry she got in the front seat with him and he had to drive her home. In the apartment she began to cry and she made him come to bed with her, crying and saying she wanted to die when he had gone away.

In the morning when the alarm went off, Doris woke before he did, and reached across him to turn it off. She remained with her chest pressed against his and her cheek against his cheek and he could feel her breath on his ear. "Benny," she whispered. "Johnny's coming home on furlough next week."

"Is he?"

"I got a letter from him day before yesterday. Do you want to read it, Benny?"

"No," he said. "He wrote it to you."

"He called me a whore nine times," she said, and giggled. "Don't you want to read it? He called me a bitch in heat twice."

"I've got to get to work," Ben said. "I'll get some breakfast down at the corner. You go on back to sleep for an hour, honey."

She reached down and rubbed her fingers over the scar on his leg, her chin still pressed into his neck. He thought she would stop it after a minute, but she kept tickling her fingers over the scar, breathing into his ear, and finally he pushed her hand roughly away. "I asked you not to do that."

"Benny, we're going to get a divorce. Do you want to marry me?"

He stared at her long sheaf of rumpled black hair, and then she raised her head and looked into his eyes. Her eyes were bright and strange behind the black eyelashes, and her pale mouth was twisted into a tight, thin smile. Suddenly he pulled the covers back, swung his legs out and got up. Doris sat up in bed, watching him as he got his clothes from the chair and put them on. He turned his back to her.

"Aren't you going to say anything, Ben?"

"I have to think," he said. "We'll talk about it tonight." When he went out the door she was still sitting up in bed watching him, her narrow shoulders hunched up, her chest flat and dead-white with her nipples looking like red twenty-five-cent pieces pasted on it.

He thought about it all day. He didn't know whether he wanted to marry her or not. He didn't know how he felt about her; he didn't think he felt anything toward her one way or another. He felt only a kind of blank nothingness. And it was a poor life for a wife, he knew, moving around from construction job to construction job, never knowing where you were going to live, and where a wife might be a focal point in a life that had no focal point; too often she was only a piece of inconvenient baggage. What he wanted now was to go back to Bakersfield. Something—curiosity, he told himself—had been urging him to go for a long time. He thought he would go back. Merely in being near Jack and V he had felt something infinitely larger, infinitely more fulfilling than this affair, or even marriage to Doris could ever be.

That night, to avoid a scene, he did not go back to her again. He quit his job, went home, wrote Doris a letter and asked his mother to mail it when he was gone. The next day he packed his bags and put them in his car, and when he had kissed his mother goodbye and had shaken hands with his father, he drove south out of San Jose and over the Pacheco Pass, and then down the San Joaquin Valley, ignoring the thirty-five-mile-an-hour wartime speed limit. It was late in the evening when he got into Bakersfield, and he drove slowly along the main street, looking at the familiar buildings and the red and blue neon signs that glowed and hummed in the darkness. He did not know where he was going, but finally he parked his car in front of the Hitching Post and went in to see if anyone he knew were there.

The first thing he saw was the legs of a girl who was sitting on a stool at the end of the bar nearest the door. He paused, looking at the legs; they were long and tanned and the girl's skirt had fallen away from her knees as she leaned back on her stool, her face turned from him so that he could see only her long, dark blonde hair. But he knew who it was, and then he saw Jack, sitting next to her.

Jack was leaning forward over the bar, talking, but his yellow eyes widened when he saw Ben. He grinned slowly. Then he yelled, "Ben!" and slid off the stool and was slapping Ben on the back. "Damn it, Ben," he cried. "Where the hell you been?"

"Hi, Jack," Ben said, and he could feel his face muscles pull painfully with his own grin. He had been away a long time, and now he felt as though he had come home. He squeezed Jack's arm. Jack looked taller and leaner, older, and his face was thinner through the cheeks than Ben had remembered. His slanting yellow eyes were glinting happily; his mouth pulled down at the corners and he stuck out his lower lip.

"You jug-eared little bastard," he whispered. "Goddamn it, it's good to see you."

"Hello, Ben," V said, and Ben, still holding Jack's arm, looked up at her. He didn't like what he saw. She looked older too, sleek and blonder. Her smile was sleek and sure of itself; it was a smile he had never seen before, and only her eyes held the old, grave, innocent look he remembered. She had learned the ropes. He released Jack's arm.

"How are you, V?" he said.

She looked at him levelly, smiling. Her chest was tan, swelling down into the top of her dress, and she wore no brassiere. He turned away and hit Jack gently on the arm with his closed fist. "It's good to see you, man," he said sincerely. "How's everything going?"

"Going great," Jack said. "Everything's booming, everybody's got draft deferments, everybody's happy and drunk all the time, and where the hell you been, anyway? How about a drink?" Ben sat down on the other side of him from V, and Ernie brought them a round of straight shots.

"Say, where's Peg?" Ben asked.

"Married, for Christ's sake," Jack said. "Married a lousy truck driver." They both laughed, Jack heartily, his head tipped back. Ben could see V watching them in the mirror behind the bar.

"Listen, where the hell you been?" Jack demanded sternly. "Don't you even know how to write? You're a damn checkout friend, you are."

"Been up around San Jose, mostly. You out at the air base?"

"Me and everybody else."

"How's chances of getting on?"

"Good. They're dying for skinners. Can you run a blade?"

"I've been on one about a year," Ben said. "But I'm not in your class yet."

Jack grinned and slapped him on the back. "Listen, *everybody's* out there. Push's grade foreman, and Petey's on a Turnapull, and Harry's got a big old roller about a thousand years old, and old Red's got the cat and tampers, and Toussaint's stake-running for me. Everybody. Mac, and Hugo Crane…Did you know Hugo?"

"You think I can get on?" Ben asked.

"Hell, yes! Push'll go wild when he hears you're back. He's been asking about you all along. Say, how about rooming with me?"

"I'd like to," Ben said slowly, and then he looked past Jack at V. She leaned forward toward him.

"Why didn't you let someone know where you were?" she asked. "We've missed you, haven't we, Jack?"

"Hell, yes," Jack said. "Bakersfield's been all shot to hell with you gone, Ben. Everybody moping around, drinking by themselves. Terrible."

Two men in leather jackets came in the door. One of them nudged the other and they both looked at V's legs. The second one nodded to Jack. Jack nodded shortly in return, scowled, and finished his drink.

"Where've you been, Ben?" V said. He could see down the neck of her dress as she leaned toward him.

"San Jose. Up the Peninsula. All around."

"Why didn't you let anybody know you were going?"

"Aw, you know. I made up my mind in a hurry. You know the way you do."

Jack's eyes were veiled and he slid the shot glass back and forth between his hands on the smooth top of the bar. All the gaiety seemed to have left him, and now he was morose and silent.

"What're you doing now, V?" Ben asked.

"I'm working at Deterle's."

"Car-hopping?"

"Yeah, it's a good racket," Jack broke in. "She wears a short skirt and a tight sweater and all the jerks and dogfaces break their necks tipping her." He flipped the shot glass upside down and sat staring at it moodily. V put her hand on his knee and laughed and winked at Ben in the mirror.

"Jack gets awfully jealous," she said.

Ben jerked his head around as the jukebox began playing, and then he slid off the stool to his feet. He had not touched his drink and, remembering it, he tossed the liquor down his throat, coughed, and wiped his mouth on his shirt sleeve.

"Everything's all right then?" he asked. He didn't look at V.

"Everything's fine," she said. Jack turned toward her curiously and she smiled at him, her hand still on his knee. Ben wondered how she had managed it. She had won, some way, he saw, and he wondered how she had done it. He thought suddenly of Doris, surprised that he had hardly thought of her all day; already, in the trip down from San Jose, she had faded as far into the past as she had ever been before.

"Well, I've got to hit the sack," he said. "I've had a long trip. You still at the same place, Jack?"

"Yeah. You know where the key is. Can't you stick around awhile?"

"Have another drink with us, Ben," V said.

But he shook his head. "I'm pretty tired. I'll see you tomorrow, maybe. So long."

"So long," Jack said.

As he walked past V, Ben saw her lips form words. "Everything's fine," she said with her lips, and he nodded to her and kept on walking. He didn't want to see her smile again.

11

He had thought he would be glad to see V win, like this. But he was not glad. He hated the price she seemed to have paid for the victory, and he hated the price she was making Jack pay. He remembered the cold determination he had seen etched on her face the night before he had left for San Jose, and although she kept it hidden now, he knew it had remained with her and had grown and held her firmly on a track like the blinders of a horse. Yet, in a way, she had not won; the grip she had on Jack could easily be broken, and she must know it. Because of this, and because of what she had made herself become, he pitied her, yet he wondered if V, knowing that as yet she did not really have Jack, was hurting him just for the sake of the hurting.

For, sorry as he had been for V, and sorry as he was for what she had made of herself in her desire to have Jack, he was sorrier now for Jack. Her hold on Jack was jealousy, he came to see; he would see her with others beside Jack, and he did not know how far she went to keep Jack jealous, and he tried not to care. But he was personally ashamed to see Jack losing, in jealousy, his dignity. Rooming with him Ben saw it going gradually, and on a few occasions completely gone, stripped off like a shirt from a deformed body.

One night Ben took V to a show and after the show to the Hitching Post. He had stopped at the drive-in where she worked one evening when he was riding around with Red Young, and she had as much as asked him to. But he didn't like being used to make Jack jealous, and he told her so. He didn't like the way she sat at the bar with her skirt up around her thighs and he told her that, too, and when he went home Jack had known where he had been, and had embarrassedly tried to make conversation to show Ben it didn't matter. But Ben knew that it did matter. It was something else now between the two of them that could not be spoken of and there was too much of that already.

The next day on the job Red came over to talk to Ben about V. Ben knew by the sneering grin of his face what he was going to say.

"Hey, you look all shot this morning. Get much last night?"

Ben shook his head silently, telling himself that Red did not mean anything, this was just Red's way. But Red said, "What the hell's the matter with you? Everybody else in town's getting it off that little teaser," and Ben felt rage burst weakly in his chest, as though, in some way, the whole trouble were Red's fault.

"Have you?" he said.

Red scowled. "Aw, hell, no. The bitch won't have nothing to do with me." He raised his water bag to his lips, drank, then corked it up. His cat, with the tampers behind, was drawn up next to Ben's grader, and Red stood beside the cab with his elbows resting on the floorboards, scowling.

"She's no bitch," Ben said.

Red looked up, squinting his eyes against the sun. "Okay," he said. "She's no bitch. What's the matter, you gone on that dame too?"

"She's no bitch," Ben said again, softly. "She's not letting everybody get it off her, either."

"Oh, hell, no!"

Ben leaned down toward him and said through his teeth, "Who?"

"Aw, how the hell should I know?" Red said. "But you can

sure as hell tell it by the way she flashes her legs and wiggles her tail. That dame's been around plenty since you was gone."

"Listen," Ben said. "Don't say anything like that till you know it, you hear? I mean it. Goddamn it, Red. I don't know what kind of bastard you are, but if you want to shoot off your mouth just don't come shoot it to me." He stopped. He was trembling, and he braced his hands on the edge of the seat, tightening his arms and staring down at Red.

Red stared back at him narrowly for a moment. The tip of his tongue came out and wet his upper lip, and Ben wondered if he were going to have to fight him. But suddenly Red made a wry face, lifted his hands in a gesture of resignation and turned away. "Gee-zus, Kee-rist!" Ben heard him say, as he walked back to his cat.

Jack drove his grader over from the fine grade for lunch, with Toussaint on the seat beside him, and they all sat in the shade of Harry's roller to eat; Harry, Ben and Red, and Jack and Toussaint. Jack was sullen and quiet and Ben saw Toussaint looking at him with his head tilted to one side. "Jack mean today," he said. "Look like Jack got woman trouble."

Red laughed loudly, unscrewing the top of his thermos. "V giving you a bad time, Jack?" Jack didn't look up, seeming not to have heard, and Harry glanced at Ben quickly.

"Well, it's a good kind of trouble," Red said. "Your trouble can stick her shoes under my bed any time she's got the itch."

Jack's yellow eyes flickered at him, then away. He looked bored, and he stretched his legs out. Toussaint was shaking his head. "How's the rolling going, Harry?" Ben said casually.

"Aw, it's rough. Damn thing wanders all over the grade. That damn thing's so old…"

But Red raised his voice. "What's the matter, Jack? Can't you handle it anymore?"

"Goddamn it, shut up!" Ben yelled. He jumped to his feet. But Red was looking at Jack, his thick lips drawn back in a tight grin, and turning, Ben saw Jack rise slowly. Knots of muscle had climbed on his cheekbones, and he stood over Red with his thumbs hooked on his belt. "Get up," he said.

Red laughed and started to get up, but Ben took a step forward and stood between them.

"Cut it out, Jack," he said. He tried to push Jack away, but Jack stood solidly, his chest pressing back against Ben's hands, his thumbs still hooked on his belt. Ben pushed at his chest. "Cut it out," he said gently. "You guys're acting like a couple of kids."

Jack said nothing, staring over Ben's shoulder; his face was blank, but through the mask Ben could see frustration and futility and blind rage. "Get Red out of here, Harry," he said. "Go on, beat it, Red!" He stood in front of Jack until he heard Red and Harry moving away. Jack's eyes followed them; a muscle was twitching in his cheek. Toussaint whispered, "They gone now, Ben."

Ben turned. Red was walking stiffly across the grade to his cat, his arms swinging, fists clenched. Harry stood beside the front wheel of the roller, lighting a cigarette and looking after him. Ben saw Jack suddenly grimace; he swung around and moved off toward his grader. Toussaint hurried after him.

When they had gone, Harry said, "They're going to have it out."

"Yeah."

"Jack'd kill him," Harry said. "Not that I'd blame him. That bastard; why can't he ever let go of anything?"

"Red's pretty rugged. He's done some boxing."

"He's fat. Jack's got muscles even in his ears."

"He just looks fat."

Harry shook his head, his lips pursed, his forehead wrinkled.

"He's got twenty pounds on Jack," Ben said.

"Jack'd kill him," Harry said.

After work Ben rode home with Jack in the roadster. Jack was tense and quiet, concentrating on the road, his black hair standing on end in the wind that swept over the top of the windshield. Finally he said huskily, "Sorry about today, Ben."

"Forget it."

"I made a clown out of myself. I shouldn't let that bastard get under my skin like that."

"He rode you too far. I would've done the same thing, Jack."

"No. You wouldn't've," Jack said. His knuckles were white, where they gripped the wheel, and he was driving too fast. Ben bent down to light two cigarettes, then straightened up and handed one to Jack.

"Thanks," Jack said, and he slowed down a little. "I don't know what the hell's the matter with me lately!" he burst out. "I get the redeye too damn easy. All the time."

"Jack," Ben said.

"Yeah?"

"Why don't you check out of that league?"

"You mean V?"

"Yeah. Why don't you check out, Jack?"

They were in the city now, and Jack stopped for a red light behind a bus. Gas fumes drifted back at them. Suddenly Jack turned toward him; his face was blank, but it looked like the face that had stared over his shoulder at Red. "I can't," Jack said.

Ben didn't say anything more. He had known that, and he should not have said anything. He watched the bus pull away as the light clanged and changed colors, and Jack shifted into second and swung around it. "Let's forget it, unh?" he said.

"Yeah," Ben said. "Let's forget about it."

But he did not forget about it, and when Jack was in the shower he went out and got into his car and drove downtown to Deterle's drive-in. He was thinking that he had never felt anything so acutely as what V and Jack had done and were doing to each other. First, what Jack had done to V, and now what V was doing to Jack. They could have had something fine and good, something of the power he had glimpsed that night at the Hitching Post so long ago, and which he felt now even more strongly. He wanted it for them; desperately he wanted it for them. But instead they did this. Instead, Jack had made V cheap and calculating; instead, V was torturing Jack until, like a dog, he turned on the person nearest him. He had to make them stop it. They had to stop mutilating and destroying each other, for they were mutilating and destroying him too, and he could not separate himself from them.

There were no other cars in the service area, and he saw V come out of the grill as he parked. She walked over to him, her order pad in her hand, then seeing who it was, she waved and stuck the pad back in her belt. Her short blue skirt flicked back and forth over her thighs as she walked, and she had on a white sweater, white boots, and a blue scarf tied over her hair.

"Hello, Ben," she said. She came up to the car and put one foot on the running board.

Ben said, "Get in a minute, V. I want to talk to you."

"Why, Ben!"

He looked down at his hands. They were shaking, and he gripped them on the wheel. This was what he hated now; this was part of her new shell he hated. The V he had known before he had gone to San Jose would not have said that. "Don't get cute with me, V," he said quietly. "I want to talk about Jack."

Her red smile faded and she walked around to the other side

of the car and got in beside him. Her eyes were round and inquiring. Ben looked down at his hands once more. "What're you trying to do to him?" he said.

"What do you mean?"

"You know what I mean. What is it you want?"

Out of the corner of his eye he could see her bare knees, and then he saw her reach up and flick the pink celluloid cupid that hung on a string from the rear-view mirror. It swung back and forth, clicking faintly against the windshield. "It was your advice," V said.

Ben clenched his teeth and looked out the window. An old Plymouth sedan full of soldiers pulled into the service area, and the other car-hop came out of the grill and hurried over to it. The cupid clicked against the glass.

"I did what you told me to," V said.

"Okay," Ben said. Then after a moment he said, "I didn't think you were going to like taking it out on him like this. You've got him now. I came over to ask you to quit it."

"How do you know?"

"Know what?" He turned toward her but her eyes avoided his. "Know what?" he said angrily.

"You said I've got him now."

"I just know. You know it too. I thought that was what you wanted."

Her voice came suddenly low-pitched and intense. "See...I have to be sure. I want to know how you know, Ben."

"I live with him."

She put her hands over her face and laughed softly, and when she let them drop her eyes were bright and for a moment he thought the old smile was back on her face. But he couldn't be sure. It was growing dark. The red neon sign over the grill had come on.

"Why doesn't he tell me?" she whispered.

"How can he? Damn it, how can he? The way you're piling it on." He shook his head savagely. "How can he, when you're running around with every bastard comes along, making him think you're easy and ready. He's too proud. Anybody'd be too proud." He stopped as his voice became thick.

"Ben, do you think it's been easy? Do you think this is the way I've wanted it?"

"Then why don't you quit it? Do you know what I think?"

"No," she said, and then she said, "What?"

"I think you get a kick out of seeing him crawl. Not crawl. Trying to keep from crawling."

"No," she whispered. "No, that's not true." She put out her hand and clutched the sleeve of his shirt. "You don't think that," she said. He could feel her hand trembling.

Finally he said, "Well, you've got him now. Do you want him, V?"

"Oh, yes!" Her voice was deep again. "That's all I ever want," she said. She put her hands over her face and her fingers looked tight and bloodless where they pressed against her forehead. But she was laughing, almost hysterically, when she put her hands on his shoulders, and she kissed him on the mouth and slid over to the door.

Ben put his fingers to his lips as he watched her get out. She stood on the asphalt, holding the door open. Her face was soft and completely beautiful. In the rosy light of the neon sign it looked like Arlene's face, the night she had shown him the gold football Bill Rasmussen had given her.

"I'm going to see him tomorrow night," she whispered. "You'll see what happens now, Ben. You'll see!" She slammed the door shut and ran over to the grill.

He sat motionless for a long time, before he started the

Chevrolet and drove out. He parked in front of a bar in the next block and went in and got drunk.

When he went home it was after midnight and Jack was asleep. Ben didn't turn on the light, standing looking down at Jack, swaying slightly, sick in the pit of his stomach. Finally he kicked off his shoes and lay down on the bed in his clothing, his hands clasped under his head, staring up into the blackness of the room. Things whirled in the darkness, and the room swayed from side to side. Jack and V were caught up in it, as he was. He felt sweat break out all over his body for he was sitting alone in the rumble seat of the roadster, and in the front seat Jack and V were entangled and wrapped in each other's arms until he could not tell one from the other. The roadster was swaying back and forth across the road, not in time to any song, but in deadly silence, the arcs wider and wider and the pace faster, and he sat rigid and sweating in the rumble seat, gripping the sides and watching the couple on the front seat with fascinated, frozen horror.

12

The next morning he felt hot and thirsty and tired and he was thinking of going away again. He had heard someone say they needed cat skinners up in Canada. They were paying big money, whoever-it-was had said, but you had to sign on for a year. He drowsed on his way to work with Jack, trying to picture what Canada and Alaska were like. He didn't say anything to Jack about V; he didn't want to have to think about V.

When finally the lunch hour came, he lay down with his head against one of the drums of Red's tampers to try to sleep. The rest of the job was out of sight and they seemed to have the whole, wide, hot, dusty valley to themselves. Red and Jack and Toussaint and Harry were shooting craps in the shade of Harry's roller and he could hear Toussaint chattering as he shook the dice: "Speak for Toussaint, dice…Stay away from me old seven… Come on eight, come on you double four…Hallooo, eight!"

The sun was hot and soothing on his face. He could feel it hot on his eyes beneath his eyelids, and then he was dreaming, an ugly confused dream in which there was no vision but only shouting sound. Toussaint's voice was crying out shrilly; there were other voices…He jerked awake, not knowing where he was at first, then knowing, and knowing what was wrong as he looked toward the others.

He grasped one of the long spikes of the tampers and pulled himself up. "Cut it out!" he yelled hoarsely. His feet were heavy, stumbling, as he ran toward them. "Cut it out, Jack!" he cried.

He saw Jack swing and Red dodge back. Harry and Toussaint

stood against the side of the roller; there was a grimace on Harry's dark, Indian face.

"Come on," Red said. "Come on, big boy." Jack stripped off his shirt and flung it from him. Harry took hold of Ben's wrist, pulling him up short as he ran toward them.

"Let go," Ben panted. "We got to stop it. Goddamn it!"

"You can't stop it," Harry said.

"They gone have it out anyway," Toussaint said. His eyes were wide open and rimmed with white. Ben heard the quick splat of fists behind him. Harry released his arm and he swung around.

Jack's nose was bleeding; a splash of scarlet covered his upper lip. He moved toward Red cautiously. "Come on," Red panted. "Try it again, blade man." His left lashed into Jack's face, lashed again.

"Cut it out, Goddamn it!" Ben cried. He took a step toward them.

"Keep away," Jack said, and suddenly Red jumped in toward him, his arms pumping, their four feet shuffling in the dust and the dust rising. Ben could feel it prickle on his face.

Jack staggered back and away and then slid forward to hit Red in the side. They were moving slowly now, awkwardly, stumbling in the dust, their mouths open and gasping. Ben closed his eyes, grimacing, listening to the terrible, dull sound of their fists.

"Jack'll kill him he nails him with that right," he heard Harry say. The voice seemed to come from very far away. He opened his eyes. Jack swung the right; Red had his hands up but the blow drove them back into his face. Crouching, Jack followed him.

Red stopped, feinted. Jack came forward. Red jumped to one side as he lunged and slammed his fist down like a club on the back of Jack's neck. Ben heard Harry whisper, "Rotten son of a bitch."

Jack fell forward into the thick dust that rose and swirled over him. He pushed himself up slowly, turning to face Red. "That filthy rotten son of a bitch," Harry said, and Toussaint was whispering, "Jack. Jack. Jack. Lookout, Jack."

He cried out, "Look out, Jack!"

Red moved in. His right flashed like a piston at Jack's face. Jack caught the fist with his left hand. The fist drew back again. Then Ben saw the long looping right swing up from Jack's side.

There was a sound like a dropped watermelon and Red was sitting down. But Jack let out a stifled cry and clutched his right hand to his face and bit it. Ben could see the corners of his mouth twisted down in agony.

But when Jack let the hand drop his face was expressionless. He watched Red push himself up. Ben could see Red grinning. Red staggered back toward Jack but Jack leaned away from him and hit him with his left, bringing it up from his knees, swinging it with his shoulders like a scythe, and the fist crashed against the side of Red's head.

Red fell forward, his arms around Jack's waist, and Jack stepped back to let him drop, then stood over him, sobbing with exhaustion, wiping the blood from his face with his left hand. After a moment he leaned down and tried to pull Red upright. But he had not the strength and he lost his balance and staggered back, almost fell.

"Quit it now, Jack," Ben heard Toussaint cry. "He had enough now." But Jack hitched at the top of his pants as though to stop himself from falling and stumbled forward and tried again to pull Red to his feet. Toussaint ran up to him, holding his arms, pulling him away, pleading with him; "Quit it now, Jack. He had enough now. He out, Jack."

Jack jerked away and fell to his knees. When he got up the face he turned to Toussaint was terrible. He raised his fist. "Keep your nigger hands away from me!" he whispered.

Toussaint stared at him. He took a step back, turned. Then, hurrying, he got his lunch pail and disappeared around the roller, and a moment later Ben saw him again, walking jerkily, his knees seeming to bend both ways in his faded dungarees. He began to run. His thin legs pumping up and down, his arms flapping, he looked like a scarecrow running.

When Ben looked back Harry had jumped forward and was holding Jack away from Red. Jack was struggling feebly, but then he went limp and Harry half-pulled him, half-carried him away and sat him down against the rear tire of Jack's grader. Jack leaned his head back, panting ceaselessly. His face was bloody and bruised and blood and sweat had muddied the dust that matted the hairs of his bare chest.

"For Christ's sake, Ben," Harry called. "Go take a look at Red, will you?"

Ben started. Moving in a trance he got his water bag and went to where Red lay sprawled, one arm pinned under his body. He rolled him over. Red's face was a mask of dust, bloody around the mouth, and Ben poured water into his hands and tried to wash the blood away. Red's eyes opened and looked up at him, glazed, unseeing. "Take a drink," Ben said. He put the snout of the water bag into Red's mouth. Red guzzled it noisily.

Ben helped him up and helped him over to the cat. Red stopped and leaned his arms on the track and his head on his arms.

"You better take the rest of the day off, Red," Ben said.

"M'all right. Just gimme minute. Gimme drink." After he had washed his mouth out and spat, Red probed in his mouth and brought out a tooth. Cursing unintelligibly he flung it away.

Ben turned. Jack had risen and was squatting beside the starting motor on the frame of his grader. Ben saw that he was coiling the rope around the flywheel with his left hand. He snapped the rope and the motor popped, slowly, then faster. Jack waited, shifted in the Diesel and climbed heavily up to the seat. The roar of the Diesel thickened gradually and Jack sat stiffly erect, staring out at the grade where Toussaint had disappeared. Finally he shifted into gear and the grader pulled away.

Red raised his head and watched it move off. He took a few experimental steps along the side of the cat, holding onto the tracks. He had moved to the front of the cat when Harry came up.

"You better knock off, Red," Harry said.

"I'll go get your car and run you home," Ben said. "You better call it a day."

"I'm okay," Red said. He began to crank, grunting with each stroke of his arm. Harry reached over and turned on the gas cock. "Thanks," Red said. "Forgot."

"Listen, Red; you're in no kind of shape."

"To hell with me," Red said. "You guys go on back to work." They stood watching him for a moment, then Harry scowled and shook his head and the two of them walked silently toward Harry's roller. There Harry leaned up against the frame, brought out a sack of Bull Durham and rolled a cigarette. They heard the uneven clack of tracks as Red set the cat moving, the drawbar screeched as he turned too sharply, and the huge, heavy, spiked drums of the tampers clanked as they rocked in their frames. Red was crouched low on the seat, both hands clamped on the right friction clutch.

"That son-of-a-bitch," Ben said. "He couldn't let Jack alone, could he?"

Harry shrugged, lighting his cigarette. He raised his head, shaking the match out, and Ben saw his eyes widen. The cigarette dropped from his mouth. "Oh, Christ!" he yelled. "*Oh, Jesus Christ!*"

Ben jerked his head around. Red's cat was a hundred yards away, moving slowly in low. The tampers rocked behind it, spiked feet punishing the ground. The seat was empty.

Already Harry was running after it. "Where the hell is he?" he cried, his face twisted and white as he looked furiously over his shoulder at Ben. Jack's grader was tearing over toward them from the fine grade.

As they ran laboriously through the loose dirt, they saw Jack stop the grader and jump off. He ran forward a few steps and halted, looking down at the grade. He took a step back, another, and then, as though he had been kicked in the stomach, bent over, retching. He looked as though he were going to fall as he ran back toward his grader, and Ben knew what had happened. Red had fallen off the back of the seat. The tampers had run over him.

Ahead of him, Harry stopped. "Oh, God!" he whispered. "Oh, look at that! Oh, God, Ben!"

Ben caught up with him, looked down, and then quickly away. He didn't look again at the crushed, bloody, dirt-covered thing on the grade. "Jesus, God!" Harry breathed.

"You better try to catch the cat, Harry," Ben said.

Harry didn't speak immediately, didn't move. Then he said, "Yeah," and began to run again.

Ben saw Jack looking at him. Jack's face was dead white, his mouth was open and pulled tragically down at the corners, twitching as his chest heaved. His left hand clutched tightly the frame of the grader, the other hung limp and half-open at his side. They stared at each other and Ben knew he should go over to him.

But he did not, and as he watched, Jack moved slowly along

the side of the grader and climbed up to the seat. He drove away in the direction of the timekeeper's shack, standing up and leaning forward against the controls, his shirt tail flapping behind him.

Ben never saw him again.

13

The note Jack had left trembled in V's fingers as she handed it back. Her other hand was at the side of her face, tugging at a strand of her hair. "But why," she whispered. "Why, Ben?"

Ben shrugged tiredly. "I guess he didn't want to stick around to face it."

She almost screamed it at him, "He didn't kill Red!"

"He helped. We should never have let Red get up on that cat, so I guess it's our fault too. But I can see how Jack feels."

He stood just inside the door of V's room, V close to him. She turned her face to the wall and slowly hit her fist against the edge of the open door. "What happened?" she said, talking into the wall. "Tell me what happened."

"Jack didn't know when to quit hitting him," Ben said. "Afterwards Red tried to run his rig and he fainted, I guess, and fell back off the seat. The tampers went over him." He almost said, "Jack was hitting you, V, when he was hitting Red," but he stopped himself.

"What's a tamper?" V whispered.

"It's a kind of drum. A steel drum full of water that rolls on a whole bunch of spikes that're shaped kind of like feet. There was two of them in tandem."

She turned to face him, her mouth forming a circle, eyes round. Perspiration shone on her upper lip.

"Each tamper weighs about five tons," Ben said, and then he watched her silently as she stepped back, slumped into a chair and covered her face with her hands. Her fingers protruded through the blonde hair at the sides of her head. Watching her, he felt nothing. He had felt anger, anger at no one, at nothing in particular, anger only that this thing had happened; he had felt sorrow, sorrow for Red, for Jack, for V, pity for Jack; but now he felt nothing. Whatever was in him capable of feeling, was bruised and overworked and shocked, and he felt as he had when he was in the hospital after Bill Rasmussen and Arlene had been killed.

"Well, he'll be in the Navy pretty soon," he said. "I wish I was with him." And since he had found Jack's note in their room, Jack gone, he had been wishing desperately he could be in the war. He wanted to participate in something, instead of always being on the outside, caught up only in the ripples, feeling only vicariously, affected only indirectly, for even with Doris he had not felt part of it, feeling that as soon as he was involved with her, some piece of him had dropped out and had stood to one side, watching.

"He must hate me for this," V said.

Ben nodded abstractedly, staring at her and trying to bring her face, which he loved, into focus, in his eyes. "He must hate me for what I've done to him," V said.

He nodded. "Ben," V said. "Don't just stare at me. Help me, Ben."

He turned his eyes to the window, and he was surprised at the coldness of his voice. "I've done enough," he said. "I should have kept out of it. I…" He frowned as he forgot what he had been going to say, and then he looked at her once more. "I'll bet he hates you, V," he said.

She was bent forward, her shoulders hunched like an old woman's, her hands clenched into fists like a little girl. Her white blouse was stretched tight across her back. "Ben, please, I had to get him back. You saw…Ben, remember what you told me!"

He felt himself nod. She'd had the tools. He'd told her she

had the tools, if she only knew how to use them. He said, half to himself, "I didn't know you'd learn to use them this well."

"What? *Oh, Ben!*"

"You didn't know when to quit hitting him," he said, and then he went out and gently closed the door because he couldn't bear to hear her crying.

14

It was late in the summer before he even saw her again. When finally he did, one night at the Hitching Post, he began seeing her often, running into her at a movie, or at a ball game, or glimpsing her blonde head moving among the other dancers at the Chamber of Commerce Hall. Then one night he took her to a movie himself, and stopped the next day at Deterle's to see her, and all at once he was stopping at the drive-in every day after work, and making a date with her whenever he could.

After the first few times she dropped the mask she had put on for her battle for Jack. One night it was gone completely, and she never again put it on when she was with Ben, as though she had felt him out and knew he was to be trusted, or as though he did not matter enough for her to go to the trouble of wearing it. She was more sure of herself now, more wary, as though the stubborn, desperate singleness of her purpose had tempered her to a hardness she could not throw off. But the honesty remained, her straightforwardness was still there. The new, sleek smile he hated was gone with her pose, for Ben she smiled her old smile, and for him her eyes held the round, grave, innocent look he could never forget.

He couldn't stay away from her. He had to see her even though she looked upon him as Jack's friend more than her own, even though the few times she kissed him he had the jealous revulsion afterward that it had been Jack she was kissing. Finally she seemed to know what was the matter with him and he began to understand he was being handled, gently and carefully. Somehow he did not mind.

One afternoon when he had stopped at Deterle's after work, she was talking to an old man in a black Lincoln convertible. She waved to Ben but stayed and talked to the old man while he waited impatiently, drumming his fingers on the steering wheel and watching them.

The Lincoln was new and the man's head was small and gray, sticking up over the edge of the door as though he were a turtle peering out of his shell. He was smoking a cigarette in a long holder, and Ben didn't like the way V was talking to him.

"Who was that?" he asked, when the Lincoln had gone and V came across the asphalt to him.

"Roger Denton. He has a ranch out near my father's."

"That the guy you go see every Sunday?"

V nodded. "He's my best friend. He and you, Ben." She seemed happy about something. The color was high on her cheeks and her eyes shone.

"He's old, isn't he?" Ben said coldly.

"What? Oh. Yes, I've known him since I was a little kid. He gave me a quarter-horse when I was sixteen."

"I didn't like the way you were talking to him."

Her smile faded and she looked at him anxiously. Suddenly he felt foolish and tried to grin it off. "Guess what I've got," V said.

"What?"

"Guess."

"I can't. What is it?"

She took a letter from the pocket of her skirt and showed him the return address on the envelope. "From Jack, unh?" Ben said, and he felt lonely and tired. "What's he say, V?"

"He's on Guam in the Seabees," V said, and her voice was deep and happy. "He sent me a picture and he says he's sending me a souvenir he picked up. It's a wonderful letter, Ben."

He fished a cigarette from his shirt pocket and stuck it between his lips, fumbling for a match. "I guess our boys get lonely out there," he said.

"Please, Ben, don't go sour like that."

He cupped his hands around the match and lit his cigarette. "Was it what you wanted, V?" he said.

"Yes," she said, looking at him strangely. "It's what I wanted."

He switched on the ignition, kicked the starter and raced the motor. "Haven't we got a date tonight?" V asked.

"You don't want to go out with me."

"What do you mean, Ben?"

"I thought you'd want to go to bed with that letter."

Her eyes clouded and he was instantly sorry. He hadn't meant to say that. "I'm sorry," he said. "I didn't mean that. I'll see you at eight, V."

She nodded and, without speaking, turned away. He watched her walk across the pavement, the short blue skirt flicking across the backs of her bare legs.

He was early that evening, pausing to smoke a cigarette outside her apartment house before he went up. When he knocked she called to him to come in. Her apartment was a two-room affair, with a davenport and an easy chair and a false fireplace in the living room. Ben lit another cigarette and found himself an ashtray and sat down in the easy chair. "Do you want me to put my hair up?" V called from the bedroom.

"Why don't you leave it down?"

"Where are we going?"

"Somewhere and talk," he said.

He smoked his cigarette, looking around him at this room, which had nothing of V in it, and then, on the mantelpiece, he saw a small photograph propped against the wall. He went over to look, bending forward but not touching it; Jack was standing with two other men beside a slanting palm tree. They all wore dungarees and sailor caps and their faces were indistinct and heavy with shadow. Ben went back and sat down again.

"What're you going to say to Jack when you write?" he called.

She didn't answer, and coldly furious, he knew what she was going to write to Jack. He waited silently, staring across the room at the photograph on the mantel. From where he sat he could not make out which of the three was Jack.

When V came out she had on a plain black dress with padded shoulders, and her hair hung loosely around her face. Her face looked very white, her lipstick very red. She carried a cigarette and an ashtray and she sat down on the davenport, crossed her legs and arranged her skirt over her knees. Ben knew what she was going to write to Jack.

"Well, you're going to keep it up, aren't you?" he said slowly, through his teeth.

"I have to make sure," V said, and she bent her head to re-arrange her dress over her knees. "I have to…"

"You damn fool."

She shook her head. "I'm afraid. I know this works." She took a deep breath and said, "Till he gets back."

"Okay," Ben said. "But just don't use me. Keep me out of it or I'll write and tell him you're a liar!"

She didn't speak, she didn't look up, and he said, "You don't care how much he hates you and hates himself, do you? Just so you get him."

"I can fix that when I see him again," V said. "I can't take a chance now." When she raised her head her face was wooden and stiff, and she smoked her cigarette nervously, tapping it into the ashtray each time she took it from her lips.

"Well, you're a fool," Ben said.

He snuffed out his own cigarette, waiting for her to speak.

But suddenly he said, "I don't know why I give a damn. I don't know why I give one Goddam, how you ruin it," staring at the photograph on the mantel. But he was lying; he did know. He hated to see her ruin it because she was killing something that was now rooted irrevocably in him. Together she and Jack had killed it, or would kill it. He knew the goal she had stubbornly kept in sight was marriage to Jack, but the getting and the marriage would be built upon and cursed by hate and jealousy and distrust, and it would be cursed now, too, by the death of Red.

I know this works, she had said, but if it did work, what would she have? He wished he had let it alone, let it alone from the beginning, so that now it might be dead instead of alive and rotten with disease. He wished he could have let it alone.

"It's just that Jack's my best friend," he said, and he got to his feet. "I'm pretty sick of the whole thing, V."

She was looking at him, and she said quietly, "I've hurt you, too, haven't I? You've changed, too. You're not...Everyone I like I hurt some way," she said, and she closed her eyes tiredly. "I'm sorry."

"It's the way I feel about you," Ben said. "You know. It's pretty rough."

She rose, stepped across to him, and laid her hand on his arm. He could feel it, soft and light, through his coat. "I guess you know how I feel, don't you?" he said. "I think you've known for a long time."

"Yes," she said.

"I guess you can see how it's pretty rough, unh?"

"Yes," she said. "I can see. I'm sorry, Ben."

"Well, it's pretty impossible, I guess."

"I love Jack. I always will. You know that."

"I figured it out." He moved toward the door, but she tightened her grip on his arm. Her eyes probed his, liquid and pitying. He hated the pity in them.

"You want me, don't you, Ben?"

"That's why I'm going."

"I don't want to hurt you, Ben. I don't want to hurt anybody."

He laughed bitterly, thinking about Jack, but he didn't understand what she had meant until she caught his eye again. Then he knew, and it shocked him. He felt his face flush painfully, felt anger, felt the anger leave him. He touched her hair.

"No," he said, and he said it not merely because Jack was watching this from the mantelpiece, and Jack was his friend, not merely because this would only be borrowed temporarily and would soon have to be returned to its owner and after it there would be nothing else. He had to say no because of his whole life, because of what he had always been and had always tried to be, and because of Jack, and because of V herself, and because of Doris, and, strangely, Arlene. But mostly because of himself, he said, "No." V's hand left his arm. He didn't look at her as he stumbled out the door.

15

He had carefully avoided any place he might meet her, and it was almost two years later and the war was over before he saw her again. But one day he got a letter from Slim Farley, and Slim had seen Jack in San Diego.

Somehow he was sure V did not know Jack was back and out of the Navy. He cursed Slim for ever writing, for now he did not know whether he should tell her or not. He did not know what was right, and he had no way of knowing. He did not know what had happened between them. He sweated over the decision, telling himself over and over again to stay out of it. Stay out of it; he should stay out of it, and at first he determined he would.

But all he had wanted for them came back to him; he became half-convinced that if he told V now, he might be giving them the one more chance which they all needed. Jack was back, and maybe V did not know. Maybe it was his duty to tell her, and then leave it up to her. One day he looked for her name in the phone book to see if she still lived at the same place. She did. He stared down at the name—"Baird, Vassilia Caroline"—as though trying to discover in it whether he was doing the right thing or not. But it told him nothing, and so, finally, he drove over to her apartment.

He walked up the green-carpeted steps to the second floor. There were thirteen steps, he remembered, but he counted them as he climbed. At the top was a railing and a round-topped newel post and across from the newel post was V's door. He stood motionless in front of it for a long time before he knocked.

She was in a blue bathrobe when she opened the door, and her face lit up and she put her hand out to him. He pressed her hand, and released it. It was cold. She looked older, more than two years older, her face had lost its youthful fullness, and her eyes and mouth looked larger in it.

Ben stood at the door, his hat in his hands, staring at her. She had just come out of the shower and her hair was damp and pinned up on top of her head. Her mouth was pink, without lipstick, and shining beads of perspiration dotted her upper lip. "Won't you come in, Ben?" she said.

"There's something I guess you ought to know, V," he said, and then he said quickly, "Heard from Jack lately?"

She shook her head and repeated, "Won't you come in, Ben?"

"I can't stay but a minute. Jack's in San Diego, V."

She put her hand up to the edge of the door and her eyes became smaller. "How do you know?"

"I got a letter from a friend of mine down there."

"From Jack?"

"No."

"How long…? How long has he been…?"

"I guess two or three months," Ben said.

"Oh." She inclined her head and he could see her throat working. "Are you sure?" she said shakily.

"Yeah."

"Why didn't he tell me he was back?" she whispered. "Why didn't he write and tell me? Why didn't he come back here? He said he was going to. Oh, damn!" she almost sobbed.

Ben said, "He's working for an outfit called Hogan and Griffith. They're on a job at Kearny Mesa, north of Dago. That's all I know, V."

She nodded.

"Well, that's it," he said. "So long, V." She still did not speak and he turned to go. He put his hand on the newel post, sliding it around as he stepped down the first step. V stood motionless; she had raised her head and was staring past him. He took another step, still sliding his hand around the newel post. He could see the beads of perspiration on her upper lip, her round, brown, staring eyes, her down-bent mouth. A wisp of hair had come loose and curled down over her forehead. He took another step and let his hand drop. She was still staring past him when he lost sight of her.

A few weeks later he read in the paper that she was marrying a man named Roger Denton, and he realized with a shock that Denton was the old rancher he had seen that day in the drive-in. The news startled and confused him. He tried to understand it, but he could not. And then she tried to phone him. The landlady gave him her name and telephone number, and said he was to call her back. But he didn't, and the next day she called again while he was gone. This time there was a message. She wanted him to give her away at her wedding.

But he didn't call her, and he couldn't bring himself to go to the wedding.

He always wondered if she had gone to San Diego to see Jack. He had thought that was what she was going to do when he had seen her the last time. He had thought she was planning it when she stared past him.

He couldn't stop himself from thinking about her, wondering what had happened, and one day after he had gone to work for the local, he telephoned the Denton ranch on the sudden impulse that he had to talk to her. But she wasn't there, he was disgusted with himself for phoning, and he didn't ask where she was.

And then Slim had written him from San Diego, enclosing the newspaper clippings. Among the clippings were photographs of Jack, of a dark-haired girl with big eyes, and a blurred, unrecognizable photograph of V smiling, and under it the caption that was blatant, and meaningless, and without dignity: "Murdered Blonde in Love Triangle."

Part III
MARIAN HUBER

1

Marian put two slices of toast into the toaster. Waiting for it to pop up she pushed the sugar bowl and the cream pitcher over toward Arch, who was eating his egg with a fork in one hand and a piece of buttered toast in the other. He had on a clean dungaree jacket and his khaki shirt was buttoned at the neck, and Marian could tell by the way his forehead was wrinkled that he was thinking hard about something.

Arch was easy to read. In the seventeen years they had been married, Marian had come to know him much better than she knew herself. She knew when he could be managed, and she knew when he was going to be stubborn and she had better not push him too far. She knew when he was contented, and when something was bothering him, and something was bothering him now.

"What's the matter, Arch?" she said.

He didn't seem to have heard. "Arch," she said, but he didn't look up, forking egg into his mouth and following each bite of egg with a bite of toast.

"Arch Huber!"

He raised his head; a slight, brown man with a narrow long face, the plainest man she had ever known. Not ugly, just plain; sometimes so easygoing and sometimes mule-stubborn. He certainly had his faults, but she wouldn't trade him for any man she'd heard of yet; certainly not for that Mr. Foley. Mr. Foley, who lived next door, was an insurance salesman, and when Marian had told Mrs. Foley that Arch ran a grader, and then what a grader was, Mrs. Foley had acted as though Arch were a common laborer. So Marian had told her how much Arch made a week and asked her how much Mr. Foley made, and since then they had only nodded to each other. She wished she had told Mrs. Foley that Arch was a man and a damn good operator, and not a miserable pot-bellied little suck-up of an insurance salesman.

She scowled and said, "What're you thinking about, Arch?"

"Nothing." He glanced at his watch and his throat worked as he took a swallow of coffee.

"You're thinking about that Jack Ward."

"All right," Arch said. "If you knew, why'd you have to ask?" He finished the last of his egg, took another piece of toast from the toaster and began to butter it.

"Arch, you're not going to see him. I thought we decided that."

He broke his toast in half and scraped his plate with it.

"Arch!"

"Well, maybe he needs something. Cigarettes or something. Somebody ought to go see if he needs anything."

"He's going to get what he needs. Now you leave him alone."

Arch grunted and Marian saw he was not going to be stubborn about this. Evidently he had not made up his mind. He was still frowning, however, and he said, "Say, you suppose Gene goes to see him, hon?"

"I should hope not. She's just lucky it wasn't her."

"Well, somebody ought to."

"There's no reason for you to. He doesn't want to see you. You told me yourself you hadn't said two words to him since…"

"Damn it, somebody ought to," Arch said, and his voice took on a stubborn tone. "He's a cat skinner, isn't he? I stood up for him when he got married, didn't I? Maybe I ought to go see if I can do something for him."

"Please, Arch. You stay out of it, won't you? I'd be real upset."

Arch looked at his watch, wiped his mouth on his paper napkin and got to his feet. His legs were bowed and skinny in his levis. He came over, kissed her absently on the forehead and started for the door.

"Arch, please!"

"Oh, okay," he said, without looking back. The door whuffed shut behind him, she heard him swinging the garage doors open, and, after a moment, the erratic grind of the starter of the Studebaker.

When he was gone she lit a cigarette and sipped her coffee, thinking about the murder. The murder had confused her; Jack, whom she had known and liked, murdering someone, confused and frightened her, and seemed in some way to involve her personally. She wondered how she had known that it was wrong for Gene to marry Jack. She had known that then, but she had never conceived of anything like this. And even if she had, she knew she would have foreseen Gene killing Jack, or Jack killing Gene, but this made no sense to her.

She did not feel as strongly about the murder as she did about what Jack had done to Gene. Mrs. Denton had probably deserved what she got. Marian had only seen her twice, and then not closely, seeing only a tall, blonde, overdressed girl, the kind who always looked as though she were walking into the wind.

Marian had immediately despised her, because of Gene, she told herself; because right away she had known this woman was Jack's mistress. But then, uncomfortably, she remembered that when they had been seeing a lot of Jack, she had thought she wouldn't mind going to bed with him herself. She wondered if she really would have, had the chance arisen. She supposed not.

He had affected her that way, though; he had made her feel like she wanted to stretch; those tiny hips and big shoulders, those yellow slanting eyes, and the way he looked at you, politely but thoroughly, as though he didn't miss a thing, and the way he talked, half-shy, half-bold, so you didn't know whether to try to make him feel more at ease, or to spit in his eye.

But when he had started cheating on Gene, she had hated him. Gene was so helpless, not at all able to take care of herself or to hold onto Jack—she had told Arch that all along. Just from the two times she had seen this Mrs. Denton she had known Gene didn't have a chance, but this had seemed to her all the more reason why Jack should have been scrupulously faithful.

Arch had met Jack on the job at Kearney Mesa. They had been living in the auto court near Five Points then, and whenever she wanted to use the car, Arch had ridden to and from the Mesa with Jack. She remembered that Arch had felt they should ask Jack to stop by some night and eat steaks with them.

He had come on a Friday night with a bottle of bourbon and they had had a good time, and after that he had come over to dinner almost every week. She had been immediately attracted to him. Before she had married Arch, she had always liked wild, hell-raising men, and she was certain Jack had been one of these in his time. And she remembered the strange combination of jealousy and gratification she had felt the night Jack told them he was thinking about getting married.

2

She had been in the kitchen starting dinner. The kitchen was separated from the other room by a low partition and she could talk to Arch and Jack while she skinned the potatoes. Jack was sitting on the studio couch with his long legs stretched out in front of him and a highball in his hand, and he and Arch were talking about the job.

Then, after a silence, Marian heard Jack say, "Well, I'm thinking about getting married, Arch." He said it casually, and she craned her neck to see him.

"What's that, Jack?" she called.

He flushed and turned toward her and repeated the words.

"Good move," Arch said. "Who's the girl?" He was sitting stiffly in a straight chair, with his arms folded and his legs crossed.

"Gene Geary," Jack said. "She works down at the H. and G. office."

"Did you ask her yet?" Marian said. She peeled two onions and began slicing them into the pan with the potatoes. Her eyes were watering and she brushed a strand of hair back from her forehead. "Did you ask her yet, Jack?"

"Yeah, she's thinking it over."

"Well, don't worry about it," Arch said. "They always do that." Marian made a face at him when he came out into the kitchen to get the bottle.

"I wondered if Arch would mind being best man," Jack said in an embarrassed voice. "See, I haven't been here very long and…"

"Of course he wouldn't mind. He'd be happy to. Am I invited too, Jack?"

"Sure. Well…I don't know if she's going to or not."

"Of course she will," Marian said. "A big good-looking boy like you." It was hot in front of the stove, her face was hot, and she felt a little tight.

"When'll it be?" she heard Arch say.

"Right away, I guess."

"What's she like, Jack?" Marian called.

"Oh, she's little. She's got brown hair."

Marian wondered if this girl were a virgin; probably not. None of these girls were nowadays. Probably Jack had attended to that already. She felt a sudden, jealous dislike for this girl, and she stepped to the door to watch Jack, who was moving his glass from side to side, studying the flat tilt of the liquor. She saw that Arch was drinking with great ceremony, and she knew he was a little tight too.

Jack raised his head and grinned at her. "Smells good," he said.

"It'll be ready in a minute," Marian said, and then she said, "So you're going to get married."

Jack grinned again and looked down at his glass. Arch started to tell the story about how he and his best man had both dropped the ring at their wedding, and Marian picked up an overloaded ashtray and took it back to the kitchen.

Jack helped her to her chair when she called them to the table, and she thanked him and looked reprovingly at Arch. But Arch was shaking his head and blinking his eyes, and she smiled. She saw that they were waiting for her and she picked up her fork.

"Is your girl pretty?" she said to Jack.

"Sure, she's pretty," Arch said. "I've seen her down at the office. She's a good-looking girl. Jack's lucky to get her."

"Well, it's about time you got married. Arch and me were married when we were twenty. Fifteen years now."

"How about eating, hon?" Arch said.

Marian didn't pay any attention to him. "How is it you never got married before this?" she asked. "Now, don't try and tell me you never went in for girls much."

"Jack's played it smart, that's all," Arch said.

"Now you stop those snotty cracks, Arch Huber!"

"I just never got around to it," Jack said.

"Well, I think those girls up in Bakersfield missed a good thing. The girls in Glenwood wouldn't've let you get away this long. Would they, Arch?"

"How about eating?" Arch said.

Jack didn't say anything, rubbing his hand over his chin. His slanting yellow eyes were narrowed and insolent. Marian felt herself grow a little more sober, and she frowned and looked at Arch, who was cutting his steak. "Eat your steaks now," she said. "Before they get cold."

When Jack was gone Arch unfolded the couch, got the bed-clothes from the closet and made it up, while Marian stacked the dishes. When they were undressed and in bed he set the alarm, kissed her, sighed and turned away, drawing his knees up toward his chest as he always did. Marian slid her arm under his neck so she could jiggle him if he tried to go to sleep.

"He's a nice boy, Arch," she said. "Don't you think so? Is he a good cat skinner?"

"Yeah, he's all right."

"He's terribly attractive."

Arch grunted.

Marian giggled and worked her arm up and down under his neck. "He's got that something women like," she said. "Those eyes and those big shoulders and those little-bitty hips, and when he looks at you sometimes you know you ought to slap him but you don't really want to."

Arch grunted disgustedly.

"I wonder why he hasn't got married till now, Arch?"

"If they all feel about him the way you do, he didn't ever need to."

She punched him in the ribs and jerked her arm up and down. Arch turned over quickly, pushed her arm away and began tickling her. She giggled, finally gasping for breath. "Stop!" she gasped. "You stop it, Arch Huber!" He stopped, turned over again and hunched up his shoulder when she tried to get her arm back under his neck.

"Great," he said. "You're ready to run off with the first good-looking skinner comes along. After fifteen years."

"Oh, Arch!" she said, thinking about Jack Ward. She wondered what he was like, but then Arch started to breathe regularly and she punched him in the ribs again.

"Go to sleep," he said. "Sleep now."

She smiled at the back of his head. She loved him, and though he never said so anymore, she knew how much he loved her; he would be lost and helpless as a child without her. She supposed some people might think they weren't much, but they were happy, and they couldn't get along without each other. She supposed their life was nothing very special, but it was the way they wanted it, and she doubted if there were many who could say as much. They both knew what they were, and, content with that, didn't pretend to be anything else. She smiled at the back of Arch's head. "Arch," she said. "Remember that time we were coming back from Rosarita Beach?"

He chuckled sleepily.

"Remember, Arch?"

He put his hand around and patted her hip. She smiled at the back of his head and ran her hand over his thinning hair.

"Come on, Marian," he said. "I've got to get to sleep. I'll be knocking grade stakes all over hell tomorrow."

He never did seem to know, and she could never bring herself to ask him. She sighed and said, "Arch, is this girl nice?"

"Sure, she's nice. Sleep! Sleep now!"

"Does she have any other boy friends?"

"She used to go around with Charley Long, I think."

"Who's Charley Long? Do I know him?"

"Surveyor boss."

"Is he attractive?"

"He's three foot tall and he's got four arms and only one leg and a glass eye and a purple goatee and a dose and…"

Marian punched him in the ribs. "I asked you a civil question."

"Oh, hell, damn it. He's a pretty good-looking guy about our age. He's got a good job and he makes a lot of money. Okay?"

"But he's not as attractive as Jack, is he?"

"Christ, I don't know, hon. Sleep! Sleep! Sleep!"

She snuggled up close to him. "I hope he's marrying the right kind of girl, Arch. It would be too bad if he didn't; if she can't handle him right. You've really got to know, with…"

"Gene's okay," he interrupted. "She's all right. For God's sake, let's go to sleep, Marian. I've got to get up at six!"

She didn't say anything more, smiling at the back of his head in the pale light that came through the window from the street lamp on the corner. She yawned, pushing down on her thighs with her hands and stretching her shoulders deliciously. Already Arch was asleep and he would be snoring soon. She pressed herself against his back, curving her body and legs to fit his.

3

Throughout the wedding, which was at Gene's mother's house, Marian studied Gene carefully. She was always a little jealous of anyone younger than herself, and she was sure these girls of Gene's age had been around much more than she had when she had been married. Gene looked nice enough; but girls always did at their weddings. She had no striking features, dark hair and eyes, an animated way of speaking, but a suggestion of a pinched, nervous look around the eyes. Her figure was all right, Marian thought, although a little flat-chested and a little narrow across the hips.

Marian and Arch, the Tullys and Smitty, the grade foreman, left as soon as Jack and Gene had driven off in Jack's Mercury. After half-promising to come over to the Tullys', Arch and Marian walked on down the street to where Marian had parked the Studebaker.

"Well, nobody sure paid any attention to us," Marian said. "I wasn't going to go thank that Mrs. Geary. I certainly don't think much of her."

"I guess she was just as embarrassed with us as we was with her," Arch said as he pulled the car away from the curb.

"They had another steak set. Did you see it? I didn't think it was as nice as the one we gave them, though."

"I should hope not. You shot our wad on the damn thing."

"Did you think the wedding was as nice as ours, Arch?"

"Nobody dropped the ring," Arch said. "No, it was all right, though."

She sat silently as they turned corners and finally came out on the streetcar tracks. Pepper trees hung over the street and the streetlights were coming on. Arch was frowning.

"What's the matter, Arch?"

"Nothing."

"You're thinking the same thing I am, aren't you?"

"How do I know what you're thinking?"

"What are you thinking, then?"

"Oh, Jack got a telegram down at his place before we came up. I was wondering what it was."

"When? You mean before the wedding?"

"While he was getting dressed. He looked like he'd got hit with a dragline and bucket when he read it."

"Somebody congratulating him or something. Arch, don't you…"

"No," Arch interrupted, shaking his head. "He looked really snowed. He tore it up like he was sore as hell."

"You should have read it when he wasn't looking. Arch, don't you feel sorry…"

"I asked him what it was," Arch said. "He said a friend of his was getting married, too. Now why do you suppose he got all upset like that?"

"I don't know. Arch, don't you feel sorry for that girl? I sure do."

Arch guided the car through a traffic signal, and then turned toward her. He looked annoyed. "You don't need to feel sorry for her," he said. "She's all right. What do you mean you feel sorry for her?"

"She just hasn't got it, that's all. She should have married that other boy."

"What the hell are you talking about?"

"She can't hold him."

"What do you think you are?" Arch said angrily. "A prophet?"

"I don't need to be a prophet to see that. You saw it too, only you always take the other side whenever I say anything. She should have married that other boy."

"Will you tell me what the hell you mean?" Arch cried. "I'm so stupid I only saw Jack Ward and Gene Geary getting married, but you seen the preview or read the plot in a movie magazine or something. Why don't you tell me what you mean?" He stopped for a red light, which changed as soon as he had stopped, and he rasped gears getting started again.

"Oh, she's nice enough," Marian said. "She's sweet and she looks like a doll and all that, but she hasn't got the stuff. Jack's going to get sick of that sugar candy and go hunting some roast beef, and you remember I said it…"

"Jesus!" Arch said.

"You just remember I said it. And you know what she's going to do? She's going to think up some way to get him back, or read a book about how to get your husband back, or something, and you can't do it that way. Not that Jack Ward. She's going to be real sweet and forgiving when she ought to claw his eyes out and then get him in bed and show him what he can't get anywhere else, only she hasn't got it, that's all."

"Oh, Jesus!" Arch said.

"You just remember I told you."

"We better start playing the horses, you know so damn much about the future," Arch said irritably.

He drove into the auto court and parked the Studebaker in the shed beside their cabin. Inside, he went to the icebox, chipped some ice, and made them each a drink. "You want to go over to Tully's, hon?"

"I certainly don't," Marian said. "I can't stand that dumb Liz Tully." She took off her coat and hung it on a hanger in the closet. She had spilled punch on the sleeve of her dress and she ought to get after it with the spot remover. Arch sat down in the easy chair, hung one leg over the arm, and switched on the radio. It began to hum and the light glowed behind the dial.

"He knew it when he was marrying her," Marian said, sipping her drink and looking at Arch accusingly. "He knew he was going to give her a bad time when he stood up there with her. You could see it on his face."

"Okay," Arch said. "You know it all."

4

A month or two after the wedding Arch and Marian had the Wards over to dinner, and everything seemed to be fine. Marian had to admit that what Arch had been telling her might be true.

Gene seemed wonderfully happy. It was obvious to Marian in her manner, in the way she talked, in the way she looked at Jack, and Marian had to admit, although grudgingly, that Jack seemed happy too. She watched him critically, watched him help Gene to her chair when they sat down for dinner, saw that he never neglected to light Gene's cigarette, watched him help her into her coat when they left and take her arm going down the steps. She had to admit to Arch that she might have been wrong, but she didn't admit it to herself. She was going to wait and see.

When, after Christmas, Hogan and Griffith got the new contract down near the border and Smitty was moved up to superintendent, he made Jack grade foreman in his place. Marian was angry at first because she thought Arch should have had it, but Arch didn't seem disturbed. He pointed out that since they were working two hours overtime a day, plus Saturday, and that Jack was on a salary instead of wages, he was making more money than Jack. When Gene called him up to ask them over to dinner, Marian guessed it was to celebrate the new job.

Jack hadn't come home from work yet when they got there, and Gene made them a drink. She and Jack had furnished their apartment themselves, with a good-looking maple living-room suite they had bought on payments from Montgomery Ward's, a three-way lamp and a maple dining-room set. Gene had made

the drapes and the spread in the bedroom and she invited
Marian out into the kitchen to look at her new stove and refrigerator, which were both gas-operated. The two of them dis-
cussed the relative merits of gas and electricity, Marian leaning
against the sink and Gene working over the stove, while Arch
sat in the living room with his drink.

When Marian went in to look at the bathroom she closed the
door behind her and combed her hair. There was a blue-and-
white chenille cover on the toilet seat, and Jack's shaving things
were arranged neatly on a glass shelf below the mirror-fronted
cabinet. Making sure the door was locked, Marian searched the
cabinet and the closet and the drawer of the washstand beside
the tub to see if she could find any birth-control equipment,
and finding none, wondered if Jack and Gene meant to have a
baby right away. When she looked at herself once more in the
mirror she was scowling, and she carefully smoothed out her
face and turned off the light when she went out.

Arch was in the kitchen with Gene, mixing another round of
drinks. It was seven-thirty and Gene looked worried. She
peered into the oven at the roast and turned the gas low.

"Why, I don't know what could be keeping Jack this long,"
she said.

"He's probably working late," Arch said. "Probably something came up at the last minute." Gene looked at him grate-
fully and Marian went into the living room and lit a cigarette.
She pulled the drape back and looked out the window at the
dark street, wishing Arch would come out of the kitchen so she
could whisper, "I told you so." She knew he did not come out
because he knew she would.

"I'm afraid the roast will get dry," she heard Gene say, and
she snubbed her cigarette in a polished silver ashtray and returned to the kitchen, kicking Arch's foot as she passed him.

She leaned against the sink again with her arms folded, watching Gene and pitying her, and suddenly liking her. She was prettier than Marian had thought at first, with the big worried dark eyes, and dark hair clustered in curls around her head, and red lips that folded softly out of the thinness of her face. She wore an apron with frills over the shoulders and she scratched her nose as she leaned down to look into the oven.

"Oh, he'll be along in a minute," Arch said, refusing to look at Marian. Finally he scowled at her, and she raised her chin and looked back at him triumphantly.

"Maybe we'd better go ahead and eat without him," Gene said. "What do you think, Marian?"

"I don't know, honey. Arch, why don't you go call up Smitty?"

"I don't know his number."

"I have it in my purse," Gene said, and Arch went to the phone with her. He returned to say that Smitty didn't know where Jack was.

"He's probably out having a drink with some of the boys," Marian said. "There's always a first time, honey. I wouldn't worry about it." Arch was making frantic faces at her.

"But that's not like Jack," Gene protested. "He knew you were coming tonight, and why wouldn't he have phoned?" She wandered aimlessly around the kitchen, finally taking off her apron and hanging it behind the door. "I'm afraid something's wrong," she said, nervously running her hand up and down over her bare arm. "Well, I guess we'd better go ahead and eat."

They ate an awkward and silent meal. Afterward Marian insisted on helping Gene with the dishes while Arch sat in the living room looking at a *Life* magazine. Gene was sniffling and Marian was beginning to be angry with Jack, even though this proved she had been right. She kept talking, telling Gene whatever came into her head about her married life with Arch. But when she had stopped for a moment, Gene said, "Marian, don't you think we ought to call the police or something?"

Arch called from the other room, "Oh, he'll be along, Gene."

Marian patted Gene on the shoulder. "This always happens, honey. You're not really married till this happens." She thought fiercely what she would do if Arch pulled a stunt like this.

"He's just out having a drink with the boys," she continued. "Don't you worry about it, honey." She raised her voice. "Fix us a drink, Arch!" Arch came out to make some drinks. Gene was sobbing and Marian made her go into the living room and sit down in the easy chair.

"Oh, I'm afraid," Gene said, looking up at her. "Something's happened!"

Arch came back with the drinks and stood uncomfortably beside Marian. She took one of the glasses from him and made Gene swallow some liquor.

"Listen, honey," she said fiercely. "Don't you ever cry over a man, you hear! They're not worth it. You just let Jack get up and fix his own breakfast for about…Arch, you go in the bathroom and get some Kleenex!"

When he had gone she lowered her voice and said, "Honey, don't you let him get away with this. You give him hell. If you just forgive him and let it go I'll never speak to you again. Now, you listen to me: you give him hell so he won't ever forget it…" She stopped as Arch came back with a handful of Kleenex. Gene was looking up at her with wide eyes and tears were running down her cheeks, and Marian knew she had scared her. She tried to smile and patted Gene's shoulder. "Oh, he's probably just working late," she said.

At eleven Marian made Gene go to bed. They turned off the lights in the living room and the kitchen, Arch silently helped her on with her coat and they went out to the car. The night was cool and the fog was beginning to settle over the streets so that the streetlights glowed greenishly.

"I'll bet she's sitting up waiting for him," Marian whispered.

"Well, I'd be sitting up. I'd be waiting for him with a meat cleaver."

She flounced around in the seat to get comfortable, pulling her coat about her, while Arch tried to fit the key into the ignition. "Or I'd be down at the corner bar finding myself somebody else to sleep with!" she said loudly, as they drove away.

Arch drove slowly through the fog, his forehead creased, leaning forward against the steering wheel. He didn't say anything.

"I told you," Marian continued savagely. "That Jack Ward's out tomcatting, and how long they been married?"

"About five months," Arch said carefully.

"Five months! Arch, I want you to tell him what I think of him. Married five months and he can't leave it alone."

"I thought you liked him. You used to tell…"

"I did! Do you like him? That poor kid. I want you to tell him what I think of him, Arch."

"All right," Arch said.

"I told you this would happen. That poor kid doesn't have the stuff to fight it. He'll break her heart before he's through. You tell him now, Arch!"

"All right," Arch said. She knew he wouldn't but she was slightly mollified at the thought of Jack knowing what she thought of him.

5

It was only a week or so later, one noon when she was going out to La Jolla to have lunch with Milly Crawford, that she saw Jack and the woman. Marian had taken Arch to work so she could have the car and was stopped in traffic in front of the Orizaba Hotel when she saw them.

They were walking slowly out of the hotel. The woman was tall, although she looked short beside Jack, blonde, and Marian immediately hated her violently. She had only a glimpse of them, then the car behind her honked and she had to drive on. She circled the block as quickly as she could, but they were gone.

Marian didn't tell Milly about Gene and Jack and the woman, and she left soon after lunch and drove back to the Orizaba Hotel on the chance that she might see the woman again. She sat in the lobby of the hotel for over an hour and had almost decided it was hopeless when there was a quick tapping of high heels and the woman passed her and got into the elevator.

Again it was just a glimpse, but Marian had already planned what she would do. She rushed over to the desk where a man with sleek black hair was writing in a ledger.

"Who was that?" she cried, leaning over the counter toward him. "I'm sure I know her!"

The man looked up and raised an eyebrow and Marian had a moment of panic. "Who?" he said.

"That young lady in the blue flowered dress. She just got her key and went up in the elevator."

"That was Mrs. Denton. Shall I ring her room?"

"No. No, never mind that. Mrs. Denton? Oh, I remember, she did get married."

The clerk looked at her coldly.

"Thank you," Marian said, looking back at him defiantly. "I shall have to look her up." She hurried outside into the sudden sunlight, feeling a little foolish, but proud of the way she had handled it, and she drove home as quickly as she could.

Arch was already at home and in the shower when she came in. She could hear the water beating on the zinc walls. She hammered on the bathroom door. "Arch! Arch!"

"What?"

"Come out of there."

The sound of the shower continued and Marian walked up and down before the door impatiently. Arch was whistling in that tuneless way that irritated her so. "Arch!" she cried.

"What?"

"I saw *her*, Arch!"

The whistling continued, but finally it broke off and he called back, "You saw who?"

"Jack Ward's—*girl!*"

The shower was turned off and after a moment Arch came out. He had a towel tied around his waist and his hair was plastered down over his head. Steam followed him out of the bathroom.

"You what?" he said.

Breathlessly Marian told him all she had seen and found out, and he whistled sharply. "The Orizaba—that big white one? Money, unh?"

"She's married, too. Arch, I'll bet she's one of these rich bitches can't live with their husbands."

Arch raised his eyebrows and walked into the kitchen, gripping the ends of the towel. He came back with a bottle of beer and sat down on the studio couch. "You sure it was Jack?"

"I was right there, I tell you! I wasn't ten yards away. Of course it was Jack."

Arch grunted and sucked on his beer.

"Arch," Marian said grimly. "We've got to tell that poor kid."

"Who? Gene?"

"We've got to tell her."

"We don't have to either!" Arch shouted. "It's none of our damn business. We're not sticking our noses in where it's none of our damn business!"

"Shhhh, Arch, you want everybody in the auto court to hear? Arch, it's not butting in. We've got to help that poor kid out. I'll bet she doesn't have any idea about this."

"By God," Arch said stubbornly. "She's not going to get it from us."

"You talk to Jack tomorrow then."

"By God, I will not! I'm not going to talk to Jack tomorrow or any other time. I'm keeping my damn nose where it belongs."

"Honey, we're the only ones that know. I'm going to tell Gene if you won't talk to Jack."

"I'm not having anything to do with it."

"All right, I'm going to tell Gene. I'm going over there and tell Gene tomorrow."

"The big nose," Arch said.

"Don't you talk like that to me!"

"Go ahead and tell her," Arch said. "I don't give a damn."

"I'm going to," she said firmly. "I'm going over and tell her tomorrow."

And she had. She had gone over to Gene's the next day and told her.

Now, as she finished her cigarette and put it out and rose and carried the breakfast dishes to the sink she smiled grimly, remembering it. Gene had had more spunk than she had given her credit for. Gene had told her off, and properly. But she considered that she had done her duty, even if Arch had been mad at her, even if Gene had said, "What right have you?" in a way Marian grudgingly had to admire, and had told her to mind her own business. But somebody had to tell the poor girl.

She couldn't remember when it was Gene and Jack had come back to San Diego again. Arch had told her, but she had not felt she could go to see Gene after what Gene had said to her, and after a long time she had almost forgotten the Wards. But the evening they read about the murder in the paper, of course it had all come back, and she and Arch had argued in bed until late at night. Arch had said he wasn't blaming Jack any because he didn't know all that had happened, and neither did she, and that it looked to him like the kind of thing where somebody blew up sooner or later and Jack seemed to be in the middle. Something about the way he said it had made her mad and she had quoted the commandment that said, Thou Shalt Not Kill, and Arch replied that he didn't know much about the Bible, but he thought in there somewhere it also said, Judge Not Lest Ye Be Judged.

But she did judge Jack, and she condemned him, not so much for murdering his Mrs. Denton, because she had not known her, but for what he had done to Gene.

She was filled with pity for Gene. She wished there was something she could do for her, but she knew Gene would not want to see anyone now. She shook her head sadly and said aloud, "I knew she shouldn't have married that damned Jack Ward."

Part IV
GENE

I

Gene looked at the faint lines of her body under the blankets. With drugged interest she looked down at the twin ridges of her legs, the lumps of her feet, the two white hands lying, palms up, outside the covers. The hands had the fragile look of tinted porcelain. She closed her eyes.

She heard the soft closing of the front door that would be Dr. Phillips leaving, going to the hospital. And she would be going to the hospital too, where they would try to make her well. Maybe they could fix her, fix her like an automobile that is sent to the shop, repair the torn, broken parts, clean out the filth and stains. Maybe they could put back in her what was gone.

She felt a presence in the room and with a conscious effort she opened her eyes. Her mother was crouched stiffly in the chair next to the bed and she took Gene's hand in her own cold bony ones. She stroked it silently.

"Has he gone?" Gene asked.

"Who, darling?"

"Why, the doctor."

Her mother stroked her hand. "He left this morning, dear."

Gene frowned. She hurt when she tried to move. "When am I going?"

"Tomorrow morning, dear. Do you want some broth now?"

"Mother, what did he say? Is it going to be all right?"

"Of course it is. He's the finest doctor in San Diego. Everybody says so."

"You talked to him a long time."

"No, darling. That was somebody else. You stop talking now and I'll get you some broth."

Gene felt the hands leave hers. She looked up at her mother, who had risen. "Was it Charley Long?" she asked.

"No, dear," her mother said. "Charley hasn't been here today," and Gene closed her eyes again and heard the quiet footsteps pass from the room. She wondered who it could have been. She had thought it was Dr. Phillips leaving, but now she remembered. The doctor had come that morning and had given her something and she had been asleep since. It must have been somebody about Jack.

It must have been somebody about Jack, she thought, and she saw him standing before her, with the barred door between them, gaunt, unshaven, fierce: a stranger with a face she had never seen before, a voice she did not recognize, saying, "Not for you." When had that been? Yesterday? The day before? Had she dreamed it? No; because after it she had gone home and gone to bed, sick and broken and too weak to get up. It must have been somebody about Jack, she thought, and slowly, painfully, heartbrokenly, she began to cry.

2

The first time she saw Jack he was standing in front of the counter in the Hogan and Griffith office; tall and broad and black haired, with slanting eyes set in a wide face. He smiled at her uncertainly as she moved to the counter with one of the new-employee blanks and a pencil. Typewriters clacked behind her, a slide ratcheted.

He took the fatigue cap from his head and laid it on the counter. Dark hair curled at his neck above the top of the white sweatshirt he wore beneath an unbuttoned Navy dungaree jacket.

"Are you the new operator for Kearny?" she asked.

He nodded and leaned a hip against the counter. She poised her pencil over the blank form.

"Name?"

"Jack Ward."

"John?"

"No, just Jack Ward. No middle name."

She wrote it down. "Social Security number?"

He extracted a dog-eared blue-and-white card from his wallet and pushed it over in front of her. She copied the number, finished filling out the form and had him sign it. Then she gave him a yellow badge from the cardboard box under the counter. "Just out of the service?" she asked.

He nodded and grinned, straining his neck to watch his fingers pin the badge to his collar. "Yesterday," he said.

"You're in a hurry to get to work."

"You bet I am."

Gene laughed and said, "I'll bet you're broke. Big party last night?"

He shook his head. "I've fooled around too long. I sat on my tail on enough islands to get to thinking I ought to get busy."

"Oh. Ambitious?"

"I guess," he said; his eyes narrowed and he looked down at the counter. "Thirty came up and tapped me on the shoulder a while back. You know." He put the Social Security card back in his wallet without looking up, and Gene saw he was embarrassed. The wallet had an aluminum oblong fastened to it, on which was printed, "Betio, 1943."

Gene pointed to it. "Marines?"

"Seabees."

"My father was in the Navy, too."

He looked at her expressionlessly, replacing the wallet in his hip pocket. "He was a Chief," Gene said. "He was killed in the Philippines in '41," and she immediately wondered why she had bothered to tell him that.

He only nodded. "Well, thanks," he said. "I'll see you again." She watched him go, standing behind the counter and tapping her pencil on its top and feeling a little foolish. He paused outside the door, looked both ways, looked back briefly, and was gone. I'll see you again, he had said, and somehow she knew he would. She discovered she was smiling after him. She liked to see them come back. It was late in 1945 and a great many of them were returning from the Pacific. Charley Long had been back six weeks now.

As she walked back to her desk she looked up at the clock on the wall above the door to Mr. Griffith's office. It was almost twelve and Charley would be in soon, to take her out to lunch.

They ate in the streamlined diner around the corner. It was crowded and as they waited for seats Charley put his mouth close to her ear and asked her to marry him. She laughed and shook her head, frowning at him, but he asked her again when they sat down on the leather and chrome stools.

"Charley!" she whispered, laughing. "This is hardly the place."

The counterman came with a plate of rolls and stood in front of them, wiping his hands on his apron, while Charley gave their orders. "You want coffee now, folks?"

"Yes," Charley said. The sleeve of his chamois jacket brushed Gene's arm as he replaced the menu, and he turned his long face toward her. "Why not?" he said.

"You don't want everybody to hear."

"Well, I have to keep working or you'll never make up your mind. You keep forgetting to think it over."

"I don't forget," Gene said. The counterman brought two mugs of coffee and Gene mixed sugar and cream into hers.

"Well, how about it?" Charley said.

"Don't be so impatient."

"Impatient! You're supposed to've been thinking it over ever since I went in the Navy. Is that impatient?"

"It's an important thing," Gene said. "You have to be sure."

"Yeah, but how long's it going to take before you get sure?"

"You just have to be careful," Gene said, and the counterman came back with the two platters. The hollow mounds of mashed potato were overflowing with dark gravy.

"You got to be careful, all right," the counterman said. He was a balding youth with a red, shining face.

"Yeah, yeah," Charley said. "Get us some catsup, will you?"

But she had always been careful and maybe that was why she was twenty-six and still unmarried. And maybe, too, it was because of her father. He was dead now, and she had not seen him since her graduation from high school; a small man in a black uniform, with a big head and a deeply lined, unhealthily white face. She had hated him. When he had had sea duty she did not see him often; whenever he came into San Diego she had dreaded it. He kissed her sloppily and smelled of liquor and he seemed always to be drunk. When he was especially drunk he would curse her mother and call her an old straw mattress. After he had gone away Gene would feel as though she had to take baths over and over again to get rid of him. She had hated him, and hating him she had pitied her mother, and pitying her mother she disliked her, and so she had always been lonely. Although she liked people and got along well enough with them, she had gone to movies by herself and read by herself and never minded it, and maybe because she had never minded being lonely she was twenty-six now, and unmarried.

She supposed she would marry Charley Long. She had known him almost from the time she had come to work for Hogan and Griffith, and he had proposed to her when he had gone away in the Navy as a Lieutenant j.g. There was no reason why she should not marry him. He was a good man, she liked him well enough, he had his own surveying company now, and there was nothing about him she did not approve of. She did not know why she kept putting off telling him she would marry him.

3

It was more than a month before she saw Jack Ward again. Then late one Saturday afternoon she looked up from her typewriter to see him leaning over the counter, grinning at her. He wore a plaid sport jacket and a sport shirt, open at the neck. He waved the check in his hand at her.

"Hello," she called, and she got up and went over to him. "What's the trouble?"

"You gave me too much money."

"Oh, really?" She got the timekeeper's pink sheets from the file, found his name on them and held her finger on the line. "How much did you get?"

"$63.38, with all the graft off."

She added his time and did the multiplication on a scratch pad. "Thirty-four hours straight time and four hours overtime," she said. "No, that's right."

"It rained Monday. We didn't work."

She smiled at him. "You get two hours pay for going out, whether you work or not. Didn't you know that?"

He stared at her boldly, and then he looked down and folded the check and put it in his coat pocket. "Oh, yeah," he said. "I guess that's it."

"How's the job?" Gene asked, clasping her hands on the counter.

"Rough. They got me dozing up gravel for the hot plant. Takes me the whole weekend to get the asphalt out of my ears."

Gene laughed, and he said suddenly, "What's your name?"

"Gene Geary."

"Listen, there's a good band at Pacific Square tonight. What do you say?"

"What do I say to what?"

"How about our going?"

Gene smiled and shook her head. "Sorry."

"Got a date?"

"Yes. I'm sorry though, Jack."

He stared at her coolly and impudently for a moment, then just as she began to grow angry, shook his head sadly and moved away. "So long," he said. Again she watched him, smiling, as he went out and past the front window. This time he didn't look back.

A few days later she noticed on the work slips from Kearny that he was operating a grader instead of a bulldozer. "Making grade," his slips said, in his heavy scrawling handwriting, instead of, "Pushing gravel." It was not long before he came to see her again, and one Saturday night they went to a dance at the Pacific Square.

Gene wore her brown tweed suit with the white jabot, and on an impulse she had bought herself the pair of alligator shoes she had always wanted. At first she smiled to herself because Jack's coat was tight and too short, but for some reason she didn't really mind. And she had never liked the Pacific Square, but this night she didn't mind that the band played too fast, that the floor was crowded, and that they did not dance well together. But she was glad when Jack took her arm and guided her into the bar. They found a table and a sweating waiter brought them two Old Fashioneds.

"Hot," Jack said, unbuttoning his coat and flexing his shoulders. It was close and smoky in the bar, and the pulse of music from the dance floor was loud. Jack's leg touched hers under the table and he drew it quickly away.

"Where are you from, Jack?" Gene asked.

"Bakersfield. Before that Lodi. I keep dropping down the state. You always lived here?"

"I was born here. We lived in Norfolk for a while."

"This town's all right," he said, nodding. "I think I'll stick around."

"It was nicer before the war," Gene said. Jack looked at her silently, boldly, and his eyes made her nervous. She looked down at her drink and said, "Were you overseas long?"

"Long enough."

There was a silence and Gene felt she had to say something. Finally she said, "I've been thinking about you. Remember that first time you came in? You said you were ambitious. I was wondering…"

"You said I was ambitious," he interrupted.

She flushed. "Well, I've been wondering about cat skinners. What…"

"Not much," he interrupted again. "See, we can do something pretty good, but what else? I don't want to be a skinner all my life, and maybe I can get to be a grade foreman. But that's nowhere. Or superintendent…"

"That's somewhere, isn't it?"

"Yeah, but you got to know a lot more than just about making grade. You got to know some engineering and I'm not kidding myself I'm anything but a stupid skinner. That's okay; I know it."

She looked at him, thinking about Charley Long. Jack was bent over his drink with his shoulders hunched forward. His lower lip stuck out and his forehead was wrinkled.

"Yeah," he said. "That's why I got a little sore when you said you'd bet I was broke. Hell, I'm fairly well loaded for a guy just out of the Navy. When I got in I got to thinking about this. I began saving my dough, and I'm making a good lot right now and I'm saving it, too. You know what I'm going to do?"

He looked up at her with his eyes squeezed almost shut and she saw he was embarrassed again. She smiled at him.

"I'm going to buy a couple of cats. I think I can save about four or five thousand bucks in about three years and then I'll get a loan and buy me a couple of cats and let them work for me. If I'm smart and can keep them up and keep them working, I'll buy some more equipment. Then I'll have something, maybe."

"I think you'll do it," Gene said.

He grinned self-consciously and finished his drink. "Well, let's have another," he said, and turned to call the waiter.

Gene decided she liked Jack. She liked talking to him and she liked him because she had been sure he was going to try something with her on the way home that night, and he hadn't. She had been so sure she was almost disappointed. As the weeks went by and she saw him often, she began to think he was just putting it off so she wouldn't be on her guard, that he would ask her to go to Los Angeles for a weekend with him, or ask her down to his room, and she made up a little speech of reproof to deliver when he did. But still he didn't, and somehow it put her on the defensive.

Then when she had come to the conclusion that she had misjudged him, she determined to tell him she was more or less engaged to Charley Long. But she didn't, and as time went on, a little guiltily, she began to worry less about Charley finding out she was seeing someone else. And one night she broke a date with Charley to see Jack.

They hadn't been together many times when Jack asked her to marry him. She could count the times on her fingers: twice to the Pacific Square, once on a picnic to the mountains, one Sunday in Tijuana, dinner at her house and dinner at La Jolla.

He had asked her to marry him that night in La Jolla. She had had a premonition about it, considering the possibility a little humorously, but feeling sorry for him, and she had tried to push the thought from her mind. Yet it had shocked her when it came. She had not known what to say, and then she had surprised herself by saying she would tell him what she decided the next time she saw him.

The next time she saw him was on a Sunday night in the Sky Room at the El Cortez Hotel. She told him she would marry him, trembling with excitement, thinking to herself that she must be crazy, that she should marry Charley Long, that she couldn't hurt Charley this way, that this was a terrible mistake. She didn't quite believe herself when she said the words, but she was trembling with excitement.

She couldn't meet his eyes. She was embarrassed and afraid of them, and she felt cold and shivery and completely alert, as though she had just come out of an icy shower. She sat looking out over the black shape of the high school and the lights climbing the hill, a little disappointed at the lack of romance, but savoring the sharp, cold, new feeling of excitement that made her tingle all over. Then as she looked back at Jack, she was in love with him; she had been in love with him all along, she had not realized it, and it was why she felt the way she did. She felt it was a tremendous discovery and she wanted to tell him.

She laughed shakily and said, "I guess I've been in love with you all along, but I didn't know it."

"I knew we ought to get married that first time I saw you in the office."

"Did you?" she said, and she laughed nervously again. "Did you, Jack?" she said.

His face became serious and he looked down and rattled the

ice in his glass. "Do you want a regular wedding or shall we just take off for Yuma?"

"I think we'd better have it at my house," Gene said, and she thought for the first time about her mother. She felt herself grimace. "Do you mind?" she asked.

"No. However you want it."

"It's just—my mother," she said. "I don't really care."

"I can get Arch for best man," Jack said.

"Arch?"

"Arch Huber."

"Oh, yes," Gene said. "I think I remember him."

They were silent for a long time. Jack was not looking at her and she studied the shadows on his broad face. His hand was a thick brown shape on the edge of the table, holding a cigarette. She realized with a shock that he was a complete stranger to her, but she didn't care. She searched his face, trying to read him, trying to find there what she wanted, what was hers now by right.

"Jack," she said.

The carved brown hand clenched, then relaxed and he grinned at her, his yellow eyes looking straight into hers. He put the cigarette between his lips and reached across the table and took her hand in his.

"Did you really know?" she said. "Did you really know that first time in the office?"

4

For Gene, the wedding had an unreal quality, as though she had not really lived it, but had dreamed it, or read it in a book: her mother disapproving of Jack; Charley Long being a good sport and wishing her happiness; walking down the aisle of blue ribbon on her Uncle Alvin's arm, with Mary Ellen playing the wedding march on the piano; so many people watching whom she knew only slightly or not at all. Seeing Jack and Arch Huber waiting before the minister, she had a moment of cold, knotted terror, and she had thought she could not go through with it.

And Jack had been strange that day. He had seemed shaken and unsure of himself. His face was pale under his tan as they drove up the coast to Del Mar.

He drove silently and she watched his hands, which were clenched tightly on the wheel. He still did not speak when he had parked the Mercury in the lot in front of the hotel and carried their bags in under the porte cochere. Gene waited at the elevator while he signed the register and received a key with a red, numbered tag on it, and they rode up in the elevator with the bellhop. In their room Jack tipped the boy and stood facing the door after he had gone.

Gene went over and put her arms around him. "What's the matter, darling?"

"Nothing," he said seriously, running his hand over her hair. "I guess I was just thinking I was pretty lucky." He put his arm around her waist and they walked slowly across to the window.

The room was large and square, with ugly wallpaper and a huge bed that jutted without subtlety from the inside wall. There was a bureau, a closet with a mirror in the door and another door that led into the bathroom, and the window looked out over the lawn and the gardens and the tennis courts to the ocean that was darkening in the early evening, with a lace of surf flickering along the white beach. A long, stilt-legged pier ran out into the water. The piles made flecks of white against the heavy blue of the ocean, and the sun, like half an orange, was crouched on the horizon. Gene felt Jack's hand move up and press her shoulder against his arm.

"Hungry?" he asked.

She smiled and shook her head. "I've got to unpack."

"I guess I'll take a walk. Do you mind, Gene?"

She shook her head. "Don't be long." She stayed at the window as he turned and left the room.

After a moment she saw him come out on the terrace below her and stride down the path across the lawn and past the tennis courts. He took long steps, his arms and shoulders swinging. She lost him where the hotel gardens fell away to the road, but leaning forward with her hands on the windowsill, she finally caught sight of him again, standing on the boardwalk by the fence that bordered the beach.

He was standing with his elbows resting on the top of the fence, staring out at the ocean. The sun had sunk to a reflected gold line on the water that pointed toward him, and Gene watched until the color was gone. Then she turned and began to unpack the bags, fingering Jack's unfamiliar belongings as she laid them in the drawers or hung them in the closet.

After she had combed her hair and retouched her mouth she went to the window again. A breath of cold air came in on her face and the beach was dim in the twilight, but she could still see the dark shape that was Jack. She saw him strike a match and light a cigarette, and then he slowly walked toward the hotel. She waved as he came up the path to the terrace, but he didn't see her.

5

When she looked back on it she could remember that they had been happy, wonderfully happy, for a while. But that happiness had become so tortured and racked that now it seemed it could not have been happiness at all. She couldn't remember when the shadow of V appeared, although it was before Marian Huber had come to tell her about Jack and his Mrs. Denton, but she couldn't detach any of it in her mind from all of it, so suffused with it had her mind become.

She had been unable to know Jack completely. From the beginning there had been something standing between them, although it had been vague and phantomlike. But then, the night Arch and Marian had been invited over to dinner, Jack hadn't come home. He had not even phoned, and Gene had cried herself to sleep, worrying about him.

Gray light was streaming in the window and across the tangled bedclothes when she heard someone moving around in the apartment and she jerked awake. She blinked the sleep from her sodden eyes and raised herself on her elbows, calling Jack's name. The morning was cold and there were goose pimples on her arm as she reached for the clock. It had stopped. She had forgotten to wind it. She called again, and then Jack was standing in the doorway, his face haggard, his features wooden and indistinguishable.

"I didn't mean to wake you up," he said.

"Oh, Jack!" she cried. "Where were you?" She knew her face must be ugly from crying and heavy sleep, and she dug her knuckles into her eyes. The tears started again.

"I had to work till just now," Jack said. "I'm sorry if I worried you."

"Oh, Jack, I nearly died!"

"They trucked the hot plant down from Kearny. I had to stay down till we got it unloaded. We had a lot of trouble."

"But couldn't you phone? Couldn't you even have phoned to let me know?"

"I didn't have a chance." He said it brusquely, but he came over and kissed her on the cheek. She put her arms around his neck and pulled him down to her, but he was stiff and resisting. She had never felt so separated from him.

"I'm sorry I jumped on you like that," she whispered. "But I was so scared. I know you must have been working hard."

He pulled away and stood erect, looking down at her. His bare chest was enormously wide, hairy, wrapped in hard, flat muscles. "I'm sorry you got worried," he said, running the palm of his hand up and down over the hair. He had his shaving brush in the other hand and behind him in the gray hall was the thin, yellow outline of the bathroom door. As he retreated toward it, he said, "Go on back to sleep, Gene. I'll see you tonight."

"Don't you want any breakfast?" she called after him. "Let me get you something to eat, Jack!"

There was a sound of rushing water from the bathroom and his voice was muffled: "I'll get something in town. Go on back to sleep, honey."

But she didn't go back to sleep, and as the gray turned lighter in the bedroom and the hall she lay awake and looked at the ceiling with wet, frightened eyes. She heard Jack finish shaving, heard him tiptoeing down the hall, heard the front door close, and then the apartment was deathly quiet. When it had been too quiet too long she got up and made herself some coffee.

6

She thought at first Jack was just tired of her, that something had happened to their marriage that happened to all marriages, and that it would soon pass, change, like a car shifting into another gear. Then, fighting with herself, she tried to believe that he really had to work late many nights because of his new job. And after all, he had been a bachelor for so long, it was only natural he would want to see his old friends sometimes without her. But she couldn't explain away the fact that he lied to her. He lied to her with words, with looks, with silence, and he lied to her the rare times he made love to her.

It was Marian Huber who caused her to make the decision to confront Jack. She could go on swallowing her hurt and waiting for Jack's conscience to win out as long as it was only between the two of them. But her pride would not permit her to play the wronged, forgiving wife in the eyes of anyone else.

She spent the afternoon at her mother's, ashamed that she would have to seek support there, and she left without asking her mother for advice, as she had meant to do. In the apartment again, she waited for Jack to come home from work, steeling herself with self-pity and righteousness, but dreading his arrival, dreading what she would have to say, and fighting the tears back. She was afraid their marriage was lost and she still loved Jack, and she was afraid that what was happening was somehow her fault.

He came home at six, unshaven and tired, and his eyes turned toward her dully as she faced him from the kitchen door. She did not speak, holding herself tightly and watching him as he dropped into the easy chair and put his feet up on the ottoman. Then she went to the refrigerator for ice cubes and mixed two highballs. She took one to Jack and sat down on the couch, and carefully placed the other on the end table.

"Thanks," Jack said. He raised the glass and drank deeply. Then he looked around at her. "What's the matter with you?"

Still she did not speak. She took a drink and then lit herself a cigarette. Her hand was trembling and she waved the match until it went out, and dropped it into the silver ashtray.

"Do you want a divorce?" she said casually.

Jack didn't move. He didn't seem to have heard. He sat motionless, turning slightly away from her, his head bowed between his shoulders, so the collar of his coat hunched up on his neck. Finally, he said, "No."

Gene waited for him to go on. She could feel the tears aching in her eyes. Jack said, "We're going away." He leaned forward in the chair until she could not see his face.

"What do you mean?"

"We're going away. We're getting the hell out of this town."

"You didn't answer my question, Jack."

"I answered it. We're getting away from here."

"Where?"

"Pendleton, Oregon. I know where I can get a job up there."

Ash from her cigarette spilled down her skirt and she brushed it away. She opened her mouth wide and rubbed her wrist over her eyes.

"We'll leave this weekend," Jack said.

"Aren't you going to say anything to me?" Gene cried. "Don't you even care enough to tell me anything? If you're in love with someone else, I want to know. I don't want to go on like this."

Jack finished his drink and shook the glass in his hand, still leaning awkwardly forward. The ice clinked. He didn't speak, and Gene felt the tears slipping from her eyes.

"Don't you think I deserve an explanation?" she said. "Even a lie. Even a lie would mean you cared enough to say something! You can't just come in here and say we're going away. I'm a person, Jack. I'm beginning to think you don't know that I've got to have something to hang onto."

"Why can't you trust me?"

She sobbed aloud at that, angrily. "Have you given me any reason to trust you?"

"I guess I haven't."

"Jack, please, why won't you say something? If you'd just tell me…If you'd just tell me, maybe I could trust you!"

Jack's head turned slowly toward her. His face was white. His eyes met hers impersonally then moved away. "Don't cry," he said, and when he said it she sobbed aloud.

"I can't help it," she sobbed, covering her face with her hands. "If you'd just say something."

"All right," he said huskily. "I'm ashamed. I'm ashamed as hell. Do you want me to crawl some more?"

She let her hands drop from her face. She said, "Do you love me, Jack?"

"Yes."

"I don't want you to crawl. You don't have to crawl at all. I just want to know about it. I have to know. Can't you see that?"

"All right," Jack said. "All right," he repeated, half to himself. He took his feet from the ottoman and let them drop to the floor, leaning forward once more with his elbows on his knees and his head sunk between his hunched shoulders.

"Is it this Mrs. Denton?" Gene said.

His head jerked toward her and the cords in her throat stood out like taut wires. "How do you know about her?" he hissed. "Did V…?"

"Marian Huber saw you with her. She asked at the hotel."

He stared at her and she saw his tight lips move before he

turned his head again. He was cursing Marian silently; finally he said aloud, "It's a girl I used to know. In Bakersfield. She's married to some old guy from the valley now. I ran into her a while ago."

He leaned back in the chair and put his hand to his cheek, running it slowly up and down. "I don't know how to tell you this," he continued. "I don't know how to explain it very well. See, it's hard for me to stay away from her.... V. Her name's V." He turned toward Gene when he said it, as though this were important. "See, it's all right if I can stay away from her. That's why we have to leave San Diego."

"Do you love her?" Gene whispered.

"No," Jack said. "No, I guess I hate her."

"Were—were you in love with her before?"

"Goddamn it, I don't know!" His hand dropped from his cheek to the arm of the chair. The tendons stood out on it. "Listen," he said softly. "I told you it was hard to explain. But, see, it was a bad kind of thing. It got started wrong. We hurt each other. I guess it got to be a kind of game. Whoever hurt the other one worst won. Just like a game. I'd hurt her and she'd hurt me and whoever hurt the other worst won. You see?"

Gene's lips felt dry and cracked. "Jack," she said. "Was I part of that?"

Again his head jerked around and his eyes blazed into hers. "No!" he shouted. "No, Goddamn it! Don't you ever think that, Gene!"

Gene shut her eyes and pressed her elbows in tight against her sides. "You don't still want her?" she said.

"No."

"Does she still want you?"

"She doesn't know what she wants. She just wants me because you've got me."

"Have I got you, Jack?" she whispered.

"If you want me."

But she shook her head and went on, "If it's no good, say so, Jack. If you want this other girl, just say so and I'll go away. I don't want to go on like this if you…"

"Stop that!" he interrupted. "That's no good. Listen, I want you. I want you for my wife and I don't want anybody else and we're getting to hell out of this lousy town." He started to get up but she pushed herself forward and knelt beside his chair and threw her arms around his neck.

He pressed his face against hers, his beard scraped her cheek and his arms were hard and tight. When she started to speak he kissed her so that she could not speak, and she clung to him, the arm of the chair hurting her breast. She strained against him but the chair was between them. Her heart beat wildly against the arm of the chair.

7

Those six months in Oregon, the remembrance of them, was the only part of her life with Jack that had no stain on it. Those months were the reason she could never hate Jack; those months when she had realized that every moment he was trying to make her happy, to make up for what had happened, perhaps for what was still to happen, those months when there was no confused, nagging fear in her, when she did not feel like a fugitive, when there was no hand clawing at the window to get in.

They had taken a trailer. Houses in Pendleton were too expensive to rent and apartments were impossible to find. It was a beautiful trailer, new and clean, with porthole windows rimmed with chrome. There was a bedroom with a double bed in the back, a couch in the front, a stove, icebox, cupboards, closets, a table that folded up against the side of the sink and two tiny chairs.

Later it seemed to her that it had rained almost every day. There had been many days when it had rained too hard for Jack to go to work, and then they would sit around drinking beer from quart bottles and playing cards with the Purdys, who had the trailer next to theirs. It all had a dreamlike quality to Gene, far away now, and sweetened and made hazy by time; the six months in Oregon spent in a trailer, where it had rained almost every day and she had to walk a hundred yards through the rain to the lavatory, where there was nothing to do while Jack was at work except listen to the radio with Suzy Purdy and sew and do the housework—the little movie house, the B.P.O.E. ballroom, Mrs. Anderson's Tea Room, The Steak House, playing cards with the Purdys and going for rides in the green countryside on Sundays. Jack had tried so hard, so almost pitifully hard, to make her happy.

But June came, the work was almost done, and Jack would soon be out of a job. And then there was a letter from Smitty, saying that Hogan and Griffith had a big contract on North Island and he wanted Jack to come back as grade foreman. Jack showed her the letter. She read it through twice, slowly, and then she looked at him.

"Do you want to go?" she asked.

He was lying on the couch with his head propped up on the red bolster she had made, cleaning his fingernails with a matchstick. "I don't know," he said. Gene sat down beside him.

"Well, I guess so," he said. "We might as well. It's a lot better job than I can get around here."

"Do you want to go?" she said again.

"It'll be okay," Jack said, still without looking at her. "It's been six months."

Holding the letter, Gene rose, stepped across to the stove and lifted the cover on the string beans. Steam drifted up into her nostrils and the cover burned her fingers, but she did not put it down right away. Finally she replaced it and turned around. "What about V?"

"She's probably gone back to Bakersfield. The guy she married's got a ranch up there."

Gene sat down beside him again and looked around the trailer. It was so small. Everything was in its place. It was as though its smallness had thrown them into a closer relationship, as though in living so intimately they had become more intimate in all ways.

"It's been nice here," she said, matter-of-factly. "I hate to leave our trailer."

Jack raised himself and put his arm around her back. "Listen, do you want to say here? I can get on as a skinner, maybe."

"Oh, no. Not if it's a better job."

"The money doesn't matter that much."

She took a long breath and turned her head and smiled at him. "I didn't mean I didn't want to go," she said. "It's just that we've been so happy here." She got up again and returned to the stove; there was nothing for her to do there, but she moved the pots around on the burners. Jack came over, turned her toward him and put his arms around her. He looked worried.

"Listen, damn it, Gene, if you don't want to go, we won't." She leaned her head against his chest. He held one hand in the small of her back, pressing her to him, and she could feel the warmth of his body. She could feel his heart beating steadily against her cheek. "I love you, darling," she said, into his chest.

Jack lifted her face and looked down into her eyes. She put her hand up to smooth his forehead. "Honey, are you worried about going back?" he said.

She shook her head, smiling at him.

"Aren't you? Honest?"

"No," Gene said. "Remember that night in San Diego when we talked about it before?"

"Yeah."

"Well, I trust you. I always will now. You've been wonderful, Jack."

He was silent, holding her in his arms, and she leaned against him contentedly, feeling him breathe and trying to find with her ear the place where she had heard his heart beating.

So they went back. They stayed in a hotel until they found an apartment and could get their furniture out of storage. Gene wondered why she had dreaded this returning. She was sure V had gone, and V would never be able to find them again. She got her old job back with Hogan and Griffith and she and Jack were able to save two hundred dollars every month. In two or three years, with a G.I. loan, Jack would be able to buy the tractors he wanted.

8

On their first anniversary they drove out to La Jolla for dinner, to the Casa del Mar, where Jack had proposed to her. They went early and sat at one of the tables by the tinted, out-slanted windows, where they could watch the day fade and the waves moiling over the black-wet rocks beneath the window.

They had steaks smothered in some kind of honey sauce, and wine. The dining room was dark, each table lit by a cone of light from a shaded candle, and Gene watched the light flicker on Jack's face; the shadows deep in his eyes, his chin and forehead highlighted, the thin, relaxed line of his mouth sharply etched. They talked about her job and his and about the tractors they were going to buy. They argued about the exact amount of money they had in the bank and Jack's leg was pressed hard and tight against hers under the table, and she had never loved him so much.

When they had finished their steaks and had fallen silent, she said softly, "Jack, it's been a good year."

He put his hand across the table and she laid her hand in his and he closed his fingers around it. "Do you think so?" he asked.

"Don't you?"

"We got off to a bad start," Jack said, and he moved his head to one side so that the light lost his face.

"That doesn't matter anymore. Everything's perfect now."

Jack took the wine bottle from the sweating bucket and filled their glasses. "Everything's perfect now," Gene said again. "Jack, I'm awfully glad we're married, aren't you?"

She saw him nod. After a moment, he said, "Gene, you've been damn fine."

She closed her eyes and smiled and took a drink of her wine. She could feel herself getting tight but she didn't mind tonight. When she opened her eyes the waiter had wheeled a table over next to theirs, and on the table was a huge crystal bowl of cherries. They had ordered Cherries Diablo; they hadn't known what it was, but it was the most expensive dessert on the menu.

The waiter struck a match and lit the liquid around the cherries, and blue flames leaped up. The flames danced weirdly and sent shadows shivering across the ceiling and lit Jack's face until he looked like a devil, and as they slowly died and the room was dark once more, Gene heard footsteps brush past and stop behind her.

When she had finished her cherries, she looked up at Jack. His leg had moved away and in the light of the candle his face looked hard and twisted and ugly. His lips were pulled back against his teeth and he was staring past her.

"Why, Jack, what's the matter?"

His eyes flickered quickly to hers. He stared at her as though he hated her, and suddenly she was afraid. "Don't you feel well, Jack?"

"Let's get out of here," he said harshly.

"But don't you want any coffee?"

He flung his napkin onto the table. "Those damn cherries," he said. "Let's get out of here." He pushed his chair back and got to his feet, knocking against the table so that the cups rattled in the saucers.

He waited impatiently, almost angrily, until she rose, and then he followed her to the lobby, treading on her heels. In the lobby she turned and put her hand on his arm.

"Are you sick, darling?"

"Let's get the hell out of here," he said, and now his eyes avoided hers. His cheek muscles were bunched tightly, his mouth was thin and bloodless; she looked at him worriedly and then she went into the powder room to put on lipstick. When she came out he was gone and she waited in the lobby, watching the door to the men's room. But suddenly he was at her side and he grasped her arm roughly and pulled her toward the door.

In the car he still did not speak, and he would not look at her. He was driving too fast and he cursed under his breath when they had to wait for a stop light. "Please, Jack," Gene said. "What is it? Won't you tell me?"

"It's nothing."

"Was it something I said?"

"It's nothing," he said. "It's nothing, damn it. Nothing!"

And at the apartment he did not undress when she did, sitting in the big chair in the living room. He picked up a magazine, paged through it rapidly, and threw it down when she came in from the bedroom to turn on the light so he could see better. She had put on the nightgown she had pressed before he had come home that evening and carefully combed her hair, and she stared down at him, biting her lip. He sat slumped in the chair, his body somehow sunken in it, and his trousers were pulled tight over his knees. She knelt beside the arm of the chair; she could feel the tears pushing at the backs of her eyes.

"Tell me what's the matter, Jack," she pleaded.

His voice was harsh, and his glance was angry but at the same time ashamed. "Nothing," he said. "Goddamn it, I told you there's nothing wrong. Just leave me alone."

The phone rang. He jumped up and snatched the receiver from the cradle. "Hello?" he said. He waited. "Yeah, yeah... Okay. Yeah, I'll be right out." He hung up and turned toward Gene as she slowly got to her feet.

"I've got to go," he said, almost defiantly.

"Where? Out to the job?"

"Yeah." He moved toward the door and Gene took a step after him.

"Jack, what's the matter? Jack, it's our…" She stopped as blue, flickering terror gripped her heart and she felt as though she could not breathe. He had been talking to V; he was going to V.

He snatched his coat from the back of a chair. It skewed across his back as he thrust his hands at the armholes. The door slammed shut behind him.

Gene stood motionless, frozen. She heard the quick grind of the starter. She heard the motor race and the car rush off. She bent her head to look at the smooth silk of the nightgown that covered her body, and ran her hands down over her chest until they fell naturally to her sides. When she turned away from the door she was crying. Terrible sobs shook the body he did not want, and she stumbled toward the bedroom, weak with help-less rage and self-pity and hate.

9

When her anger had passed she was able to think coldly and clearly. She would get a divorce. She would get a divorce as quickly and with as little trouble as possible. She would go to Las Vegas and when it was over, if he would still have her, she would marry Charley Long.

But a thought nagged at her. She tried to thrust the thought from her mind but it kept returning and she had to consider it, and considering it she could not think coldly and clearly. She grew to like it more and more. It appealed to her: Jack was depending on her to save him from V. He needed her as a shield, if she left him she would be failing him, and somehow, with this, her dignity and self-respect were safe.

Each morning she got up and went to work and came home again to the often empty house, not because she was waiting for Jack to speak, but because she was turning the matter over in her mind. Gone was the cold determination she had had at first, and the more she thought that Jack must need her desperately, the stronger she felt. She liked the role she would soon be playing. And Saturday when the phone call came she almost welcomed it, although she was frightened and demoralized by the voice that came over the wire.

The woman's voice was smooth and self-assured, strange to her, and yet she had known that voice for a long time. It was as though she had lived with that voice as long as she had lived with Jack, and hated it as long as she had loved him.

"This is V," the voice said.

Gene held the phone away from the sudden loudness of her

breathing. Her fingers looked white and lifeless against the black instrument.

"*Hello?*" said the phone.

"Hello," Gene said.

"*Is this Gene?*"

"Yes."

"*Could you meet me at three at the El Cortez? I think...*"

"Yes," Gene said. "Yes."

And they arranged a meeting, as though they were two old friends who hadn't seen one another for a long time. She was to meet V at the Sky Room of the El Cortez Hotel, where she had told Jack she would marry him.

She had never known fear as she knew it then. She tried, as she had already tried so many times, to imagine what V was like. Now she would know, and she told herself it was always easier to fight something you knew. But she was afraid, and then she tried not to think about V as she pressed her black suit and carefully dressed and fixed her face and combed her hair. She put on her black hat with the short veil, her black gloves and her Chesterfield, and then she called a taxi.

But in the ascending elevator, staring at the tightly tailored back of the elevator operator, she felt completely alone and shabby and inadequate, with too much and too many against her, and her courage was almost gone. The elevator stopped, the doors opened on sunlit glass and she walked dazedly across the room to a table in the farthest corner. She ordered a straight bourbon and looked at her watch. It was ten minutes to three, and she should have been late. In ten minutes V would come.

Then her courage was completely gone and in its place came utter panic. What was she doing here? What could she ever gain by seeing V, whom she hated too much and feared too much and who was so much stronger than she that she had made of her, Gene's, marriage a hateful and rotten thing? What could she do but lose, and losing now lose altogether the dignity and self-respect she thought she could save? She couldn't face it; as though it were a dark night and she could not turn to face the demon that followed her, as though if she did not turn the demon could not be there. She fumbled a dollar from her change purse, snatched up her bag and gloves and fled toward the elevator.

The burnished arrow circled the burnished arc and stopped. The elevator doors opened and she brushed against someone as she blindly thrust herself forward. A hand touched her arm, the voice said, "You're Jack's wife, aren't you?"

A cry of terror almost pushed from her throat. She forced herself to look at the source of the voice, feeling the muscles pull tight at the corners of her mouth and in her throat. She could not separate the details of the face she saw from the whole, she saw no eyes, mouth, nose, hair, as such; she saw only a face that had known always what she was only now learning, learning now in this moment, and what she would learn in years to come, and knew too what she could never learn and would never want to learn. The face was beautiful and ruthless and was all to Gene that she herself was not and could never be, and then she saw the pity in it and her knees turned to liquid and she felt as though she must faint.

"No," she whispered. "No, I have to go. Let me go, please."

She almost cried out as she saw the elevator doors close, the arrow arch down. Her eyes, bright and hot with tears, searched for the call button; she found it, pushed; the arrow continued to arch away. She looked wildly for the stairs.

"Wait," V said.

"No," she whispered. "No. Let me go," but paralyzed, she

made no move. She saw Vs face turn hard and white. The gold choker around her neck sparkled dazzlingly in the sun and Gene's eyes were caught and held by it.

"You've got to divorce him," V whispered. "We can't go on like this. None of us. You've got to…"

"He hates you," Gene said. "He hates you. I can't."

There was no pity in V's face now. "You must!"

"No," Gene moaned. "Let me alone, you…" She saw the bronze arrow swinging up. It stopped and the doors slid open. People pushed out past her and she stumbled against V. She sobbed aloud as their arms touched.

"Wait, Gene," V said, but sobbing, she covered her ears with her gloved hands and ran into the elevator. The operator stared at her with impersonal curiosity. "Down!" she cried at him. "Take me down!"

As the elevator doors slid together she raised her face. Through a hot, salt film she could see V shining in the closing rectangle, the sun bright on her blonde hair and gold choker, and in her brown eyes pain, and the horrible pity. Then the doors clanged softly shut and the floor dropped away beneath her feet, down and down, and she pressed her hands to her face and sobbed with humiliation.

10

The next day when Jack came home she told him she was going to get a divorce.

He sat slouched in the big chair, his feet crossed on the footstool. His arms lay outstretched along the arms of the chair, his head was bent forward and Gene could see a muscle twitching in his cheek. She sat stiffly on the couch, watching him. The anger and hate and self-revulsion that had filled her the day before were gone, and all the tears had already fallen. Now she felt a curious, empty nothingness.

"Half the money's yours," Jack said finally. "You better take it out and put it in your own name."

So this is the way a marriage ends, she thought. Out of all it had been or could have been, there was left only the money in the bank and the things they owned together. That was all there was left to talk about even, a kind of residue of marriage.

"I don't want any of it," she said.

"Yes, you do. Anyway it's California law, I think. Are you going to want any—alimony?"

"No," she said. "I don't want anything." She shook her head and clasped her hands in her lap. "I don't want anything," she repeated.

"You been to a lawyer yet?"

"I'm going to Las Vegas."

"Oh," he said. "Yeah."

"I'll leave next week. I think I'll fly."

"Yeah," Jack said, and then he sat silently, sullenly, his eyes brooding at her. "Well," he said. "I'll check out. You may as well stay here till you get ready to go."

"I'll go stay with mother. That's standard procedure, isn't it?"

"No," Jack said. "Stay here. I'll move out."

"Oh, I see," she said. "You'll want to go stay with your V. I thought she was married. Isn't she married? Her husband must be very forgiving."

"He's dead," Jack said. Suddenly he grimaced and said, "Gene, I guess it wouldn't make you feel any better if I told you…"

"Do you want me to help you pack?" she interrupted, and she got to her feet, holding her clasped hands at her belt.

"No," he said. "Thanks. I'll come back this afternoon and get my stuff." His cheeks bunched, hiding his eyes, and he stood up slowly, his clenched fists pushing down on the arms of the chair. He was so big. "When do you think you'll go to Las Vegas?" he asked.

"Next Saturday. I'll work next week."

"Okay," he said, without looking at her. "I'll see you before then."

That afternoon she went over to tell her mother, dreading it, for her mother had never liked Jack, and she did not want to be pitied. The pity she had seen in V's eyes had made her physically ill. She was afraid she would turn on her mother: at least she had the courage to divorce her husband, and her mother had never had; and at least Jack was a man, and not a sodden little animal, as her father had been. Riding out to Mission Hills on the streetcar, dreading the afternoon, she began to despise her mother, and she didn't want to show it.

"You poor thing," her mother said. "What has he done to you?" Her eyes were little and hard and she put her hand to her forehead and brushed back a strand of gray hair. She had on the gray, man's sweater she always wore when she was cleaning the house.

Gene put her purse down on the davenport on top of her coat, and sat down beside it "We just couldn't get along," she said, with an effort to speak lightly. "It's just one of those things."

Her mother took a step toward her and looked keenly down into her eyes. "He's hurt you, hasn't he?" she demanded. "He drinks, doesn't he?"

Gene almost screamed at her: what about your husband? At least I'm getting out, at least I'm not going to spend my whole life being a martyr and feeling sorry for myself like you have, at least I'm salvaging myself out of this. But she managed a smile and shook her head gently. "Oh, it's nothing like that. We're still friends." The understatement of it seemed melodramatic and she hated this necessity to lie. She wanted to go back to the empty apartment where no one would intrude and make demands upon her, where she could stretch out on the bed and think. Her mother's hands were clasped in front of her, the fingers dovetailed; her mouth was pinched and hurt, white around the edges of the lips.

"I'd think you could tell me, Eugenia. I know that man has done something to you."

"No," Gene said. Looking at her mother she thought: if you say I told you so...If you so much as think it...She wouldn't take any pity.

Finally she said, "Really, there are no hard feelings at all," and she looked around the room, chilled at the shabby, manless familiarity of the place. She stood up and said, "I have to go now, Mother."

"But aren't you coming back here? You're not going to stay in that apartment by yourself!"

"Yes. I am."

Her mother stared at her angrily. "Oh, I'll be all right," Gene said. "I have to get rid of the furniture and there's a lot of cleaning to do. There's a lot to do when you break up housekeeping."

"Why can't *he* take care of that?"

Gene shrugged tiredly and gathered up her coat and purse. "I don't mind," she said as she walked out into the hall. She pushed the screen door open and turned around. "Goodbye, Mother."

Her mother came into the hall behind her. "I told you that Jack Ward was no good. You never should have married him."

Gene's hand clutched the edge of the door tightly, the feeling of weak and helpless anger came back and nauseated her, and she felt the floor dropping away beneath her feet. She clutched desperately at the edge of the door while the nausea pitched in her stomach. Her mother and the hallway whirled grayly.

"If you must know," she said loudly, "it's my fault. I'm frigid. I'm sterile. Like you are. Does that make you happy?" She almost laughed as she saw the words she had thrown strike her mother in the face, and then she turned and stumbled out into the sunlight. The sun was bright on the grass of the lawn, bright on the white stucco and red tile of the houses that lined the street. In the next yard a lawn sprinkler was rotating, sending out a round flower of shining spray. As she hurried down the walk Gene wondered if anybody anywhere had ever hated anyone as much as she hated V.

11

She even felt vaguely resentful toward Charley Long when she saw him on Monday. He stopped by the office before he went out on the job, as he sometimes did, and he watched her cautiously when she told him about the divorce.

"That's too bad," he said. He stood beside her desk with his hands pulling down the pockets of his chamois coat, looking very lean and tall. The usual good humor in his brown, horse face was restrained, and Gene saw he was seeking her mood.

"It just didn't work," she said. "That's all. Nobody was hurt."

Charley took his pipe from his pocket, filled it and lit it with irritating slowness. "I'm sorry," he said presently. "I don't know what else to say, Gene." He folded his tobacco pouch and replaced it and his eyes, looking up, searched hers.

Mr. Griffith came out of his office, holding a letter in his hand. He let it glide into Gene's inbox and said, "I made some changes on this, Gene. Would you type it over and shoot it back?"

"Of course," Gene said. Charley nodded to Mr. Griffith, looked at Gene again, then walked slowly around the end of the counter. He raised a hand toward her as he went out the door, and she saw him look back again before he got into the station wagon with his surveyors.

She had already given the landlady notice and during the week she made arrangements for selling the furniture, and the stove and refrigerator. She prided herself on the efficient way she was handling everything. She had intended to work the week out at the office and then leave for Las Vegas, but Wednesday morning the strain of it all seemed to hit her. The nausea came again and she was violently ill. She didn't go to work that day and in the afternoon she felt much better.

But the next morning it recurred, and Friday she went to the doctor. She knew what it was and at first she was not angry, only tired and frightened and confused; she knew she had missed her period, but she had never been regular and had never worried when she skipped. But now she seemed to know. The doctor confirmed it. The baby that was hers and Jack's would be born in April.

Jack had phoned that he would come by to see her that night, the night before she had been going to leave for Las Vegas. He came a little after six and she didn't get up to answer the door, remaining motionless on the couch and watching him as he sat down in the straight chair by the radio.

He had on the suit he had worn when they were married. His shoes were shined and he carried his tan corduroy hat in his hand. Watching him sit down and hitch his trousers up and cross his legs, Gene felt ugly and swollen and hateful. For the first time she hated him. She hated his slanting eyes and his broad face and big body. She hated his false smile.

"How are you, Gene?"

She didn't answer. She sat watching him, hating him and his V, who was part of him.

"Well, everything's all set," he said. "I've got a cashier's check here for twenty-two hundred bucks." He leaned forward and laid a check on her lap.

She glanced down at it and moved her leg so that it floated to the floor. She saw Jack's lips tighten. He said, "Do you need any cash to tide you over?"

She reached for the humidor to get a cigarette, wondering if she only imagined it, or if it really were hard to bend her body.

She turned farther than was necessary to see if there was any stiffness or pain; there was none, but she held her body uncomfortably twisted as she tamped the cigarette on the top of the humidor. She tamped one end and then the other, slowly and listlessly.

"What's the matter?" Jack said.

She looked back at him. She smiled with the strong, exultant knowledge of how she could hurt him now, and she said, "I went to the doctor today, Jack."

"What's the matter?" he said. She saw him lick his lips, but then he was no longer focused in her eyes. He seemed to circle in the chair, fading and returning, and she felt as she had as a child when her cousin had spun her around on a piano stool. She put her hand out to steady herself, staring intently at the blob that was Jack's face. It was sharply white in the vague room and finally it fixed itself in her eyes.

"I'm going to have a baby in April," she said. She almost laughed aloud, but the room began spinning again and she closed her eyes and let her head rest against the back of the couch while the nausea mounted in her body. When it receded she opened her eyes and looked down at the cigarette in her hand. It was flattened and bent and she tossed it to the end table.

"I guess there's only one thing to do," she heard Jack say.

"Yes."

"We'll have to start all over. We'll have to forget…"

Laughter broke from her with a tearing sound that hurt her ears. Jack stopped, his mouth still shaped for the next word. His face seemed to have broken up into white lumps of flesh and he was sitting very straight with the hat clenched in his hands. Gene leaned toward him, feeling her face twist painfully, and she said, "Do you think for one minute I'd do this for you?"

He stared at her, and she saw he did not understand.

"Do you think I'd let this happen?" she said. She shook her head, savagely. "No," she said. "I won't have your baby. Oh, no, Jack," she said and she stretched her arm and turned her body to recover the cigarette from the end table. She brought it to her mouth with a jerky motion.

"Listen, Goddamn it," Jack said. "You can't do that, Gene! Listen…"

"Can't I?" she cried. "Can't I? You just watch me do it!"

"Listen! Gene!"

"I don't want anything of yours!" she screamed. "Get your filthy V to have one for you. I don't want your money, either; I don't want one bit of you. I don't want one thing to ever remind me of your filthy, dirty, cheating…" She stopped and rubbed her hand over her eyes. Tears burned like acid in them and her face felt hot and tight, her body tight and full and spilling over with hate.

She saw Jack shaking his head. She fixed her eyes on the hat he gripped between his hands; crumpling it as he had crumpled her. "Don't go off like this," he said doggedly. "We'll have to forget everything else. We can do it. This is bigger than…"

"It's not bigger!" she cried, and then she tried to speak reasonably. "No, Jack, I'm going through with it."

He leaned toward her. "Don't," he said. "Don't do it, Gene. You can't. I swear it won't happen again. You've got to see I mean that."

"You're crawling," Gene said. "Remember that time you asked me if I wanted you to crawl any more? I said I didn't, but I love it now." The tears ran down her cheeks, out of her burning eyes, as she tried to laugh. "Oh, Jack," she said. "You had something I wanted so badly, and do you think I ever got it? Do you think I ever did? You've hurt me and hurt me and made me hate you and your V and myself till I can't hate enough…" She stopped, panting, for all at once she was afraid that she had gone insane.

She felt the fear grip her tightly as she lit the cigarette and drew into her lungs smoke that made her head spin again. But she couldn't stop herself, and she said, "Now I've got something you want. I hope just as badly. Worse. And you're not going to get it." She laughed again, shaking with it. "You killed something inside me, Jack, and now I'm going to kill something there too." She liked the way that sounded and she repeated it, watching Jack's throat work and watching him rub his hand over his black hair.

"Listen," he said. "Let's talk about this later. I know how you feel, but you can't do this. We shouldn't talk about it when you feel like this."

"I'm going to do it!" her voice rasped. Her throat tasted sour and dirty from the cigarette. "I'm going to do it!" she cried, and her voice rose and broke and she pounded her fist on the arm of the couch. It made a small, thudding sound. "I'm going to," she said. "I'm going to."

She saw Jack snatch up his hat from the floor, rise and take a step toward her. He stood there for a moment and she could see written on his face how this had hurt him. She could see fear and anger on his face and she whispered, "I'm going to," leaning forward so that her face almost touched him, and saying it over and over again as he turned and half-ran out the door. And when the door slammed shut behind him she slumped down on the couch, sobbing and laughing and gasping for breath.

12

And she went through with it. Afterward she would wake up in the night sometimes, saying over and over again, "Oh, God! Oh, God! Oh, God!" not waking from a dream, but from the remembrance of the smell of blood: her legs up on the bandaged racks and the animal screams that had come from her, and the smell of blood; a smell like no other, like everything ever smelled and nothing ever smelled, hot-smelling, salt-smelling, sweet-smelling; the Mexican doctor with the blood like paint on his rubber gloves and the steel, bloody hook in his hand. And the anesthetic that hadn't worked and hadn't worked and hadn't worked again, so that she had to have her consciousness and her eyes when she would have cut them out with a dull knife not to have them; the pain, the dull, insistent pain, and the sharp, tearing, killing pain, and the basin. If only she had not had to see the basin. She had fainted when she had seen it, but the fainting had printed the sight with acid somewhere inside her.

Waking in the night with it she would ask herself why she hadn't died then. She had asked herself that a thousand times; why hadn't she died? Coming back to the border in the car, leaning her head against the glass, her head hitting against the glass of the window as her mother drove the car slowly over the rutted road, the road rutted so deeply that at each jolt she thought she would die, hoped she would die; why hadn't she died?

It was her mother who saved her. It was her mother who stood by her, found out about the little Tijuana hospital where a Dr. Mendez would perform the operation for two hundred dollars, American; who took her down in the old Hudson and held her hand through the nightmare of pain and blood and anesthetic that hadn't worked, who brushed the flies away from her eyes when she thought she would go insane because of the flies, whose hand was the thin, bony grip of reality that held hers and pulled her back when she was on the edge. When she thought she would die, had no reason not to die, wanted to die, it was her mother who fought with her and talked and pleaded and ordered her back to life, knowing when to use harshness, when kindness, and who nursed her night and day until fatigue and worry were painted on her face with coarse, cruel brush-strokes.

Then came the weak, lucid feeling when pain and all emotion had dropped from her body like discarded bandages, and only remorse remained. Remorse over the loss of the child, the killing of the child, swept over her and beat into her head until she thought she could not bear the realization of what she had done. And then remorse too was gone, and there was nothing except remembered pain and grief; those hours, so long, when nothing would stay on her mind, as at first nothing would stay on her stomach, when there was nothing to do but stare at the outline of her body in the bed, and the tapestry chair and the white bureau and the mirror. And slowly what at first had been only a vaguely aching lack gathered shape and crystalized. She still loved Jack. She did not want to give him up.

And Jack had come to her.

She heard him first arguing and pleading with her mother. His voice sounded louder, nearer, and then he had come, huge, through the doorway. His shoulders were slumped, the flesh of his face was tight over the bone, his cheeks dark with beard. She called out to him.

And when she heard her voice say his name and saw his eyes, she was sure he loved her with everything that was decent in him. She was sure of it, and it was what she wanted desperately now; he loved her with everything in him that was not cursed by V. With an awkward stumbling motion his arms were around her and his rough, tobacco-smelling, liquor-smelling face was against hers. He whispered words she could not understand into her ear and suddenly she found that it was she who was comforting him, trying to give him strength, and it was she who asked him to forgive.

She saw her mother standing in the doorway. Her hands were working in her apron and her face was twisted savagely. She was screaming at Gene, but Jack was talking hoarsely and Gene looked down and smoothed his hair, saying over and over again that it would be all right; it was all right and they could have another baby as soon as she was well; and when she looked up again her mother was gone.

Jack was half-kneeling beside the bed and half-lying on it. His heavy arm hurt where it pressed against her chest, but she did not try to move it. "You need me, don't you, Jack?" she whispered.

"Yes."

"You needed me and I failed you, didn't I? But I won't again."

"No," he said thickly.

"Yes, I did. But I won't again."

"You didn't. That's not it."

"You married me to get away from her, didn't you? No, I don't mean that like it sounds. I know you love me. But you wanted someone to keep you away from her because she's a devil, didn't you?"

He raised his head and looked down at her. His forehead was creased. He moistened his lips as though he were going to speak, but he did not, and she pressed her fingertips on his mouth.

"I know now," she went on. "It doesn't hurt me, Jack. I'm proud."

He stared down at her, frowning, pain deep in his eyes, as though she did not understand. But she knew she did and when she took her fingers from his lips he did not say anything, and she smoothed her hand over his crumpled black hair, sobbing now, but smiling and talking to him.

13

The winter of 1947 was a bad one in San Diego. It was cold and it rained so much, and Coronado, where they finally found a furnished apartment, was a bleak, cheerless place when it rained.

Gene did not go back to work. She was weak and half-sick, her appetite was gone and she lost weight, but she was happy. She felt a new strength and she felt she had a new relationship with Jack. He needed her now, and he was looking forward to the child they would have as soon as she was well. But she did not seem to be getting well very quickly.

Hogan and Griffith had transferred Jack to the new Mission Bay airport, where he was grade foreman. It was a much bigger job than he had had working under Smitty, and the pay was better. He began talking about taking some correspondence engineering courses, and one night they wrote for a brochure.

Jack looked older now, and Gene, who was not yet twenty-eight, could mark gray hairs at her temples when she looked in the mirror. The gray hairs were new, and her eyes seemed to have sunk into her head, eyes that hurt with constant headaches.

Her health did not seem to be improving at all, and once after she had had to spend a week in bed she went to Tijuana, to see Dr. Mendez. He assured her that nothing was wrong, that it was only after-effects and shock, and that it would soon pass. But it did not pass, and a month later she went back again. This time she could not find Dr. Mendez and there was no one about who could speak English.

And finally she had the pains, and after a night spent crying with fear, she made up her mind to go to a doctor in San Diego.

She did not tell Jack. She was afraid of worrying him and he was working hard lately. He no longer had time even to come home for lunch. She knew he was trying his best to make good in the new job, his face had a constant strained, harried look, and she did not want to worry him when there might be no reason for it. She went to the general practitioner who had been her mother's doctor for as long as she could remember, and he sent her to a Dr. Phillips in the Medical-Dental Building—a specialist.

The visit to Dr. Phillips' office was now only a haze of horror in her mind. Although she had seen him since, she remembered him only as the stocky, hearty man with freckled hands, in a spotless white tunic that buttoned down one shoulder, whom she had seen that day. She had been too shocked to cry, too terrified to think, too dazed at first to understand, and all she could remember was the pity in his eyes when he told her she had an infection. She would have to have an operation soon. She would never be able to have a baby.

She did not take a taxi home. She walked slowly down to the ferry slip and waited for the ferry to bump and fit itself in among the creaking piles. Aboard she still did not cry. The tears seemed dried up in her. She climbed to the top deck and stood clinging to the rail, feeling the salt wind blow the hair around her head. The water of the bay was a deep blue, speckled with gold motes of sun. Lean, gray, numbered prows leered at her as the ferry passed three destroyers herded together, and porpoises wove in and out of the water beside the ferry in an endless procession of plump black bodies and triangular fins.

Her hands were clenched fiercely on the wet, sticky rail. With revulsion she looked down at the body that was outlined against the wind beneath her dress. What had they done to it? A life torn and hacked apart in it, the only reason she, a woman, had for being, bludgeoned to death in it; diseased, now the disease to be hacked out like the other. She retched weakly as she looked down at herself. What had they done to her? Inside her the flesh was slashed and mutilated and diseased; it was her body, and she was chained to it like a dog to a fence-post, until she died.

At home she lay down on the bed without removing her hat. She opened her mouth wide, straining her jaws, expecting that now the tears would come. But nothing came. Her eyes felt as though they had been dipped in sand.

She lay for a long time without moving, waiting for Jack to come home. She had to tell him. How could she tell him? Why hadn't she died? A dry sob convulsed her, and inside her the pain cut sharply.

When the phone began to ring she opened her eyes to the dark whiteness of the pillow. She could not loosen her clenched fists. The phone rang again. She let it ring still again before slowly, wearily, she raised her body from the bed and went in to answer it.

Part V
JACK

I

When Jack had been in his early twenties the relationship between men and women seemed very simple. It was not something he had ever sat down and thought through. In a way it had just developed, and it seemed, among his friends, to be pretty generally accepted.

Men wanted to go to bed with women, and women, in turn, wanted to go to bed with men. But for some reason, perhaps because of the way they were made, women had to put up a fight. So the man's part was the attack, the woman's was defense. It was a struggle, with the odds on the side of the man; he realized that. But there was nothing really lost either way. If the woman lost, well, she enjoyed it as much as he did, because, underneath, it was what she had really wanted too. And if he should lose he had only to look elsewhere.

Before he left the CCC camp he had never had many opportunities to play the game. He had gone to whores a few times, but he had not liked that much; it was as though you were going deer hunting and there was some way you could pay the deer to walk up near you where you could shoot it. But in Fresno there had been a waitress at the café around the corner from his rooming house, where he and Ben ate every night. She had been fat and much older than he, but she was his first real conquest, and he learned much from her. From her he learned about the second struggle.

The second struggle came always after the man had won the first one, and in this the positions were reversed; the man went on the defensive and the woman pursued him. The waitress

had talked about getting married, and he had been so frightened he had almost left town. But after the original fright was
over he had known intuitively how to handle her. At first he had
stayed away, and when that hadn't worked and she had come
up to his room once, and another time bothered his landlady,
he got to talking to a truck driver who ate in the same café, and
discovered that the truck driver had been sleeping with the
waitress too. He picked a fight with her on this count, and that
had finished it.

Then there were others; a girl who worked in the cannery, a
redheaded girl named Mary Ann MacNicoll, whose father owned
a big furniture store and who had gone for a while to the college
at Fresno, Peggy, the waitress at the Hitching Post, and Ruth
Adams. It was a simple and exciting game with one goal and no
rules that he knew of, and he was good at it. He played it with a
great many women in Fresno and Bakersfield and Visalia and
Porterville; he nearly always won, and he always got out of it
when they wanted to hang onto him, or tried to get him to
marry them. He was attractive to women and he knew it, he
liked playing the game and he didn't want to get married and
drop out of it for a long time yet.

The fact that V was a virgin did not seem to exempt her from
playing the game. It meant that he would be the first, but
someone had to be the first. He had seen her a great many
times around the Baird ranch before he had a chance to talk to
her; he would look up to see her sitting motionless on the
copper-colored horse on the top of the far hill behind the ranch
buildings, watching him. She would watch him for a long time,
sitting up very straight on the horse, and then when he would
look up again she would have disappeared, as suddenly as she
had come. She was blonde, young, and she had a nice build,
and he liked the way she sat on the horse, but he had never
seen her closely until she rode down into the bottom one day

when her father was talking to him, and that night after work he got her to let him ride the horse.

She was standing at the corral gate when he returned. His legs were stiff and his hands ached, because Tony had got the bit in his teeth and had run all the way back to the corral. Tony was panting and sweating and V grabbed the reins from him when he dismounted. Her face was flushed. Her hair was done up in two short braids tied with blue ribbons, that swung out when she jerked her head toward him.

"You know a lot about horses!" she said fiercely.

"Boy, you've sure got him spoilt," Jack said. She pulled on the reins and Tony clopped past him. He stepped over to the fence and leaned on it, grinning, as V threw a blanket over Tony's back and walked him around the corral. She looked at him angrily from time to time. Her levis were tight over her bottom, the legs rolled up around her brown ankles.

"Aren't you going to give him his bottle?" he said.

"Shut up!"

He watched her, leaning against the fence, till she had rubbed Tony down and led him into his stall. When she walked out toward him, he said pleasantly, "That's a good horse, V."

She said nothing, sulkily wiping her hands on the seat of her levis. Jack slapped at a fly. "How come you want to spoil him like that?" he said.

"Oh, shut up!" V said. She started past him, but he grabbed her arm, swung her around and kissed her, hard. She relaxed for a moment, as though she didn't know what he was doing, but then she stamped on his foot. When he released her arm she hit him in the face.

The blow made his eyes water. He put his hand to his mouth and looked at it to see if he was bleeding. "Oh…" V said.

"You pack a mean right."

Her eyes narrowed and she rubbed her hand roughly across

her lips. "You get out of here!" she cried. "I ought to tell my father on you."

"Okay, okay," Jack said. "Just don't hit me again." He pretended to be staggering as he went around the shed to his car, and when he drove past the corral she was still standing in the gateway, her fists doubled up on her hips and her legs braced apart, glaring at him. He could see her breasts tight under her white shirt. He waved at her and laughed to himself, racing the car around the jutting corner of the house.

He didn't think she'd stay mad. The next day he brought her a box of candy and apologized, and when he had finished dozing the stumps in the bottom she invited him up to the house for iced tea with her and Baird. And when he had the D-4 in the orchard clearing the irrigation ditches, she began packing her lunch and coming down to eat with him. They ate together every day.

One day they were sitting in the shade, leaning against the cat with their feet in the sun, teasing the glass-eyed dog. After a while Jack slid down and covered his face with his cap, listening to V chatter about Tony and about a Mr. Denton. But finally she stopped, and after a pause, said in a low voice, "Why did you kiss me that day, Jack?"

Without moving he peered out at her from under the brim of his cap. Her face was turned down and she was sitting with her legs crossed, intent on plucking out blades of grass, one by one, and arranging them in a pattern on the blue cloth of her knee. "Because I wanted to," he said.

"Do you always do what you want to?"

"Well, sometimes I don't get away with it."

He saw her frown. He pushed his cap back from his face and sat up. He said seriously, "I didn't get away with that."

She brushed the blades of grass from her knee and wiped her hands together, still frowning. When she looked up at him there was an embarrassed smile on her lips. Jack put his hand on her arm and smoothed the hairs on her wrist, knowing that she wanted to be kissed again, but that it would be best not to kiss her yet.

Her arm was warm from the sun, brown, the hairs golden. He stroked her forearm gently, ready to take his hand away if she moved. But she let it stay.

Finally he stopped and they both leaned back against the side of the cat. Their shoulders touched. The sun was hot on their legs, and they said nothing more until it was time for Jack to go to work. When he had started the cat and climbed into the seat, V walked slowly away through the trees toward the house. The dog followed her, barking and jumping at her legs. Jack saw her put her hand down to pat its head as he swung the D-4 around toward the irrigation ditch.

The next day at noon he parked the cat a little more in the sun, whistling as he cut the engine and climbed out of the seat. V came down the hill, carrying her lunch in a paper bag. She hadn't brought the dog with her, and she wore her levis and a fresh white shirt with the sleeves rolled up on her brown arms. Sitting down beside him, she opened the sack and took out two waxed-paper-wrapped sandwiches.

The day was hot and the trees left checkerboards of brightness and shadow on the cool ground. They didn't talk while they ate. V seemed shy. She thanked him stiffly when he let her drink some of his coffee.

He let his shoulder touch hers. She moved away at first, but then they touched again. When he put his arm around her she looked up at him with an embarrassed smile, and said, "Jack." He thought she was going to tell him to stop, but she said, "Who did you have a date with the other night?"

"When?"

"You know. You said you had a date."

"Girl named Peggy," he said.

"Where did you go?"

He shrugged. "To some dance."

"Where?"

"At the Chamber of Commerce Hall."

"Is it a nice place?"

"It's all right."

She leaned against him and he pressed her closer, smoothing his hand in the soft hollow of her back. He felt her shiver. "Is she pretty?" she asked.

"Who?"

"This girl. Is she prettier than me?"

"She doesn't even come close," Jack said. He could feel the heat of the sun spreading up between them. He stroked her back. Her lips parted over her teeth as she smiled, and her eyes, half-closed, shone through the blonde lashes. When she turned her face away he touched her throat with his lips. She gasped and put her hand up to the place, but he didn't kiss her again. He stroked her back slowly, softly, feeling the warmth creep up between them.

Gently he ran his hand around and over her belly; it was hard and flat and she sucked it in under his hand. When he moved his hand back she stretched, and then her arms went around his neck.

He could feel the hot points of her breasts against his chest, and he kissed her, slowly and softly. Then he kissed her harder, gradually harder, until he felt her breath quicken. Her lips were sweet and pressed back against her teeth and she made a tiny, thick sound in her throat, as though she'd known all along what it would be like, but now, although it was proved to her, it was still wonderful and new.

He had never known a virgin before and at first it was

impossible. It hurt her and she was afraid, but he realized ashamedly that she was trusting him. But she was too nervous and too scared, and he did not force himself upon her.

The next time it hurt her again, but crying, she made him go through with it; crying and laughing at the same time, her arms holding him to her with strength he would not have believed was there. And afterward she would not release him, holding him with the strong arms and crying and talking to him and to herself and to no one, and laughing hysterically, her eyes shining with tears.

Then had come the night in the shed. He heard her make a sound that wasn't the right kind of sound, he felt her body tense, and looking up, he saw the old man standing in the doorway; short and stocky, with just enough light behind him so that Jack could see his thick bush of white hair. He took a step back, and then he stood motionless, staring down at them. And then with a quick motion he turned and disappeared.

Everything was quiet. They were both silent, hardly breathing, and Jack could pick sounds out of the silence; the buzz of flies around the manure pile behind the shed, the crickets calling, the horse stamping a foot, the sound of the old man's steps as he went up the hardbeaten path to the house.

"Get up!" V whispered. "Get up!" Her face was averted, her body felt cold and she was shivering. They stood up and stared at each other in the darkness. He put out his hand toward her. He was glad he had. She snatched at it and pressed it to her cheek.

"Jack," she said, just "Jack," trembling, gripping his hand as though it were the only thing in the world she had to hold onto. Jack felt his shirt trembling over his chest; he had realized suddenly what this meant. He had been playing the game, but she was not, and now it wasn't a game anymore. She had lost, but he hadn't realized all she would lose. He took a deep breath.

"I'll go talk to him," he said loudly. His legs felt weak; he didn't want them to be weak; he tensed the muscles in his calves. He felt very young and very frightened.

"Oh, God, Jack!" V whispered.

"Come on," he said. "Let's go talk to him."

"Wait!" she said. "Wait," she whispered. "What're you going to say?"

"I don't know." He tried to take her arm but she wouldn't let go his hand. Hay crunched under their feet as they moved over to sit on the low stack of oat sacks that lined the wall. Opposite them the door was a rectangle of lighter blue in the darkness of the shed. He put his arm around her.

"Jack," she whispered hoarsely. "What'll we do?" Suddenly he was surprised she wasn't crying.

"Don't cry," he said. He licked his lips. "I don't know," he said. "We'll have to go talk to him."

"But what will you say? What'll you say?"

"Goddamn it, I don't know. You want to wait here while I go?"

"No," she said breathlessly. "No. Please don't go yet," trembling as he tightened his arm around her. When she relaxed it was all at once, and she clung to him, still not crying, but holding him fiercely, her fingers digging into his back, her face tight against his chest. "What can you say?" she whispered.

"I'll think of that when I see him. Maybe I'll tell him we're going to get married."

She was silent, pressed against him. After a long time she breathed, "Oh, yes!"

"Let's go," he said gruffly. "Let's get it to hell over with." He heard the faint whack of a door slamming.

"Oh, please, wait!" V said. She put her lips up for him to kiss.

They were cold and pressed flat against her teeth and she was trembling again. "I love you, Jack," she said. "I love you." He closed her lips with his mouth but still they moved; she was telling him she loved him. He pushed her away and stood up. He could talk to the old man now.

"Come on," he said, and holding each other they went out past the corral. V didn't look at Tony who snorted gently as they passed. She clung to Jack's arm, slowing him down. He pulled her on toward the lighted windows of the house.

Then he saw the bags. At first he couldn't make out what they were; merely squarish shapes in the darkness on the driveway. Then he saw they were suitcases and he gasped at the stupidity and righteousness of them. He hated them. He hated what they meant and he cursed the old man. He cursed himself.

He stopped as V's hand tightened on his arm. She made no sound as they stared down at the suitcases. Jack felt his breath whisper through his lips, dry and hot. "Goddamn you to hell," he whispered.

Turning, he pulled her along behind him as he hurried back to his car. They drove up beside the suitcases, he got out and slung them savagely into the rumble seat. When they passed the house through the window he could see the old man bent over his food, shoveling it in. "Goddamn you to hell for this," he whispered.

They drove down the rutted road between the trees to the highway. The Ford squeaked and jolted and V clung to his right arm with both hands, her body pressed close to his. She was silent, staring at the short slice of road ahead that was bathed in the hard, white glare of the headlights. When he turned onto the highway, she had begun to cry.

2

At first it had been fine. He had been charmed by V, by her
naivete, her complete trust. He knew she worshipped him and
she never bored him. He enjoyed teaching her to dance and to
swim and he enjoyed learning how to bowl with her; they
always had a good time together. Always, with her, everything
they did was slightly different than it had ever been before,
new, and exciting. But this newness and excitement puzzled
him, and sometimes he was ashamed of it.

Sometimes he was ashamed of it because he felt himself
being carried along in her enthusiasm for everything they did
together, as though they were children, or puppies. He had
never seen anyone so completely happy; he could feel it in her
and she told him of it time and time again, as though she had
never been happy before, and he had always thought about
happiness as being something you either had or didn't have,
and which there wasn't much use thinking about.

She had no shame with him and no false modesty; she said
always what she thought or felt, or showed him what she thought
or felt, and although many times it thrilled him deeply, as many
times he was embarrassed by it. But she must have known,
instinctively, what it took him most of his life to find out: that
especially when they made love they had something between
them they could never equal elsewhere, that lived just in them
and because of them, realized a thousand times beyond itself
because of them; a perfection to be found once in their lives
and only once. V had known—she must have known, must have

realized it deeply, or, when she had lost him, she would not have tried so fiercely and ruthlessly to get him back—but he had been unable to recognize it for what it was.

It was as though he was incapable of any kind of perfection. He had mistrusted it, had been afraid of it. He had been afraid of being moved so completely by anything, and he had to obliterate it, smudge it with dirt, shy away. He had been incapable of what they had.

And there was the nagging suspicion that he had been trapped. He had always told himself he wanted to be free and he felt himself held by something mysteriously strong. The feeling grew on him that he had broken some vague rule in the game, either in taking her, a virgin, or in the slip when he had spoken of marriage. He felt there was a debt he owed, a bill he should pay.

And the fact that he had not known about the bill until now made him rebellious. He knew the bill was fair and he didn't want to be a welsher, a poor loser, but he was not ready to get married, and he was sure it would be happy for neither of them if they did. Something seemed to demand that he not hurt her, for he was aware that she was not like the other girls he knew, but much as he liked her, he hated the bonds she was imposing on him. He felt guilty and frightened about what he had done to her, about what she might become. He felt responsible, and he hated it, for he wanted no responsibilities. They had no part in his life.

Ben Proctor had thrown them up to him one day, and Ben was the only person whose opinion he cared about. Ben's judgment of him hurt him, and he was hurt more when he came to the conclusion that Ben must be in love with V. When, without notice, Ben left town, this seemed confirmed, and he thought bitterly how it must have been for Ben to see what he had seen.

The whole thing had turned bad. He wished he had never seen V, that he had never taken the job dozing stumps for her father. It was something strange and complicated and frighteningly strong in his mouth, and it had to be spat out.

He had thought it was to be finished the night of Push's birthday party at the Hitching Post, and he was so ashamed of that night that whenever afterward he remembered it, he would feel himself flush and his eyes would grow hot and he would curse himself, trying not to think about it. He had been drunk, there with V and Push and Harry and Petey Willing and three other girls, all of them drunk except V.

He remembered arguing with Petey. Petey had wanted to play *Rose of San Antone* on the jukebox for Carol Lester, who was from Texas, and Jack had insisted on playing *The One O'Clock Jump* over and over again. Carol sat on Petey's lap, crying because she wanted to hear *Rose of San Antone*, her lipstick smeared all around her mouth and around Petey's mouth. Harry was telling jokes, and Push and the two other girls were leaning on the table, listening to him. The girls snickered from time to time. V sat silently beside Jack.

Petey had upset his glass and when Peggy came over to mop up the liquor, Jack patted her on the hip. "Hi, honey," he said. She smiled down at him and he put his arm around her waist and pulled her onto his lap.

Peggy smelled of cheap perfume and face powder. She took his face between her hands and kissed him, long and sloppily, and he kissed her back. He tightened his grip when she tried to pull away, a little sickened by the smell of her. And V was watching.

"Whew," Peggy said, when he let her go. "Your little girl'll be mad, honey."

"To hell with her," Jack said. "She's a sorehead, anyway." He didn't look around at V. Push was watching him from across the table, his eyes fixed on a point at the exact center of Jack's forehead. Jack kissed Peggy again. He put his hand up under her dress, but suddenly he felt sick. He jerked his head away. V was gone.

Push was looking toward the door, an expression around his mouth as though he had tasted something rotten. *Rose of San Antone* was playing on the jukebox. Jack thrust Peggy from his lap and got to his feet, holding onto the back of the chair.

"Goddamn you, Petey, you bastard," he said. "Did you change that record?"

"You leave him alone!" Carol said.

"Somebody else changed it," Petey said.

"You better…"

"Why don't you go away?" Carol said. "You're filthy!"

He felt himself flush. "Shut up!" he said. He didn't look at Push. He crossed unsteadily to the machine, put in a quarter and punched number 19 five times. He knew what was the matter with that little Texas bitch; she'd been on the make for him ever since she'd come to town, and he'd never even looked at her. Then he remembered that this was Push's birthday party and Push had been talking about it for a month. He wondered where V had gone. He stood punching the red plastic button, feeling sick, feeling as he had when he'd shot his first rabbit and it had screamed and jerked its mangled body around on the ground until he could get his father's old shotgun reloaded and kill it.

He started back to the table. He changed his course and made for the door. Hurrying, he bumped into a chair, and he stopped to set it on its feet again. "Oh, you bastard," he muttered. "Oh, you bastard." Behind him *The One O'Clock Jump* blared.

V was packing her bags when he came into the room. Her hair parted up the back of her head as she leaned forward over the bed, folding her clothes into one of the suitcases. The other was already closed and strapped. She didn't look up as he stood just inside the door, watching her, and finally he stepped forward and grasped her elbow and turned her around. She was limp and unresisting, but she turned her face away from him.

"Listen, V," he said. No more words seemed to come and after a moment he let her go and sat down on the other bed. V returned to her packing, and Jack stared at the bags, remembering when he had seen them in the darkness on the driveway at the ranch. V was folding the black dress he had bought her the first day she had been in Bakersfield. "Listen, V," he began again, and finally he said, "Where you going?"

"Away."

"What do you mean, away? Where?"

She shrugged her shoulders.

"Listen, what the hell's the matter with you?"

She closed the suitcase and snapped the locks and buckled the straps. She turned to face him. He looked down and shook a cigarette from his pack and lit it. He blew a cloud of smoke between them. "Well, what the hell's the matter?" he said.

"This is what you wanted, wasn't it?"

"What?"

She laughed shakily and he couldn't meet her eyes anymore. "Hell," he said. He could feel her eyes seeing him. "Listen, V," he said. "I'm tight. Let's talk this over tomorrow, unh?"

"No," she said. "You're not drunk anymore. I know when you're drunk."

His hand trembled as he raised the cigarette to his lips. He blinked smoke out of his eyes. "You're all mixed up," V said.

"Aren't you? I always thought you knew what you wanted. You always said so. But you're all mixed up."

"Yeah," he said, grimacing. "I'm tight, is all. We ought to talk this over, though. There's a lot of things I got to explain."

He lowered his head. She was waiting for him to go on, but he didn't know what to say or how to say it. After a long time she put out her hand. "Goodbye," she said.

He pretended not to see the hand and she let it drop to her side. The streamliner went by in the yards with a long sucking rush, its horn blaring. He heard it slowing down.

"Goodbye," V said again.

"Well, okay," Jack said. "If that's the way you want it. Will I see you again?"

"Do you want to?"

"Sure."

"Why?"

He shrugged. "Why not?"

"You'll see me again if you want to enough," V said.

"Oh, Jesus, now you're getting cute with me." She didn't say anything, and he added, "You're not leaving town, unh?"

"I don't think so. Maybe I will."

Jack took out his wallet and slid the bills from it. There were two twenties, a ten, and two fives, and he replaced the two fives in the wallet, and the wallet in his hip pocket. He stood up unsteadily and held the money out to her.

"Have you got any dough?" he asked. He knew she hadn't. "Here," he said. "You'll need this."

"You don't have to do that."

"Take it."

"No!" she said tightly.

He grasped her hand and pushed the money into it. "Take it, for Christ's sake! You don't have a damn cent."

She stood looking down at the three bills that lay in her hand. It was a long time before she spoke. She said, "I guess we know what this makes me."

"Oh, for God's sake," Jack said. He sat down again.

V looked at the bills. He saw that her face was flushed now, and suddenly she looked up at him. "Goddamn you," she said dispassionately.

Jack's mouth dropped open. He had heard her swear before; it had been a joke between them, because she didn't know what she was saying. But she meant this, and it shocked him.

"Aren't you even sorry?" she said slowly. "Can't you…Jack, isn't there anything in you for me at all?"

"If you need any more…"

She looked as though she were going to cry. Her face twisted to one side, her mouth was pulled down at the corners, her eyes were round. But she said, "Goddamn you, Jack," in the same dispassionate voice, her voice shaking now, and tiredly she picked up the two bags. He watched her carry them to the door.

"Wait," he said. "Don't go, V."

She dropped the bags and turned toward him. Her eyes, wide open, blazed. "Ask me to stay," she whispered. "Go ahead and ask me, Jack."

"Stay."

"Do you want me to?"

"Yeah," he said. He started to get up.

He saw her throat work and her lips jerked upward into a tight, hard smile. Then she went out. He could hear the suitcases bumping on the steps as she went downstairs.

He got up and closed the door and then he sat down on the bed again, feeling vaguely angry with himself, and then blusteringly angry at V, and then, all at once, he loathed himself.

He lay back with his hands locked beneath his head. He turned his face to one side so he could survey the empty room, waiting patiently for the feeling to leave him. After a while the thought passed through his mind that the least he could have done was carry her bags downstairs and take her wherever it was she had wanted to go.

3

He missed her. He had an immediate, sharp sense of loss, but at the same time a feeling of relief, of having got out from under. And there were plenty of other girls to occupy him.

It was a long time before he saw her again. One night he had a glimpse of her at a dance. She was with a fellow in a gray covert cloth suit and she disappeared among the other dancers without seeing Jack and Mary Ann. He looked for her unsuccessfully all the rest of the evening.

A week or so later he saw her at a baseball game eating a hot dog and laughing at something her escort had said; the escort a pimply faced Joe College with his hat brim turned up all around. The following week Jack went to the ballpark again and waited near the gate till he saw her come in with the same fellow, turning his back when they passed him, and wondering why he did it.

Then Harry told him V was working at Deterle's, car-hopping, and Jack decided to go down and see how she was getting along. When he had parked she came out of the grill and walked across the asphalt toward him, her legs long and tan and smooth between her short skirt and white half-boots. She smiled professionally in the window at him, one foot up on the running board. "Hello, Jack," she said. "How goes it?"

"Good. How goes it with you?"

"Just fine."

There was a pause, and he said, "Good," again, and nodded.

"It's been a long time," V said.

"Yeah. Your sweater's too tight, V."

She flushed, still smiling. "Is it?"

"I guess it's just shrunk. You ought to use Lux."

She laughed. She had on too much lipstick and she had changed the shape of her mouth, a thin line of her lips showed bare beyond the edges of the lipstick. "I guess I should," she said.

"How long you been working here?"

"Oh, a long time. Since January."

He nodded. The traffic light on the corner clanged and changed and cars streamed past, motors racing, gears shifting; it was Sunday afternoon and the traffic on Highway 99 was heavy.

"Lots of dates, unh?" Jack said, but the expression on her face did not change. Her smile had a confident, expectant quality. "I've seen you around a few times," he said.

"Have you?"

"Who was that with you at the baseball game last week?"

She flushed again and Jack felt better. "Clyde Bryce," she said. "He works for the gas company."

"I thought maybe he was a college boy," Jack said, grinning. He felt much better. He said, "What're you doing tonight?"

But he cursed to himself when a new Chrysler swept into the parking area, and the effect of his question was lost when V turned to look at it. The other car-hop trotted out of the grill. "Why?" V asked, as she turned back.

"How about a date?"

She shook her head. "I've already got a date."

"With Clyde?"

She shook her head again.

"How about Saturday night?"

"I'm sorry," she said. She bit at the inside of her cheek.

"Sunday?"

"I'm sorry, Jack. I can't, Sunday."

"You mean you don't want to go out with me, unh?"

"No," she said. "I don't mean that at all. I'd like to."

"Okay, let's make it Saturday night. What time do you get off?"

"I'm sorry, Jack," she said quietly. "I've already got a date."

His stomach tightened. Talking to V this way, having to ask her for a date, seemed stupid, and he felt coldly furious. He snapped on the ignition and started the motor. V stepped back. There was a dark smudge on her forehead, over one eye, that made her look worried.

"Okay," Jack said. "Go to hell, then." He raced the motor. Another car came in and honked and V glanced at it.

He backed the roadster around in a tight arc, clashed the gears and tore out of the drive-in, feeling frustrated and silly. He had to stop for the light on the highway and in the rear-view mirror he could see V walking over to the car that had just come in. She had her order pad in her hand and he saw her put her foot up on the running board. She looked as though she had already forgotten him.

He cursed aloud and drove down to see if Ruth Adams wanted to go swimming. She wasn't home and Mary Ann was in Los Angeles. He went to a bar and spent the rest of the afternoon alone, drinking beer.

He knew she had him. Worse, he knew she knew it; that was what stung him. He'd humbled himself trying to get a date with V. He'd made a fool of himself, and he had failed. She must know he would come back again, begging for a date; when he had prior rights to her, when she had been his and had been discarded. He sat drinking beer and feeling lonely and bored and angry, and wondering how hard she was going to squeeze it.

4

It was a month before he got a date with her, and after the dance he drove out the north end of town on Highway 99. The moon was showing over the Sierras, bright on the mountaintops. V's face was serene and cold in the cold moonlight, and the wind that swept over the windshield blew her hair around her face. She had bent the rear-view mirror askew when she had made up her mouth; it was what she had always done, and he had never been able to make her remember to turn it back again. He felt a strong emotion made up of nostalgia and a hundred other indefinable things, and he forced his attention on the road ahead.

They had driven the other way on this road the night they had left the ranch. V had been crying, without making a sound she had cried all the way into Bakersfield. Jack grimaced and reached up to straighten the mirror, and then he swung the car out of the traffic and onto a side road. The Ford coasted down a slope, he stepped on the accelerator to take it over the railroad levee, then guided it down two rutted, winding tracks that led across a field. At the end of the tracks a grove of eucalyptus trees loomed against the sky. He parked in their shadow, and, still bent over the steering wheel with his fingers on the ignition switch, watched V out of the corners of his eyes.

She was staring at the mountains. Her face was cleanly profiled, her hair a tangled, ghostly white, and beyond her, headlights from the highway cut across the fields, sudden swaths of white light that bathed the ground and illuminated the blonde, splotched trunks of the trees. V sat neither close nor far from him, sitting at an uncomfortable, halfway distance, and Jack pushed the spadeshaped ignition switch up and down, listening to its metallic clicking.

She didn't speak when he put his arm around her. She didn't move, didn't resist in any way, but she was merely something soft and vaguely warm under his arm. He had the angry thought that this was mechanical with her, that she was doing only what was expected; he was merely one of her friends, nothing more, he had no special qualifications, no special rights. He felt his lips tighten painfully over his teeth. He pulled his arm down hard against her neck, tensing it, forcing her against his shoulder, but she seemed not to notice.

"V," he said. He cursed her silently for not noticing the pressure of his arm, for not speaking. He wanted her to look at him. "V," he said again.

When she turned, the dark of her lips framed a calm, sure smile. She said, "Did you ever get your radio fixed, Jack?"

He waited patiently for the anger to leave him. Finally he said, "No. It's all shot."

She put out her hand and turned the knob. The dial glowed yellow. Jack quickly turned it off. "V," he said. "Come back."

"What?"

He tried to press her closer but her body seemed heavy and unwieldy. He lifted his arm and pushed her away and she looked off at the mountains again. After a moment he squeezed his eyes closed. "I guess somebody's told you you look like Carole Lombard," he said thickly. "It's a good profile, all right."

"Do you like it?"

"It's great. How do the others like it? I'll bet it creams them too."

"What?" She looked at him coolly.

"Skip it. Well, you really learned how to get along, didn't you, V?"

"You taught me, you know. I had a fine teacher."

"I did, didn't I? Well, you got to be a hell of a lot better than teacher, didn't you?"

He saw her lick her lips and she looked down at her watch.

"Well, now you've shown me," Jack continued. "You want to go on and play some more, or you want to quit now?"

"It's late, Jack," V said. "We'd better go."

He snapped on the ignition and pushed his foot down on the starter. The wheels spun in the dirt when he let the clutch out and he raced the car up the rutted tracks to the highway.

When he skidded to a stop in front of the three-story building where she roomed, V opened her door and got out before he had shut off the motor. Her heels rapped sharply on the sidewalk with their own familiar rhythm. Jack followed her up the steps. At the front door she turned. "Thanks for a nice time, Jack."

He stopped on the step below her and they stood looking at each other. When he kissed her the step made them the same height and he kept his eyes open; he looked into her open eyes. Her hand brushed the nape of his neck, and she kissed him in return. Her kiss was as impersonal as a new pair of shoes. She was just kissing someone on the front porch after a date. Dozens of girls were doing the same thing on dozens of porches all over town, and afterward they would say good night and go inside and undress and get into bed and go to sleep.

Her lips opened under his, but abruptly he moved away. He heard her say, "Good night," as he walked down to his car, but he didn't look back. Anger and humiliation made him feel incredibly lonely, and he felt as though he had been given a drink of ginger ale when he needed a straight shot. He wondered what she was thinking now. Did she feel completely indifferent? Did she pity him? He wondered if she were laughing at him, getting undressed and into bed and laughing softly, and that night, unable to sleep, he told himself he was through. He was through with her for good.

5

He stayed away from her for a month. But then, swallowing his pride, making excuses to himself, he went back to the drive-in again. He got a date with her for two weeks away, and she didn't even seem to realize it had been a month since she had seen him. She acted as though he were someone she had just met and wasn't very interested in.

She didn't seem to care whether she went out with him or not. She never noticed, or if she noticed, did not care, whether he was angry or not. But he took her out more and more often and finally she promised him she would always see him on Saturday night. He saw her other nights too, whenever he could, but Sunday night was reserved for someone else. Sunday was reserved for someone else or for the field or for herself, he could never find out which, and he was too proud to ask.

At first, except for kissing him good night, she would not let him touch her. He was tempted to force her, but something stopped him. He realized that if he did, he would have lost completely, and not only would he have lost, he would have admitted his defeat. She would not go to his room, and after being rebuffed he did not ask her again. When finally she let him have her, it was in the car, letting him undress her and sitting close to him, white and long-legged and perfect, her face dark in the shadow of the eucalyptus trees. And he had almost told her then. He almost told her how he felt, that he had been a fool, that he wanted to marry her.

But he did not, for even then she was punishing him. She

was completely passionless. She might have been made of white marble; even when she helped him put the crumpled blanket under her hips, even holding him to her with the strong arms he remembered, she was completely passionless. And when he was trembling and unsure of himself and lost, she guided him with hands that might have been old at this when he was first hearing of it in the dirty-boy talk behind the gym in school and at the CCC camp. The whore he had had once in Fresno who smoked a cigarette all the while, had not been this insulting, and afterward when he reviled and cursed V, she took that too, with the same emotionless understanding with which she had taken him.

And with that came the jealousy. From that time on there was the black, rotten jealousy that he was not the only one; the being sure, the wondering who. From that time on there was the jealousy and the strain of keeping from V the fact that he was jealous, that he cared that he was not the only one, the humiliation of knowing he could not keep it from her, and this doubled because he was sure it must be known to others that she was public property, and so he must face down the humiliation and hide his jealousy from his friends, not knowing if they knew, wondering what they thought, wondering what they said about him among themselves.

He wondered too if they considered V a whore. He wondered if they blamed him for making her one. But he saw the hypocrisy of his own thinking that he must save her from this. He wanted to have her, not to save her. Maybe the saving was part of the having, but he wanted all of her, not just her body once a week. He wanted her to belong to him again.

To make it worse, Ben had come back. Ben had to see what he had made of V. Ben would be hearing the stories and rumors about her he himself had never heard but knew must be going around. Ben would see she had learned the ropes and how well she had learned them, and would hold him responsible. And Ben would see what she was doing to him.

It had been raining lightly the night V told him she was going out of town for the weekend and wouldn't be able to see him on Saturday night, and immediately a picture came into his mind of V and a faceless man, a man he hated as he had never hated anyone in his life. Who, he wondered desperately; who? They were sitting in the roadster in front of her apartment house, the street was wet and blackly shining, and there were wide, shining pools of yellow on the curbs below the street-lights. The air smelled of rain.

Finally he said, "Going up and see your old man?"

V shook her head.

He was glad he had thought to mention her father, and he said, "You ought to go see the old guy, V. Tell him how you're getting along. I'll bet he gets lonely out there."

She didn't say anything. She turned the mirror toward her, opened her purse and took out her comb and lipstick. Jack watched her paint her mouth. Who, he wondered; who? He wanted desperately to know, but just as desperately he didn't want her to know it mattered to him.

"What's your Sunday night boy going to say?" he asked. "He'll be pretty hard up by next week, won't he?"

She turned toward him. She was combing her hair and her mouth looked black in the darkness of the car. "Why do you have to say things like that?"

"Hell, it's so, isn't it? I get mine Saturday nights, he gets his Sunday, and the rest of the week you kind of spread it around."

"Does it make you feel any better to think that?"

"Sure," he said. "Share the wealth." He puzzled over the phrase, wondering where he had picked it up. Someone was always saying it—Red was. He scowled and said quickly, "No use being a hog."

She looked at him. She made a face as she combed through a snarl.

"Say," he said. "Who is this Sunday night boy, anyway? Maybe we ought to get together this weekend."

V leaned forward to turn on the radio. After a moment music blared, then was muted and fuzzy as she tuned it down. The music crackled with the electricity in the air.

Jack took a deep breath. He knew he was talking too much but he couldn't stop himself. "Maybe there isn't anybody on Sunday nights," he said. "Maybe you're just putting one over on me. Why don't you ever go out with anybody I know, so I can check up?"

"I've been out with someone you know," V said. "You didn't like that, either."

"Ben?" he said, and tried to laugh. She must mean Ben, he thought. He knew she'd been out with Ben. She'd made sure he knew. He wondered if she'd been out with Petey Willing, or Harry. But Harry would have told him. Then he thought of Red, and he began to swear.

He told himself she wouldn't do that. He knew she hated Red as much as he did. She wouldn't go out with Red; but the thought sickened and obsessed him. He saw Red's thick, obscene body and V's long white one. He almost sobbed aloud.

"By Christ, if you did," he said, and stopped. Something in his voice made V's face jerk toward him. "I'd kill you if you ever went out with Red!" he said hoarsely. "I'd…"

"What?" she said.

"I say I'd kill you!" and he was too shaken to look at her any longer. "Both of you," he said.

"I'll go out with whoever I want to. You don't own me."

"I'm telling you. Don't you ever let Red…" The words turned to thick wool in his mouth and he almost gagged on them. He wiped his hand across his eyes.

V said, "Jack, you know I…"

"Get out," he said. He reached across her and flung open the door.

He felt her hand on his leg and her voice was strange and tender. "Jack, I'm just going up to see…"

He slapped her hand away. "Get out!" he shouted. She got out and the door slammed shut as the car shot away from the curb.

He almost fought with Red the next day. It would have been all right if Red had let him alone, for he had come to his senses quickly. He knew he had been crazy to think such a thing. But Red would not let him alone; Red would never let go of anything like that, and he wouldn't take it from Red. He could take the kidding, except Red's kidding, because he hated Red.

He did not know why he hated Red, except that something had started the time he, instead of Red, had been given a new Adams grader, and it had been building up ever since. And with his kidding and his jeering laughter, Red had slowly come to symbolize the whole degradation of what V had done to him; that there were others who had her besides himself; that he wasn't good enough to satisfy her; the admission to himself of what he felt for her when she was so indifferent. But if Red had only let him alone, the fight would not have been inevitable.

Red would not let him alone, and they fought, and Red was killed. Afterward he knew that in a way it was not his fault; he tried again and again to tell himself it was not. He tried to blame it on V. He tried to blame it on Red for picking the fight, and then for insisting on running the cat and tampers when he was groggy. He tried to blame it on Ben and Harry for letting him.

But in the end he always had to blame himself. He had not wanted to stop hitting Red. Hitting Red, he was hitting back at V, and he had not wanted to stop. He had stopped only when his strength was gone.

He drove up to the timekeeper's shack, jumped off the grader, and without checking in, got in his car and drove home. He had to hold the wheel and shift gears with his left hand. His right hand was broken; he could feel the bones grate together when he pulled at the two middle fingers.

In the room he packed his shaving kit, his suit, three shirts and a handful of shorts, scribbled a note to Ben that he had gone to join the Navy, and left for Los Angeles. He didn't look back as he passed through the southern outskirts of Bakersfield on the tree-lined highway that pointed straight toward the mountains to the south, his head bent forward to escape the punishing wind.

He didn't let his right foot up from the floorboards until the mountains separated him from the San Joaquin Valley, and in Glendale a police car pulled him over and he was given a ticket for speeding. He tore it up. He sold his car to a used-car dealer for one hundred and twenty-five dollars and went to a doctor to get his hand set.

The doctor said it would be two weeks at least before the hand healed and he could enlist. He found a room in an expensive hotel on Wilshire Boulevard, and for the first three nights he whored and stayed drunk, and slept all morning and most of the afternoons. Then, suddenly, he was through with that forever.

For the next week he lay on his bed all day and read detective magazines, rising only to eat when he was hungry and to go to a movie at night. And while he was reading, or eating, or seeing a movie, or trying to sleep, he thought about what he had done.

There were two charges that lay on his conscience like

unpaid bills. It was the start of the stack. He had seduced V. He had made her what she was and what she might become. And out of that and because of that he had killed a man. Red was dead because of the action and reaction between V and himself. And V's part in it had been only the reaction. His was the original action that had set it all off. His was the responsibility.

There it was. It pressed down on him. Even when he cursed and explained and reasoned and rationalized and exonerated himself, it was with him. It pressed down on him, and each day it grew heavier. When he could stand the thinking in the sterile hotel room no longer, he stripped the cast from his hand, cleaned off the tape marks with lighter fluid, and went down to enlist in the Seabees. Perfect physical shape, they said.

6

He got his orders for discharge on Maui, in early September, 1945. Their battalion had shipped from Guam to Maui to join the 4th Marine Division, which had just returned from Iwo Jima, and they had been making ready for the landings on Japan when V-J Day came.

The camp was on the side of Haleakala, the enormous extinct volcano that sucked up the rest of the island like a boil, and on the mountain it had rained constantly. Even through August and the first week of September it had rained almost every afternoon.

Rain came down in sheets along the front of the pyramidal, dripping in around the edge of the door, leaking in the flap at the top and running down the stanchions to make little puddles in the corners. Jack sat on his cot with his sea chest open in front of him, watching it rain.

Fergie had gone to the Marine PX and Mort was asleep, the sound of his snoring like a ripsaw in rotten wood. He twitched as Jack looked over at him, lying on his face with his arms under his body. The endless Hawaiian music tinkled from Fergie's radio.

Jack's orders lay on the unmade cot beside him, a sheaf of coarse, mimeographed paper. He picked them up and riffled through the sheets. Toward the end the orders changed to four lines of typed endorsement, signed in blue ink: "W. D. Farrington, for J. V. Smith, Lt. Cmdr., USNR."

He tossed the orders onto the cot and stared out at the rain again, locking his hands around one knee and balancing on the rail of the cot. Guitars clunked from the radio as he watched the rain fall steadily. The roofs of the warehouses below the drill field were bright silver. It seemed to be raining everywhere.

Finally he took his sea bag from the chest, unfolded it and propped it upright. He worked quickly, filling it, putting in a layer of clothing and packing it tight and bouncing the sea bag so each layer would settle. He grunted when he uncovered the Navy .38 pistol he had found on Guam. He picked it up and turned it over in his hands, feeling the grip and thinking about the last two and a half years he had considered such a waste of time.

Now he knew the time had not been wasted. He had changed, he knew; he was more than two and a half years older. He was a man, and he was ashamed of the boy that had been Jack Ward. He had seen that boy in too many of those around him.

And he knew that for him the war had been nothing terrible. Only the eternal boredom had been hard. There had never been any danger. The battalion had always gone in after the fighting was over, when an area was safe enough for them to build the air strips or roads unmolested. They had only once been under fire. It had been on Guam, and evidently the sniper was much more frightened than they, for there had been only the three, thin, crackling shots that might not even have been directed at them.

A fire team of Marines had gone after the Jap with a Tommy gun, and Jack had walked over to see him. Battered, blood-covered, dead, he had looked like Red Young.

He tucked the pistol in among his dungarees, remembering when they had all been excited about souvenirs. He had sent V a Jap flag he had found on Tarawa, but he was glad he had kept the .38. It was something to remind him he'd been in a war.

There was only rubble left in the bottom of the sea chest now; some paper-bound mysteries, envelopes whose flaps had stuck closed, a heap of worn-out socks and skivvies, and in one corner was the thin packet of letters he had received from V.

Slowly he picked up the packet and untied the string that held it together. The letters were on pink stationery, in pink envelopes with flowered linings. He fanned them out in his hand, staring at them and tiredly cursing the day he'd ever written her; the day on Guam when, so lonely he could feel it in his stomach like hunger, he had written her the first letter.

He had written her when he had come to feel himself completely unattached from the rest of the world, when he had felt he had nothing to go back to, no one to go back to. There was only V in his life; she was the center of the orbit in which he revolved. He had written her to be sure she would be there when he returned, a fixed point in a life that had never had a fixed point, for he could think of nothing else there was to return to. And now he wished he had not written her, because he was going somewhere else and start again.

He arranged the letters by the stamped dates of their postmarks and lay down on the cot to read them. The letters did not anger him now. That part of it was gone, but he wondered why he bothered to read them at all. They were all the same and he knew by heart what was in them; crude attempts to make him jealous and keep him in line, which he recognized as such. They told what a good time V was having, who she'd been out with, where they'd gone, what they'd done, and who else she'd heard from overseas, a few reminiscences. They were crammed full of devices planned to fit her purpose.

There were eight of them, the last dated in April, thanking him for the bottle of cologne he'd sent her for her birthday. When he finished it he crumpled them all into little balls, made a heap of them on the floor and set fire to it. They blazed fiercely for a moment, black creeping up the expanding pink balls, and then the blaze died out and the black, brittle shapes blew across the floor. He lay back on the cot again, gazing up at the slow, dark trickle of rain that made its way down the stanchion above him.

He was still lying there and Mort was still asleep, when Fergie came back. It had stopped raining, the Marines were out drilling, and Jack was listening to the rhythmic stamp of feet, the slap of hands on rifle slings, a shrill voice calling cadence: "Huhwun, hup, hreep, hup. Yerrrightflank—harch. To therip—harch. Rip, harch!"

Fergie slammed the screen door shut, shuffled his feet and hung up his poncho. He was eating an Oh Henry bar. "Hi, men," he said, and he sat down on his cot and turned off the radio. "What the hell'd you do in here?" he demanded. "Build a fire to keep warm?"

Jack lay listening to the Marines drilling. "Ripe shoulup—harms!" came from the drill field, and the smack of palms on leather.

"Hey, grade boss!" Fergie cried.

"I burned some letters. Anything wrong with that?"

"They stink."

"This place stinks anyway."

"You don't have to stink it up any more," Fergie said. He took another candy bar from his jacket pocket and skinned off the wrapper. His fat face was lowered so that Jack could see his pink scalp under his thinning blond hair.

"Well, that's sure tough on your dainty little nose," Jack said. "You don't hear the twentieth-century Rip van Winkle bitching about it, do you?"

"Christ, he'd lay there beating his ear if the whole place burned down," Fergie said. "What was you burning, anyway?"

"Letters, I said."

"Dear Jack, unh?"

"Just a bunch of crap I was all through with."

Fergie stuffed the rest of the candy bar into his mouth and wiped his hands on his pants' legs.

"All through," Jack said. Then he said, "What're you going to do when you get back to the States, Ferg?"

"First, or second? I don't believe we're ever going to get out of here, though. This points crap's just scuttlebutt."

"The hell," Jack said, and he laughed. He sat up and shook the sheaf of orders at Fergie. "Proof," he said.

"Hey, no kidding?" Fergie said. "When you going?"

"Today at eighteen hundred. Farrington wangled me a seat on the plane."

"You lucky bastard!"

"I hope you're stuck here forever," Jack said, grinning. "I can see you in about ten years, sitting here eating candy bars and counting up your points and watching those gooks get lighter-colored every day."

Fergie grinned back at him, got another candy bar from his pocket and tossed it over. "Thanks," Jack said.

"Bon voyage," Fergie said, "Going back to the valley, Jack?"

"Hell, I don't know where to go. San Diego, I guess."

"Dago? That hole?"

"That's where I get discharged."

Fergie held up a hand, cocking his head to one side. "Hey!" he said. "Hear that? That's your plane coming in now, you lucky bastard. Want me to wake Mort up?"

"Let him sleep," Jack said. "I got a couple of hours yet. I'm going out and watch that plane come in."

Outside he jumped over the puddles in the areaway until he came out on the drill field. The Marines were down at the far end: "To the rip—harch!" a corporal was yelling. "Rip, harch!"

Above them Haleakala loomed, its rim fringed with clouds, and below, the pineapple field patchwork of red earth and green plants stretched down to the ocean.

The plane was circling the Kahului air field, silver and blue, its propellers two bright celluloid discs in the sun. Jack waved at it; the plane that would be taking him to Pearl Harbor, where he would catch a ship back to the States.

7

There was a call for a bulldozer operator for the Kearny Mesa job when he checked in with the union at San Diego. He met Gene at the Hogan and Griffith office. He liked her immediately; a slender, almost thin girl with dark eyes and dark, short hair. He liked the fast, breathless way she talked, her crooked smile; there was something about her that told him she was the kind of girl he should marry.

He had lied when he told her he loved her. He didn't love anyone. He was through with that because V had finished it in him. He was through playing the game, but he was going to be sure nobody played it with him.

He was satisfied with the way he had made the break with V. They hadn't written for a long time, he was not going back to Bakersfield, and the thing would never have a chance to begin again. But he thought of her sometimes. He could not stop himself from thinking about her; it was like a wisdom tooth coming through, the pain acute for a time, but gradually the gum would grow over and there would be long periods when he did not think of her at all. V would marry someone in Bakersfield and settle down, and he would marry Gene. It was all over.

The job on the mesa was pushing gravel from the rock crusher to the hopper of the hot plant where the paving for the air field was mixed and loaded into dump trucks. It was dirty work. He had to wear a respirator and goggles and by the time he had finished his first run in the morning he would be covered with rock dust and asphalt. Asphalt stuck in his hair where it was not covered by his cap, his clothes were always stiff and black with it and his face, when he turned in at night, would be completely black except for three circles, a big one around his nose and mouth and smaller ones over his eyes.

Ordinarily he would have quit such a job the first day. In the Seabees he had been a kind of equipment boss, and Commander Smith had written him a letter recommending him as a grade foreman. But he knew it would be impossible to get a foreman's job directly, and he had not even held out for a grader because he wanted to go right to work. So he stuck with it, and when one of the other skinners quit, Smitty put him on a grader, working the fine grade with Arch Huber.

He was a little surprised when Gene said she would marry him. It had not occurred to him that she might refuse, but he was surprised suddenly at the realization that he was going to be married. He found he was pleased. He wanted to be married. He wanted it to be as soon as possible.

But one night after work he was driving down the street toward his rooming house, slowing down and pulling over to the curb to park, when he saw V.

At first he did not recognize her. She was carrying a suitcase, looking up at the numbers on the houses. He was behind her, and he only knew she looked familiar. He watched her because she was blonde and had good legs, but he had the confused feeling that she was someone he knew who was completely out of place, that she was a person connected in his mind with somewhere else and had no reason for being here.

He frowned, letting the Mercury idle along behind her, studying her legs, and the square shoulders in the white coat, and the familiar hair, and then he was conscious of the pattern of the rapping of her heels. His legs seemed nerveless as he raised his foot to the brake pedal.

The car slowed, jerking along in high gear with his foot off the accelerator. His mind was blank. The world was silent except for the unmistakable sound of V's heels. He watched her pass the telephone pole, the two garbage cans on the curb, and then she turned and saw him.

She stepped off the sidewalk and came over to the car. She opened the door, lifted her suitcase in, and sat down on the seat beside him. They sat and looked at each other, the Mercury nosed into the curb, the motor dead; V incredibly sitting beside him and looking exactly as he remembered her, her breathing uneven and beads of perspiration sparkling on the curve of her upper lip, looking tired, her eyes round and a little bloodshot and most of her lipstick gone. He compared her with the image in his memory; the tiny mole above her nose in the vertical crease of her forehead, the soft down on the undersides of her cheeks, the blonde hair that almost met her eyebrows at the sides of her head, the minute bare ridge around the edges of her lipstick. Her lips seemed larger than he remembered and instead of in the middle, her hair was parted now on one side and held with a silver clip. She was a picture he was studying, trying to determine its authenticity. And she sat staring back at him.

Slowly, wonderingly, he began to feel what she had always made him feel, as though he had been plugged into an electric socket, or as though there were a sun suddenly in the car, with the special kind of warmth the sun had had when they were sitting against the D-4 caterpillar in the orchard at the ranch. He reached down and pressed the starter button. He picked up her suitcase and pushed it into the back seat. It was a new suitcase, tan, with dark brown stripes. The motor whirred silently. V still stared at him, smiling, her eyes round.

"What the hell are you doing here?" he said. It was a comment, he expected no answer, and she gave none, arranging her skirt over her knees. There was a run in her stocking. He pulled the gear lever into low and the car moved forward. When he looked at her again she leaned toward him and put her hand on his leg.

Night came while they were in the cabin in the auto court. From yellow, the shaded west window had gradually merged with the darkness of the room, and Jack sat on the edge of the bed beside V, staring down at her. He could see the thin, glinting lines of her open eyes.

He put out his hand. Carefully, almost shyly, he touched her arm. Her arms were outstretched above her head, the wrists crossed, and he moved his fingers down over her arm. He touched her breast. He touched the nipple. He felt the sudden hard hollow between and below her breasts. He moved his hand to touch her stomach and her thigh and when he could reach no further down her leg without moving, he withdrew his hand. She was perfect, all of her was perfect, and dumbly he felt that it was her perfection that hurt him, for he had never been so shaken, and shaken he had soared and fallen achingly beyond the limits of his understanding.

But the perfection was not only of her, it was of the both of them. This feeling that, when he lay with her, was emotion powered and expanded a thousand times beyond itself, was almost too big for him to be capable of feeling, and was enormously too big for him to express; it left him tottering on the lip of a valley filled with the musically screamed answers to all the questions he had never been able to ask, or had only vaguely felt, or had never known he had felt until he heard the answers. It tore at him with a torment of seeking, and in an excruciating light had almost let him see. But somehow it had all destroyed itself and he feared it now as though some hideous, perverted evil had tricked him and trapped him.

V was speaking to him but he did not hear her. His mind had been wrenched and now he felt drained and weak and afraid. He felt completely absorbed into her, as though she were the two of them, and he, as an individual, had been destroyed. He heard her say, "Jack, it's all over now."

"What?" he said.

"I said it's all over now. We can live without hurting each other." He felt the soft touch of her hand on his slumped back, but he did not answer. The words did not connect. He tried to put them together with a mind that was groping elsewhere. "What?" he said again.

"Don't you understand, Jack?" V said patiently. He heard her move. She said, "All that's over. We can't hurt each other anymore. Do you love me, Jack?" Her voice was vibrant, and it seemed to fill the room.

"Yes," he said, and he thought of Gene.

"I love you," V said.

"If we'd only known a long time ago."

Again he felt the touch of her hand on his bare back. He shivered, and he reached around behind him and took the hand in his. He felt it carefully, the fingernails, fingers, knuckles, the crotch between the thumb and first fingers, the hard bone of the wrist, the soft hairs of the forearm. The arm was connected to V but he could not see the rest of her in the dark. "I love you now," he said.

He was trying to think clearly. He wanted to know himself, to understand this, he wanted to be truthful to himself and to V. It was more than the fact that he had made a bargain, more than the fact that he wanted to hurt V, but he did not know what all it was and he could only say when he knew.

"I love you now," he repeated. "But I love you too much and I don't love you enough. There's too much...I don't love you enough, V," he said.

She gasped and her hand was gone.

"Wait," he said. "I know what I did to you. I know that. But you've done too much to me too. There's just too much..."

"It was the only way I knew to keep you!" V cried. "Oh, please see my side! There's never been anybody but you. Those were all lies about…"

"It was Red that made it too much, I guess," he interrupted. "That happened because of us, and now…"

"Jack!" she cried again. "It's only one more reason why this has to stop now!"

"Yeah," he said.

"No! No! I don't mean that. Why we have to stop hurting each other. It can be all right if we stop that."

His shoulders ached as he slumped forward. He shook his head doggedly. He was trying, too, to shake off the instinct that now he should hurt her, for he could hurt her cruelly for those letters, for Bakersfield, for all of it. He could stab her and twist the knife and make her beg and watch her writhe. He hated this feeling of wanting to hurt her, because the feeling hurt him. He hated this way she made him feel. But it was too strong and it burst from his lips like vomit. "How do I know you love me?" he said.

He shuddered with revulsion at himself. He could hear her breath whispering through her lips. When she spoke her voice shook. She said, "It's always been that. Why do you need to ask that? Why do you think I came down here? Why…" Her voice broke off again and again he could hear her breath whispering through her lips. He wondered if she were crying.

It amazed him that he could do this. Too much hurting had been done already and he knew this was just something else stacked before him that he must pay for. "I'm getting married," he said quickly. "Next week."

Her breathing came faster, then not so fast, and then she seemed not to breathe at all. "Who?" she whispered.

"A girl," he said. "A girl from the office."

There was a movement beside him and V was sitting up.

Her hands grasped his arms, her face was thrust close to his, frighteningly white, the eyes closed as though she didn't want to see him, her closed eyes two dark, shadowed holes in the white face. Her fingernails dug into his arms. "You're lying!" she said.

"No, I'm not."

"You're lying!" she whispered. "You're lying!" she repeated, shaking her head. "You love *me*!" she said fiercely.

He didn't speak. Her fingernails cut into the flesh of his arms. Her eyes opened and seemed to touch his face like fingers. "Why?" she cried. "Oh, God, don't! Don't! We've got to stop this!"

"I'm going to marry her."

The hands let go his arms and she was gone. He could feel the pressure on his leg where she had rested, but he couldn't see her anymore. Then he heard her whisper, "Is she pretty?"

"She's all right."

"Jack! You just told me you loved me!"

"Okay. That wasn't all I said."

"Why don't you hit me if you want to hurt me so? Why don't you hit me like you hit Red?"

He felt absolved; he said tiredly, "See?"

She was crying, a painful, hopeless sound. "Oh, damn you, Jack," she whispered.

"I tried to tell you."

"You lied! You wanted to hurt me. All right, you're going to. This'll be the worst. You'll win. But you're going to hurt yourself. And this girl, too. Don't you see what you're going to do to this girl?"

"I'm going to marry her."

"Oh, yes," she said. "You will, you fool. Oh, you fool, Jack." She sounded as though she were lost somewhere, crying fretfully where no one could hear her, sobbing bitterly; he heard her say, half to herself, "You never understood what we had."

"I understood what you damn well had," he said fiercely. "Yes, but you're never going to get me again! You'd break me right down to the ground. You take the man out of me. Do you want to know? I'm scared of you, damn you! And I'm ashamed. Do you understand? You've ruined it. *You* have! *You…*" He stopped, panting, shaking, straining his eyes to see her. He was terrified that he might never be rid of her. She was a cancer in him. By sending her away he was hurting her, yes—but hurting himself, too, for he could never be through with her.

He felt her hand on his arm. It tightened, pulling him down beside her. Her leg pressed against his. "That's all over," she whispered. "Listen, we can get married tonight. We can drive…"

"No," he said through his teeth. "I meant it."

"We can drive over to Arizona," V went on. "Tonight. We can never let each other go, Jack."

He pulled away from her roughly. "It's all over," he said, and he stood up and took his shirt from the chair. She did not speak while he dressed, but when he walked toward the light-outlined rectangle of the door, she said, "Jack!"

He turned, his hand holding the knob.

"It's not over," she said. "It will never be over." She had stopped crying.

He didn't reply, standing staring toward her. He couldn't see her but he wanted to remember her like this, this the last time. He could still feel the place on his leg where her leg had touched, and he pitied her.

He turned and went out the door. Something inside him was raw and tender, and bitter in his throat.

8

He was not surprised when he received her telegram. He had accepted the fact that this had not been the last blow, that she would hit him in return. It came the day of the wedding, and Arch Huber was with him in his room, waiting while he dressed. Arch was sitting on the bed, knocking ashes from his cigarette into a peanut can balanced on his knee, and Jack was tying his tie in front of the mirror over the dresser, when there was a knock on the door. It was Mrs. Ostermann, the landlady, her dyed hair done up in curlers, a broom in her hand. "Telegram," she said. "I gave the kid a dime."

Jack got two nickels from his pocket, gave them to her and closed the door. He tore open the yellow envelope, unfolded the flimsy and read the pasted-on message. Holding his face tight and sucking at his front teeth he looked again at the name on the bottom: V Denton. He rubbed his thumbnail over it.

Coolly he tried to recall where he had heard that name. Then he told himself it didn't matter. He smiled wryly at his instinctive jealousy of this Denton, whoever he was. He should have known V would strike back like this. But this was what he had wanted; V married to someone else, himself married to Gene.

Still holding the telegram he returned to the dresser. He laid it on the scarf, face up, and looking at his reflection in the mirror, pushed the end of the tie through the loop and pulled it down. The knot came out lopsided and he took it apart again. When he read the telegram once more he heard the bed springs creak, and Arch said, "Bad news?"

"No," Jack said. Then he said in explanation, "Friend of mine just got married."

Arch laughed. "That's a coincidence."

Jack studied his face in the mirror. The muscles of his cheeks were bunched like tiny fingers and a hard grin pushed out his lower lip. Abruptly he covered the telegram with his right hand. He braced the other on the edge of the dresser and leaned forward, half-supporting himself on his hands. His face was pressed close to the mirror, distorting his image, and he felt the shoulder muscles bunch under his shirt.

The telegram tore under his weight and letting himself down he crumpled it into a ball and batted it off the dresser. He retied the tie quickly and pulled the knot tight against his throat.

"About ready?" Arch asked.

Jack took his comb from his hip pocket and ran it through his hair, staring fixedly at the hard face, wooden now, that looked back at him from the mirror. Behind him he could see Arch sitting on the edge of the bed with his legs crossed, watching him curiously.

"Yeah, let's go," he said.

9

The thought of V, married, tortured him. Waking in the night with Gene asleep beside him, he would wonder about V, imagining, playing scenes between her and her husband in his mind. He hated to think of her being as happy with her husband as she had been, for a time, with him in Bakersfield; he hated to think of her expressing her feelings and emotions to her husband as she had expressed them to him, for that had been first with him, and so, he felt, should always remain his.

He had finally placed Denton as the rancher V had talked about when he had first known her. He remembered V saying he was an old man. He tried to comfort himself with this, but somehow, at times, it made him furious. He told himself she could not be happy in bed with this old man, but thinking of that, he wanted her, and when he wanted her he would wonder if he were happy now with Gene. And he hated to wonder about his life with Gene, because he had told himself over and over again that it was right, that he was happy, and that this was the way it should be.

He tried to tell himself calmly that everything was over between V and himself, that all there was left of V was a lot of memories, and the good memories would soon be disposed of by the bad ones. He told himself that he loved Gene and that he was coming to love her more every day. He wanted his marriage to be good. It was a bargain he had made; he would stick to it and do the best he could by it. Gene was the anchor he had needed badly. She was the fixed point for him now, for gone completely was the feeling that he wanted to be free of any ties, gone with the loneliness of Tarawa and Guam and Maui.

Yet there were times when the aching need for V came back as overpoweringly strong as ever. He cursed it. He tried to shout it down, to shout down with it the dread that Gene did not, could not, satisfy. He cursed the longing and the knowledge and himself as stupid, unclean, despicable, but it was more and more with him. And it was as though V had felt it in him two hundred and fifty miles away, for she came back. She phoned him on the job one day and he went to her, coldly, and alone and defeated, and making no excuses to himself.

He stopped her when she started to tell him about her husband. Denton was in the hospital and would not bother them; that was all he needed to know. He didn't want to know anything else about Denton, he didn't want to have to think about him. So they never spoke of Denton or of Gene, and for a while, together, there were just two of them, and for a while he thought V had been right when she had said it could have been good.

But the disease was there. There was guiltiness in them both now. Even if it could have been good, it was cursed by what he was doing to Gene, by what V was doing to Denton. Anything they did, any time they were together, they were hurting someone. It did not matter that they hurt themselves; that was only of and between themselves and perhaps could pass. But there was always someone else they betrayed, or damaged, or destroyed.

He had resolved to end it before Gene confronted him. He had made up his mind to take Gene away somewhere where V could never find them again. That way it could be finished. And the fact that now Gene knew, only made him more determined. He and Gene had gone to Oregon.

There, he had felt confident it was over. He was whole at last and the evil had been exorcised. He felt that he could free himself from V by absorbing himself completely in Gene. He did everything he could to make amends to her for what had happened; he had dedicated himself to her and there was no more room for V.

It had been simple and logical that they return to San Diego. When the job at Pendleton was almost over, there was a letter from Smitty offering him more pay than he had ever earned before, and a good chance to go higher. And he was sure of himself now. Six months had passed. But still he felt a twinge of fear when Gene suggested they go to La Jolla for dinner on their anniversary. La Jolla was where V had been staying.

But it had been logical that they go to La Jolla. He had proposed to Gene in the dining room of the Casa del Mar, and they would go there again on their anniversary. And, afterward, he supposed it was perfectly logical too, that V would still be there.

The waiter had just brought them their dessert when she came in. As she passed she looked at him with no surprise, almost with no recognition, and she sat down at the table behind Gene. With her was a skinny little man with dark glasses, whom Jack took to be Denton, and when he could think again he felt angered and cheated that Denton was not old, as he had believed. Then he was angered still more at the realization that this was not Denton.

V sat opposite him, one table removed. He had to look at her when he looked at Gene, with the man's dark, cropped head between. He had to look at her but she did not meet his eyes, talking animatedly to her escort. Her hair was blonder, drawn back high on her head, and her face was deeply tanned. She looked shiny and expensive in a gold dress that was cut low to show the cleft of her breasts.

Then he could bear seeing her no longer and his fury turned on Gene because he could not get her out of the dining room quickly enough. Waiting in the lobby while Gene went to the powder room, he was sick with anger and impatience and desire. He lit a cigarette and immediately strode to the tall blue-and-white vase that stood by the door, to grind it out in the sand. He turned toward the entrance to the dining room. Helplessly he walked in.

He made his way across to the table where V was sitting. He put his hands on the tabletop, leaning forward and searching her eyes for a look he knew must be there, a flicker, a shadow, something to show she knew she had caught him again. She put her hand to her throat. A ring sparkled on her finger. He heard the man say something.

"Call me in half an hour," he said steadily, tight-lipped, to V. "Franklin 5852-R."

"I *beg* your pardon," the man said. He put his napkin on the table and moved to get up. He had on a tuxedo and a black tie and his nails had been manicured.

"Never mind it," Jack said to him. It seemed unfair that V should be attractive to men like this, who wore tuxedos to dinner and had educated accents and manicured fingers, and probably bought a new Cadillac every year. He grimaced and looked back at V and said, "Franklin 5852-R."

"See here, get out of here!" the man said, and Jack turned and walked away from the table. Gene was waiting in the lobby. She had just had a permanent and her hair was stiff and tightly curled. He came up behind her and took her arm.

Driving home, he wondered what there was in him that V wanted. For he had known she had wanted him tonight; even though she had looked at him with no expression on her face, even though she had not said a word, and he knew she would phone him. But suddenly completely conscious of what he was, he wondered why she wanted him. He saw himself as a big, cheap grade foreman who didn't know how to speak properly and had no manners, who worked with his hands and wore dirty clothes all day and had dirt permanently imbedded under his fingernails, whom she had seen drunken and despicable and cruel, who had killed a man in an animal fight, who had forced her to leave him once and had left her twice; why did she want him? He did not know, but for the first time he was jealous of her and not of someone else. She had started no better than he, but now she was better. She had money now, expensive clothes, jewelry; she was beautiful and desired by men who would not have spit on him had they even thought of him. He wondered at it, watching the streets and lampposts and houses flash by, and he was afraid to look at Gene, who sat silently beside him, staring up at his face with worried eyes.

V called him that night and he went to her. What had never stopped had started again.

10

Denton was dead.

He did not know what to say when V told him. He could only listen to her silently, for when she told him about Denton he knew she had loved her husband, just as he loved Gene.

It was Denton to whom she had gone when she left him in Bakersfield. It was to Denton she had devoted her Sunday nights. Denton had kept her till she could find a job; he had saved her when she might have been lost; he had been her refuge, father and friend. When she had found a job, not letting him get one for her because she was too proud, she had moved into Bakersfield, but every Sunday after work he called for her and took her out to the ranch, and she spent the afternoon, the night and Monday morning with him, riding his Morgan horses, and quail shooting, and playing cribbage with him at night.

She knew it was the same as being hired as a nurse when they were married. But she loved him and she was grateful; she knew what she owed him. He had had strokes before, and he suffered a bad one a month after their marriage. When he was well enough to be moved he had gone to a sanitarium in La Jolla and V had taken the apartment at the Orizaba, where she could be near him. After four months in the sanitarium he had recovered enough to go to Los Angeles on business, and early that summer they returned to the ranch.

In August he had the stroke that killed him. He had collapsed and had fallen from a horse he should not have been riding, and completely paralyzed, he had never regained consciousness.

Her voice had become lower and lower and Jack could not

be sure she had stopped speaking until he looked up at her. She was staring back at him with her arms crossed on her chest, one hand to her throat, and after a long time Jack said, "Did he know about us, V?"

She nodded silently. Then she said, "He knew all that before he married me."

"He didn't care, unh?"

"No. It wasn't like that. It was like he was my father. That was how he'd always been."

He looked at her and she raised her chin defiantly. "That was how he always was," she said.

That wasn't what he had meant. That didn't matter now. "Did he know about us, V?" he said again.

Her eyes looked dark and dull. Almost imperceptibly she shook her head.

It was only something else that must not be thought about. He supposed it was better that Denton had not known all of it, that Denton had been in the sanitarium where he could not know, and Denton was too much of a shadow for him to concern himself with. He had never met him. He had never even seen him. Denton was merely the pale, cuckolded phantom that had been V's husband.

Denton was dead, as Red was dead, and could fade into the past. But Gene was still present, and suddenly Gene was thrust forward into it again. The first time he ever thought he wanted to die, thought the only way out, the only possible solution, was for him to die, was the night V told him she had talked to Gene.

They were sitting in his car in front of the hotel. He had just parked and switched off the lights, but when he reached across V to open her door, she said, "Wait," and put her hand on his arm. He stopped and looked at her questioningly. She said, "I talked to your wife today, Jack."

He stared at her. "What do you mean?" he said. "Where?"

"In the Sky Room."

There was nothing for him to say. He saw V and Gene together. He felt drops of perspiration start, the cold, quick sweat that came when he had drunk too much and should start worrying about getting sick.

"You bitch," he said finally, tiredly seeing V and Gene. He saw Gene taking it from V, who was beautiful when she was not, in expensive clothes that Gene could not have, wearing the clothes as Gene could never wear them. Slowly he turned toward V again, but her face was averted. He pressed his hands over his eyes. His hands smelled sour.

"I had to do it," V said.

"Why did you have to do it?" he said, through his hands. "Why? What'd she ever do to you? Goddamn you, in your hundred-buck dresses and your diamond rings. I'll bet you really put them on for her, didn't you? Goddamn you, V."

When V spoke her voice was unsteady. She said, "I told her she had to divorce you, Jack." She put her hand on his knee. He saw her eyes shine in the light from the hotel door.

"I had to do it, Jack," she said. "Will you listen a minute without getting mad?"

"Sure," he said.

She licked her lips.

"Sure," he said again, hoarsely. "Take away everything a guy's got that's any good…" He stopped, panting, and then he said, "And knock him down and push his face in the mud and then push his wife down with him and tell him not to get mad.

"Sure," he said. "I don't get mad. What's there for me to get mad with? I'm not even a man anymore. I don't have anything to…" Again he stopped. He was shaking violently. He looked down at V's hand on his knee.

"Jack, listen!"

"You rich bitch," he said.

"Stop it, Jack!"

He closed his eyes, pressing them tight shut but still seeing V and Gene. V was talking but he didn't hear what she said. He couldn't think.

He opened his eyes. "V!" he cried. "Let me be the one who does filthiness like that! Let it be on me. Look," he said. "Look, I started it all. From the beginning it's been me who's done the filthy things. First you, then Red, see? Now let it be my doing about Gene.

"V," he said. "Oh, Christ, I don't know how to say it—but if it's me I can take it because I can suffer for it. I can take it, if it's my doing. But if it's you I'll…"

"Jack!" She raised her voice. "Gene's just something in the way. I didn't put her there. It seems like I've been fighting for you forever, and I've got to think of myself, Jack. Don't you see?"

"No," he said. "You didn't get what I mean. I mean…" He felt the hopelessness of ever saying what he wanted to say, but he tried to speak calmly. "Listen, V: when I think about it— when I think about it right, it's me who's done all this. Well, just let it be me. If I got to feel the way I feel about myself about you, I don't know what I'd do. I couldn't stand it. I'd have to do something. I…" He looked away from her. The light from the arched entrance to the lobby of the hotel sent a bright stripe across the hood of the car.

"You said it's been your fault," V said. "Did you mean that, Jack?"

He nodded.

"Then why don't you make it right? Get a divorce and we can get married and it's all all right."

"What did Gene say?" he said hastily.

"She didn't say anything."

"Tell me the truth."

"She didn't say anything," V repeated, nodding her head as though to confirm the statement to herself. "She just…She just ran out. She wouldn't say anything."

Jack groaned and squeezed his eyes shut against seeing it. "Don't you understand?" V said. "Don't you understand this way all three of us are going to go on living in hell? But if you get a divorce at least you and I can be happy. And she'll be better off."

"I wish it was that damn easy."

"It is that easy." And then she cried, "Jack, you've got to do it! You've got to! It's just going on and on and on and on!"

He felt his hands clench, sweating. He tightened his lips. "Oh, no, it's none of your fault," he said through his teeth. "You didn't play it for all it was worth there in Bakersfield, did you? You made old man Denton happy, did you? The old man had heart attacks because he was so happy, did he?"

"Don't you say that!" V screamed. "Oh, damn you, Jack. Don't you ever say that!"

He stared down at his hands on the wheel. The tendons made tight ridges on the backs, but the lump where the right hand had been broken had almost disappeared. He was sweating and his breath whispered drily through his lips. "Okay," he said with an effort. "I'm sorry. Forget it."

"Oh, damn you, damn you, damn you," V said brokenly. "We can't do that anymore. We can't let ourselves, Jack!"

"I'm sorry," he said. He put the palm of his hand to his forehead and pulled it slowly down over his face, pressing hard on his eyes and nose and mouth, feeling the pain as his lower lip was torn down. Finally he said, "It's just that I can't stand to think of you and Gene."

She didn't speak for a long time, her head bent forward, arms crossed on her chest as though she were cold. At last she said softly, "Why can't you make up your mind? You have to decide. You have to decide now." Her voice was suddenly hard and dull. "If you don't, it's just going on like this. I won't stop till it's you and me and nobody else. Don't you see? I want back what we had once so long ago I don't think you even remember it. I want that back, not just a wild time in bed once in a while when we can't stand it any longer, with you feeling like it's a terrible thing you're doing to your wife, and hating me for it, and hating yourself, too. I don't want that anymore; that's killing us. You have to see that."

She waited for him to speak, and when he did not, she said, "I don't want to hurt Gene." She shook her head and put her hand to the side of her face. "But she'll get hurt if she doesn't divorce you. I'm going to get back what we had. It's stuck inside me like a big hollow ball I can't swallow or throw up or do anything with. It's always there, and everything I ever say or think or do or want or don't want or have or haven't, sticks on it and can't get past it or around it. It's been there since…"

"I know about it," he said. "I know what it does."

She put the other hand to her face and bent her head forward. He put out his hand to touch her, but he did not, and finally she said, "Oh, God, Jack," and her voice broke and he could hardly hear her. "We could be so damn happy."

He wondered if they could. He wondered if anybody ever could. He remembered what it was she wanted back, but could it ever be the same? So much had happened to them since then, there were so many other people in it; everything changed and went on changing, and the hollow ball that was stuck inside him was now the fear that it could never be the same.

"Jack," she said. "One night in Bakersfield I went to Ben to ask him if you wanted to get rid of me. He said I had the tools to hold you. He said I had the tools if I just knew how to use them."

She stopped. Her fingers pulled at the edges of her skirt, arranging it over her knees.

"I didn't know about many tools," she went on. "I tried to use one; you know what it was. It ended up with Red Young getting killed and you going away and not wanting to come back. I didn't know how to use that tool. I almost killed us with it.

"Now, I've been using the only other one I know. It works, too, like the other one did for a while. It brings you back to me and every time it does I almost cry because I'm so happy. But when you're gone again I really do cry because I'm afraid it'll kill us like the other one almost did. I'm afraid it makes you hate me too; I'm afraid it's too big a thing for us to handle; I'm afraid that your wanting me so much like that is going to get so big it'll kill everything else in us, and then if it should die or get killed itself, there'll be nothing. It'll have left us nothing, and we could have had so much."

"V," he said hoarsely. "Is that the way…? Is it already…? Is that the way you feel when I…?"

She shook her head violently. "No. No, but I'm afraid. We wouldn't have anything left."

He stared at her. He had never thought of her as being wise, or profound; he knew she was not. Yet she knew him better than he knew himself. She had realized and was terrified by the danger he had only vaguely sensed sometimes in the moment of drained and saddened truth after the moment of wildness. And now it terrified him too. Was it the only thing that brought him to her?

He slid down on the leather seat until his chest was against the steering wheel and his knees pushed against the dashboard.

His coat was bunched tight under his armpits. And when he looked toward her again he knew it was more than that, immensely more, and with a quick movement he raised his hand and she was in his arms. Her hair was soft and fine against his cheek, her wet, cool face was buried in his throat, her arms were tight around him, her body pressed tight, squeezed between him and the steering wheel, her face was pressed tight; but it seemed unreal and impossible. V pressing her wet face into his throat, the feel of her back under his hands, were not real. It was only part of a dream that had been both nightmare and dream.

When she pulled herself away her hair caught the light and shone whitely. Her face was hidden in shadow and her voice was muffled. "Will you ask her to let you go?"

"Yes."

"Now?"

"Tomorrow. I'll go see her tomorrow. You go on, now; I'll be up after a while. I just want to sit here a minute."

V didn't move.

"I just want to sit here alone for a while," Jack said unsteadily. "I'll be up in a minute."

"All right," V whispered. When she got out of the car he could see the tears shining in her eyes.

11

In his helpless, horrified sorrow after he learned Gene was going to have an abortion, he had set out to get drunk. He bought a fifth of bourbon, rented a room in a cheap hotel and began the process of stupefying himself. He sat on the bed looking out on the dingy building well outside his window, drinking from the bottle and welcoming the protective insensibility that came over him. But twice he tried to phone Gene, and both times Mrs. Geary hung up on him.

When he woke the next morning, he was conscious of only one thing: he had to stop it. He was shaking when he went downstairs, and his eyes were blurred. He drove out to Mission Hills slowly and carefully, hugging the right-hand side of the road and talking to himself. He had to stop it.

There was no one at Gene's mother's house. He thought at first they were just refusing to answer the doorbell, but the garage was empty, and when he broke into the house through the window of what had been Gene's bedroom, the house was empty.

Slowly, feeling dead, his stomach gripped into a tight, sick fist, he drove out to La Jolla. He parked the car and walked into the lobby of the hotel. He didn't care that he wore no tie, that his clothes had been slept in and that he had a two-days' growth of beard on his face. He knew he looked like a tramp and stank of liquor, and outstaring the desk man and the elevator boy, he rode up to the fifth floor.

V opened the door and he pushed past her into the apartment. She was wearing a blue-figured, two-piece bathing suit and evidently she had been sunbathing on the terrace; her body shone with oil and there was a stripe of zinc oxide on her nose. Her eyes were swollen.

"What happened?" she said.

He walked over to the sideboard and poured himself a drink. "Jack, where've you been?" she cried. The straps of her bathing suit were tucked in at the sides, and holding the halter with one hand, she looped the straps around her neck and tied them. Her eyes narrowed. "You're drunk," she said.

He nodded, feeling the pleasant, cool, handful of glass, studying the warm amber color of the liquor. Then he put the glass down and leaned against the carved front of the sideboard, staring at her, pitying her, feeling how this had brought them closer, although she would never know it, but at the same time had made it completely and unalterably impossible.

She looked angry and nervous. She took a step backward, and holding her hands behind her, pushed closed the tall glass doors. The sun was bright through the glass. "Where've you been, Jack?" she said again.

"Getting drunk."

"All right. Why?"

He found a cigarette in his pocket. It was bent and wrinkled and the tobacco was stringing out one end. He put it between his lips and lit it, the hand that held the match strangely steady.

"We've killed another one," he said.

Her face turned white and haggard, suddenly old. Her hands rose slowly as though to ward something off, and then she dropped them and leaned against the other end of the sideboard. The drink stood between them. Jack snubbed out his cigarette and picked it up and felt the bourbon that warmed his throat turn to sickness in his stomach.

He tightened his lips and wiped them carefully on the back of his hand. "Another one," he said. "Two stars. Two stripes…" He shook his head. "Strikes," he said.

"What is it?" V asked harshly. "Is it something about your wife?" Her face was ugly and lined, old above her young body.

Jack spoke slowly and carefully, drawing the words out. "She was going to have a kid. That's what you have when you get married, you know. Kids. She…"

V made a sound that wasn't a sound, wasn't anything.

"She's giving it the treatment," Jack said. "She didn't want to have my kid." He moved his hand gently up and down, watching the liquor slop in the glass. He could taste grief like brass in his mouth, then the brass mixed with bourbon, then the brass alone again. V's hands crept slowly up to her face.

"Goddamn us both for this," he said.

He crossed the room unsteadily and sat down in the big Monterey chair cradling the drink against his chest. He watched V. He studied every inch of her he could see, wishing he could see her face, wondering how she felt. He wondered if she felt anything of what he did, wanting suddenly, desperately, to know how she felt about this.

"Well, how do you feel?" he said aloud, and then he said, "V, I guess this tears it. I think I wanted that kid."

She said something he couldn't understand, her voice muffled in her hands. Her fingers kneaded her forehead. "I keep thinking up names for it," he said. "I keep thinking about that."

"Do you?" he heard her say.

"Well, we fixed it up, all right," he said. "Just like everything else. We fix everything," and all at once he was surprised he wasn't blaming her. He didn't need to hurt her for this. This was their doing, the two of them together. It was not just his fault, or her fault. This was the two of them and he could never blame her for anything again.

"Red and the kid, honey," he said, to himself and to her. "Do you think we're worth it? Do you think the two of us are worth the two of them?" He was glad he had not mentioned Denton.

"Now we have to be," she said, and she turned and looked out the glass doors. It was a beautiful day—he hadn't noticed it before—the sun was shining and the sky was a hot, light blue; the kind of day on which kids pile into their old jalopies and go out to the beach and everything is beautiful. He watched V's back as she looked out at the sky and the ocean and the sandstone cliffs around the cove.

"No," he said. "We're not worth it," and she turned back toward him. Her face was like a stiff mask with two dark eyeholes in it, her nose ridiculously caked with the white paste.

"It's not your fault," he said. "It's only our fault. It's always been our fault." His glass was empty. It had left a wet circle on the dark arm of the chair.

V nodded. "I don't know what to say to you," she said. "Except...Except I know how you must feel. I'm sorry."

"I know what to say. I'm going back to her. If she'll have me, I'm going."

V put her hand on the edge of the sideboard as though she would have fallen. "No! Jack!" she cried hoarsely.

"See, I have to make it up to her," he said. "I owe her most now."

"Jack!" she screamed at him, but then he couldn't hear her anymore. He heard only her fist pounding hollowly on the top of the sideboard. He couldn't see her anymore. He knew she was talking, crying out to him, but her voice seemed to come from very far away, and he wouldn't let himself listen.

He helped himself up and made his way to the door. He turned the knob and opened it. He didn't look back at V. She was calling to him but he didn't hear. His legs were like rubber and he felt sick and hollow, but he felt strong in knowing what he had to do. When he closed the door behind him he found he still had the empty glass in his hand. He took it with him.

12

He was lying awake one night, staring at nothing and thinking of too many things. He wanted a cigarette, but he didn't want to wake Gene. He could feel the feverish warmth of her body next to his, and he lay perfectly still, searching the darkness with his eyes.

Now he could make out the dim forms in the room; the dresser below the black pool of the mirror, the lighter shapes of the windows, the darker shape of the door to the living room, the chair over which his workclothes hung, the luminous hands of the alarm clock on the bedside table. He concentrated on the slow, sleepy sound the clock made, the sound of time being destroyed.

He turned as he felt a movement beside him. He could see Gene's head on the pillow, the short, dark hair, the pale face. He felt her hand on him and her voice was blurred with sleep. "Are you thinking about V, Jack?"

He didn't say anything. He put his arm under her head so that her face was pressed against his chest.

"You are," she said, but her voice did not sound concerned. He could see the soft luster of her eyes. "Jack," she said. "Trust me, won't you? Don't worry."

"Sure," he said.

Her arm crept around his neck and she pressed her thin body against him. She was unhealthily hot under her cotton pajamas. She was not well, he knew, had not been well since the abortion. She had lost weight and her eyes seemed to have been pulled deep into her head. But she never complained and he knew it was because she didn't want to worry him.

"Honey," he said, "why don't you go to a doc?"

"Oh, I'm all right," she said sleepily. "I feel better every day," and she giggled. "Don't pretend you were worrying about me, darling."

"I was."

"Too?" She laughed again. "She can't fight the both of us, Jack. I'm too strong now. Don't worry about her. Don't worry about either of us."

"Sure," he said. "Go on back to sleep, Gene." She smiled and closed her eyes and he kissed the end of her nose, feeling false, completely false, knowing she believed she had arrived at an understanding of this thing, but knowing she had not, because there was too much she could never understand.

She seemed to have come to look upon V as a kind of evil witch, whom he hated but under whose spell he was. She was protecting him from that witch. She seemed to enjoy the prospect of sacrificing herself for him in some way, and he could not tell her she was wrong.

He could not tell her that he had never wanted her as he wanted V. He could not explain that when she pressed against him in the night, or touched him, it wasn't her he wanted. There was no way to make her know she had never satisfied him. He couldn't even try. It was not her fault and he could not hurt her by trying to explain.

Now he knew the problem. It was so basic and simple that it took his breath away, and he had been searching for the answer without even knowing what the problem was. It was that he loved V. He loved V too much ever to love Gene enough. Trying to love and live with Gene was like walking a tightrope to which he could cling with nothing but his will. He had no feet, no arms, no hands, because they belonged to V; he had only his will to hold on with, and it was neither strong enough to let him make his way nor weak enough to let him fall.

With Gene there was not enough. He had to keep striving for something else outside his life with her. She had talked him into sending for a brochure on a correspondence engineering course. He had wanted to send for it himself, but he knew he could not be an engineer. He knew what he was. He was a cat skinner who was smart enough, who could handle men well enough, to be a grade foreman. Yet he had the feeling that he should strive to be more, not merely because of Gene, but because he felt the need of something else. He must try to be what he could not be.

Even though he knew the problem, that did not give him the answer. He knew what he owed V, but now he owed Gene more. He had left the one debt unpaid to pay the other in counterfeit coin.

The cruelty of it made him groan aloud, for none of it was Gene's fault. He could love her in a way, but never completely. He wanted her to be well so they could have a child and maybe then it would be all right—it was a straw he grasped at desperately, but he knew it was only a straw.

And she wasn't well yet. They would have to wait. He couldn't have her if he had wanted her. He lay awake, listening to the clock grinding the seconds into the past, and each second came to seem to him a terrible loss that should be caught and drained of everything it held before it was gone.

13

When he went back to V again he wept for the first time since he had been a boy. He was not ashamed that V should hear him sobbing, heavy, unpracticed sounds that shook his body and left him gasping. V seemed to understand there was nothing else he could do. This feeling, that once would have found an outlet in furious anger, in a fight, in getting drunk, was now too huge, too complicated. There was nothing else he could do.

And when it was over he felt relieved. V was stroking his back and he took her hand between his and pressed it to his face, his face turned into the pillow. The end of the sobbing had brought a tired catharsis to his body and mind, and now he could think clearly, his mind washing clearly and quickly over the knots that had seemed unsolvable, like a mountain stream over the pebbles and boulders in the stream bed.

Shame was gone. Guilt was buried in the past. Everything was strange and new. This woman whom he could not see, but whose hand he clutched tightly to his face, was all that life had ever held for him, was life itself, and he was held to her by ties made up by both their lives. He realized he loved her completely and cleanly, had always, and the dirt of the guilt, the shame of the animal in himself, were washed away in the clear, cold stream of his mind. Everything he felt for her was purified and he saw the perfection he had only to close his hand upon.

Everything was simple now, turned into simple, understandable meanings and answers, and the torturing phantoms he had lived with so long were gone. The need for hurting V was gone.

Guilt was gone; the death of Red, the murder of the unborn child, had been paid for now in his and V's separate sufferings. They were separate no longer, but welded inextricably together.

The weight that had crushed him into a sobbing, grotesque caricature of himself was gone. He had felt it lift and dissolve into the air. He released V's hand. He had wanted her fiercely, but suddenly he was no longer ashamed of the wanting. There was more than that for them; he knew it, yet now they did not need more, now they had not had time for more, they had had no chance for more. All that had held him from her in fear and hate was gone and what had thrust him to her only in wildness was gone, and it was as though his brain had burst free into a place where everything was calm and serene. He wished desperately he could tell V of this discovery, this change, the termination of the sentence, but he did not have the words. He could only run his hands over her body that was long and cool and clean, had always been so clean, that belonged to him and had always belonged to him, hearing the husky sound in her throat and feeling her arms come around his neck, arms that had known always that he belonged to her. He could not tell her, he could never hope to tell her. He could only show her, and feeling the aching pull again at his throat, he showed her; knowing that this was no animal, this was all of him, all of her was all of him, the wonder and the beauty of his life, that left him washed clean now and completely whole, that was his perfection, and exaltation, and apotheosis.

When it was over she lay with her face pressed against his chest. Her face felt wet but she made no sound. He looked down at her bare back and her brown arm flung out on the pillow, and stroked her hair, feeling the warm wetness of her tears on his chest.

Finally she said, "Will you go to her now?"

"Yes," he said. "I can tell her now."

V raised her head and pulled herself upright, her hands clutching his arms. "Will you?"

He nodded, trying to smile at her. He would go to Gene now and tell her. But V's face was frightened. Her hair had slid around to cover one cheek and her mouth was trembling. She stared into his eyes and he could feel the sharp points of her fingernails digging into his arms.

"Yes," he said. "I can do it now. I understand it now. I've been crazy too long, but I'm not anymore."

She shook her head. The lock of blonde hair slid back and forth over her cheek. "I don't know," she said. "You've said that before. I'm afraid." He thought she was going to say more, but she only repeated, "I'm afraid," and shook her head again and bit her lip.

He freed his arms and put them around her and pulled her down. "Listen, V," he said, speaking very slowly and carefully. "I'm going to Gene and tell her I want a divorce and she's going to give it to me. Then we're going to get married." He shook her gently. "We're going to get married," he said.

She thrust her damp face into his throat, and he could feel her breath when she spoke. "I've thought about it so much," she whispered. "I build it up and think we've got it now—that it's finally going to *be*...and then it always falls apart again. I believe you now, when I hear you say it like that and see it in your face, but when you go away I'll die and die and die, because I know it won't be true."

"Shut up with that," Jack said. "Knock that off. I'll cut off an arm and leave it here with you so you'll be sure." He shook her again. "Listen, V," he said. "Where'll we go? Back to the Valley?"

She laughed softly. "We can go anywhere. Haven't you ever thought of that? I've got quite a lot of money. We can go anywhere and do anything we want to."

"What would you want to do?"

She shook her head, her hair tickling his shoulder. "What do you want to do?"

"Buy a couple of cats. Rent them around. After a while buy some more equipment and get a little business going."

"We could buy a lot of cats. Right away."

"Just two," Jack said. "Two big yellow D-8 dozers. I want there to be more because of my being smart enough, not because of your dough."

"Maybe they'd have a little cat," V said. She laughed breathlessly, and moved her face so that she was looking up at him. He had never seen her eyes look so big and dark. Her nostrils were stretched taut, as though she were holding her breath.

"There'll be a lot of little cats," Jack said. He laughed too. The laughing bubbled up inside him and made him shake all over. He thought of Gene; but that didn't matter now. Nothing else mattered.

V laughed the breathless laugh. "How bourgeois," she said shakily. "How completely beautifully perfect and bourgeois." He didn't know the word. His breath caught in his throat as he stared down at her; how much more did she know that he didn't know? How much was she used to that he was not? How could she want what he wanted? Suddenly he was afraid.

"V, is that what you want, too? You don't just want to go somewhere and be big time, do you? You…"

"No," she said.

He shook his head at her. "You could; I guess you know that. But I never could. You know that. You know what I am. Just…"

"You shut up," V cried. "Haven't I ever told you all I wanted?"

He nodded seriously, and then he grinned. V smiled back at him.

"You're my big time," she said. "And how I've tried to make it!"

He moved his face until his cheek was against hers and she was pressed against his chest. Her body felt tight and hard, as though every muscle was being strained, and she pushed him away again. "Is this it?" she whispered, her eyes probing his. "Really? *Really?*"

"Really, damn it!" He pulled her roughly back. Her body relaxed and she clung to him.

"Yes," she said. "Yes, yes, yes. I know it. But when you go away now, I'll die. I'll…"

He covered her mouth with his hand. "Goddamn it," he whispered in her ear. "I mean this." He brushed the blonde hair away from her ear and put his lips against it and whispered, "Something happened to me just then. Something broke. There's nothing else now. There's nobody else now." He felt her hands tighten on his back and he removed his hand from her mouth and covered it with his mouth, feeling her strong arms on his back and pulling her to him and trying to make her know that it was now; it was now, and there would never be anything that could get between them again, because now there were only the two of them, there was nothing else; because now he knew what she was to him, and he could not live without her.

He left her sleeping to go back to the job. He wanted to go to work. He drove up beside the bulldozer, called to Danny Snyder to get down, and climbed up on the cat himself. He ran it all the rest of the afternoon, working as deftly and as surely as he had ever worked, enjoying hugely the dust in his nostrils and the trembling of the clutch levers and the dozer control under his hands, feeling his own sure power, his own narrow but complete skill, transmitted through the enormous power of the cat.

When the five-o'clock whistle blew he leaped down off the cat tracks. Danny waved and when Jack came over to him, said, "Hey, Jack, you should have been a cat skinner."

14

He drove through San Diego and onto the Coronado ferry, thinking about Gene. He had not avoided thinking about her that afternoon. She was only another problem that was newly simple too, and did not bother him. Now that he knew his own mind, now that he knew himself and V, he would just have to go to Gene and tell her, as he should have told her the first time, that they had to get a divorce. He would let her keep everything they owned, for he needed nothing. She would be hurt, he knew, but hurt less than if this were to continue, and he could only try to tell her how sorry he was. And Gene was young yet and attractive enough. She would soon forget him and marry again and be happy the way he could never make her happy. He was completely confident he could make her see why it had to be this way.

But Gene was not at the apartment.

He felt puzzled and vaguely worried, he was sorry it had to be put off, but his mood was not affected. He took the ferry back to San Diego and drove out to La Jolla with the radio playing, tapping his foot in time to the music. Wind from the open wind-wing was shunted onto his face and he had never felt so completely free.

He grinned at the operator as he got into the elevator. He walked down the carpeted hall of the fifth floor with long strides. Then he heard the sound.

First it was just a harsh, echoing whack, something he'd vaguely heard before. Then it was a shot. His legs became leaden as he realized it. He stopped. He moved forward again and ran the few steps to the door. He put his hand on the brass knob, he turned it, pushed. The door opened.

Through the great glass doors light streamed into the room and stabbed his eyes and burst in his head. He stood in the doorway, holding the edge of the door with a hand that felt like a steel hook. A meaningless sound rasped in his throat as he looked down at the crumpled shape on the floor, and the blood.

His eyes were held by the blood. With an effort he pulled them away. He saw Gene. She stood motionless, her arm, pointed down, turning into gun, the gun glinting bluely in her hand. The sharp smell of gunpowder cut into his nostrils.

Gene did not move. Her face was like a lump of white dough, her eyes two dark, wild spots in it. He saw that she was panting, swaying, gasping for breath, but still holding the gun pointed down at the floor. Her face turned toward him and she whispered, "She's dead."

Jack looked down at V. One leg was crumpled under the other; he could see her brown thigh partly covered by pink slip, then the pink slip covered by her blue dress. Her arms were flung out as though she had been going to dive. They pointed toward him and her face was turned away, but he could see the red spring of blood below her breast. He took a step forward, his breath tearing at his lungs. His brain had stopped. He heard the door close behind him.

"She's dead," Gene said.

He tried to focus his eyes on Gene. He took a step toward her, another. He snatched the gun away. It was hot to his hand and he dropped it into his pocket. Gene's eyes rolled idiotically. He could see spittle at the corner of her mouth.

"I've killed her," she said, and she began to laugh. It was a high, hysterical sound that cut painfully into his ears. He slapped her face, too hard, and she slumped forward. He caught her and held her, limp and heavy in his arms. She babbled unintelligible sounds.

"Make sense," he cried. "Make sense, Goddamn you!" He was shaking, holding her. His face was wet with sweat, each drop of sweat an active pain to his nerve-ends. Everything inside him was dead with the thing on the floor, upon which the light streamed, bright and cold and mocking.

Gene hiccoughed, spit trickled onto her chin, her mouth began to work. He tried to listen to the words, forced out with harsh, deep breaths. "She called me up. She asked me to come here…" And then she began laughing again, and hiccoughing. Jack felt his fingers tear at the soft flesh of her arms. He shook her.

"Why did you do it?"

"I went to the doctor," she gasped. She stopped and his hands released her arms and reached for her throat. They twitched and shook. He made them drop. Gene said, "I can't ever have a baby. That Mexican doctor…His instruments weren't clean. I've got something all over inside me."

He put his hands over his face and took a step back. Gene said, "Then she called up. It was just then. I'd just come back from the doctor and it was just like the other time she called me, only when I knew…"

"When you knew what?" he whispered. *"What did she say?"*

"She wanted to know where you were. She asked me if you'd told me and I didn't know what she meant and then she said she had to talk to me…"

She stopped. *"Oh, why, God?"* he whispered. His eyes had turned to hot balls of iron in their sockets as through his spread fingers he watched her bend over, hiccoughing, gasping for breath. It was as though he saw her through the wrong end of a telescope. But suddenly his brain came to life. There was no time.

"Where did you get the gun?" His voice was too loud but it

would come no softer. He didn't look at V, staring fiercely at Gene; he felt the flesh of her arms twist as he pulled her upright. Oh, why, God? he thought. He shook her.

"She asked me if you'd told me," Gene said. "So I knew you'd been here again. I knew it then and it was when I'd just got back from the doctor. Jack, when I…Jack, something in me tore all apart. I couldn't stand…"

"Where did you get the gun?"

"It's yours. Jack, I couldn't stand it anymore and I took it out of your dresser there." His hands fell from her arms. "It's the one you've always had," she said. "It's always been there." He felt the weight of the gun in his pocket then, so heavy it seemed to pull him off balance; the gun he had brought home from the war as a souvenir. He sobbed aloud.

"Get out of here!" he cried. She didn't move. "Get out!" he cried. He half-pushed her, half-carried her to the door. He opened it and pushed her out. "There's a stairs down at the end of the hall." He pushed her roughly toward the stairs and she stumbled and almost fell. She gaped back at him over her shoulder.

"What're you going to do?" she whispered. "Jack!" She swayed toward him. Her dark eyes were huge and rimmed with white. "Jack!"

"Go on!" He raised his fist and she staggered away from him. The hall was empty, silent. *"Go on!"* he whispered. She stumbled down the hall. At the door to the stairs she turned again. He raised his fist again. She disappeared and he watched the door swing slowly closed behind her.

Inside the room again, he looked down at V. The gun was an immense weight in his pocket as he moved toward her, moving as though he were walking through water, seeing her in a bright, watery haze.

He dropped to one knee beside her, then, with a jolt, to the other. Clearly now, he saw the red wound below her breast. It was edged with charred cloth. Blood had soaked the blue of her dress to a sickening purple, had spilled from her waist and soaked darkly into the carpet. He put out a slow, nerveless hand toward the wound. He stopped it, changed its course and touched the other breast. He sobbed as he felt it; it was warm. He couldn't see her anymore. He tried, but she had dissolved into tears in his eyes.

He took the gun from his pocket. He thumbed the hammer back, the metal biting into his thumb, the gun too, still warm. Taking a deep breath he staggered to his feet. V lay dead on the floor before him, robbed of all beauty and cleanness, robbed of any dignity. He watched the gun as though it were a deadly snake he held. He turned his hand slowly. The muzzle turned slowly toward him, a thick ring, the barrel extending down into darkness and release. He could see the slugs in the cylinder as he watched the muzzle turn toward him. There were muffled footsteps in the hall.

There was a knock on the door. He heard it, but his nerves did not signal to his brain. His finger pressed gently, almost delicately, the trigger. He stopped. He forced his finger to press again, gently, his hand straining to be gentle.

The door flew open and slammed back against the wall. He saw them, in blue uniforms. He turned the gun toward them. *"Get back!"* he shouted. There was a flash of fire and sound from the doorway. He ducked and the gun escaped from his hand. He tried to catch it, but it dropped and he saw them running at him.

He turned toward the glass doors. His legs moved with terrible slowness. They were on him; one of them crashed upon his back, something grazed the side of his head. He went to his knees. His arm flailed out and he heard one of them scream.

There were shouts and pain and madness as he tried to stagger up with the one still on his back, and his heart tore apart with the effort. He ran toward the bright, sun-streaming squares of the glass doors.

Something hit him from the side and he fell heavily. He lay pinioned on the floor. Panting, pleadingly, he looked up at them. There were two and each held an arm, panting with him, shouting at him. Blood streamed from the mouth of the one on the right. The hotel was full of shouting, and running feet. He was lying on the floor where V was lying.

"Why couldn't you let me?" he panted. He looked at the one on his left, who was young and had a red face and his cap still on. He felt the man's grip loosen a little, and with a quick, convulsive movement he jerked his arm away. He slammed his fist into the face of the other. He clutched at hair and pulled himself up, turning and running and falling toward the source of the brightness. But there was a flashing pain in his head and he fell against the glass and slid down it to the floor, the brightness turning to blackness and then even the blackness gone.

15

Then the hours of riding, of being jerked and shoved, of people staring and people talking, and the bright steel handcuffs that cut into his wrists and the pain in his head and the aching nothingness inside him; the police shouting questions at him and then others asking him questions and listening quietly while he told them how he had killed her and why he had killed her, and then what he had said was brought back to him typed neatly and he read it and signed it; then the darkness of the cell where he wanted to sleep but could not sleep because he had to think, trying to remember what he had said, trying to remember if he had said it correctly. He had said it right and what he had done was right, and all his thinking only came back to the simple, quick judgment and decision he had made when he saw V dead.

He would see them looking at him; he wondered if they thought he was crazy. He knew they thought him a murderer, and they were right. But they should understand that he realized it too, that he knew it was his doing and only his, that his was the responsibility, that he wanted to pay for it. Responsibility; that was the only word that came near describing the enormity of it; his responsibility—Red, the kid, and finally—V. The feeling of responsibility that had grown from the passion and the rotten, corrupting jealousy, the desire and the shame of the desire, that had changed and grown, and had grown too large…

Why had it happened this way? He had not been the first man to seduce a girl. But that girl had been V. His had not been the first fight, but Red had been killed. Abortions were common, but this one had gone wrong. And he had never understood.

He had never understood what was wrong and what was right, good and bad, what he wanted and did not want; he had never been able to solve the knotted snarl of his life because of the very complexity of that snarl, because of his indecision, because of the double responsibility he felt, and when, finally he had become man enough to solve it, it was too late, and too many forces had been set in motion. V was dead.

The next day Gene came.

The turnkey brought her to the door of the cell and went away, the jingle of the keys he carried and his squeaking shoes fading to silence down the long corridor. Sitting on the cot, he looked at Gene through the barred door.

After a long time he got up, stretched, and went over to her. The black, spaced bars were between them. Gene's hands were two white knots of flesh, pierced by the bars, and between them her face was like death, her eyes huge and dark with seeing too much. Two bright spots of fever burned on her cheeks.

He stood with his legs braced apart, looking down into her face. "What do you want?"

Her white lips parted. She whispered, "Why are you doing this?"

"You'd never understand," he said. "Go on home."

"Please…"

"Get out," he whispered fiercely. "Get out and don't come here again. Get as far from here as you can, where you'll never even hear about this. Don't you ever…"

"Please. Let me take what's coming to me."

"Get out!" he said. Her hands clenched tighter. He saw her throat work. "This is mine," he said.

"No! I did it, Jack."

"*Shut up!* Listen," he hissed. "Stay out of it! You stay the

Goddamn hell out; don't tell, don't say a word. If you do I'll kill myself in the rottenest...." He clenched his fist in front of her face. "In the filthiest way I can!"

He was shaking when he turned away, and he heard her crying. The sound angered him. Around them the cell block was completely silent.

"*Jack!*"

He turned back, scowling. Her black-clad body was pressed against the bars. One hand reached through toward him. "*Tell me one thing,*" she whispered.

"What?"

"*Tell me the truth. Please.*"

"What?"

"*Jack, are you doing this for me? Or for V?*"

He stared at her, suddenly breathing hard. He took a step back.

"*Are you doing this for me or for her?*"

"Not for you," he said.

She slumped against the door and her hands relaxed. He turned and went back to the cot and lay down with his face to the wall. After a while he heard her go away.

Epilogue

When he had finished the cigarette he snuffed it out against the iron side rail of the cot and lay completely motionless for a few moments. Finally he raised his knees and clasped them tight against his chest and then released them.

He rose with an effort, stepped across to where the shards of glass lay upon the floor, squatted and carefully swept them into the palm of his hand. Sitting on the edge of the cot again he sorted through the pieces until he found a large, wedge-shaped segment that was thick and sharp at the apex, thin at the base. He pricked his finger with it.

As he watched the drop of blood form he began to sweat. But he stared at it with fascinated, unafraid eyes. It was perfectly round and dark red, and exulting and trembling, he held the hand up in front of him, massaging the finger until the drop of blood grew larger, and suddenly he doubled up his fist, clenching it and tightening his forearm until the blood vessels stood out bluely, knotted and tumescent at his wrist.

He did what he had to do quickly, with steady fingers, and then he lay back on the cot and dropped his arm over the side so that he would not see the blood. He was not afraid of it, but he did not want to be afraid. He felt no pain; only his pulse seemed to sound loudly in his ears, the palm of his hand tickled and felt hot and sticky, and when he tried to clench his fist once more, his hand was weak.

Sweat prickled coldly all over his body and he relaxed the fingers of his right hand to drop the bit of glass. He closed his eyes and thought about death. He had not thought about death *before, but he did not fear it, he only wondered about it. How did it come, he wondered. Was it only an instantaneous blotting out? But it must be more than that; he hoped it would be more. He needed it to be more.*

How does it come, he wondered. Did it come like the soft sighing of the wind across the desert, coming louder and louder, until like the last long roll of Naval guns along the beach at Betio, so loudly sighing, it filled every void and lack and aching hollowness. Was it a great rush of feathered wings descending and carrying away in a blinding rush of brightness and sound, wings like white strong arms, brightness that was the sun and everything ever seen, sound that was all the universe of sounds, all the words ever spoken by all the world of voices.

Or did it fit the person to whom it came, a mechanism created in and of himself: for him a great, spectral tractor, with a pale, black-clad operator on the seat, one gloved hand on the blade lever; and the great engine straining and roaring and shaking the world, the cable keening in the cable-channels, the great tracks clacking and biting with sharp cleats, the enormous blade shining and down with its load of black earth and at the corners the cutting edge gleaming silver; a band on the friction clutch as the monster comes closer, and it turns toward him, the engine roaring and filling everything with sound and shaking, and the gloved hand touching gently the blade lever, and the cat nearer and nearer and louder and louder...